VALLEY COTTAGE FREE LIBRARY
W9-BKH-337

Valley Cottage Library
110 Route 303
Valley Cottage, NY
10989
www.vclib.org

THE MOST FRIGHTENING STORY EVER TOLD

ALSO BY PHILIP KERR

The Winter Horses

Children of the Lamp series

THE MOST FRIGHTENING STORY EVER TOLD

PHILIP KERR

ALFRED A. KNOPF
NEW YORK

THIS IS A BORZOI BOOK PUBLISHED BY ALFRED A. KNOPF

Visit us on the Web! randomhousekids.com

Educators and librarians, for a variety of teaching tools, visit us at RHTeachersLibrarians.com

Library of Congress Cataloging-in-Publication Data
Names: Kerr, Philip, author.
Title: The most frightening story ever told / Philip Kerr.
Description: New York : Alfred A. Knopf, [2016] | Summary: "Scary-story enthusiast Billy Shivers helps out when the Haunted House of Books threatens to go out of business." —Provided by publisher
Identifiers: LCCN 2015035400 | ISBN 978-0-553-52209-9 (trade) | ISBN 978-0-553-52210-5 (lib. bdg.) | ISBN 978-0-553-52211-2 (ebook)
Subjects: | CYAC: Haunted houses—Fiction. | Bookstores—Fiction. | Ghosts—Fiction. | Contests—Fiction. | Humorous stories. | BISAC: JUVENILE FICTION / Mysteries & Detective Stories. | JUVENILE FICTION / Books & Libraries.
Classification: LCC PZ7.K46843 Mo 2016 | DDC [Fic]—dc23
LC record available at http://lccn.loc.gov/2015035400

The text of this book is set in 11-point Amasis MT.

Printed in the United States of America
September 2016
10 9 8 7 6 5 4 3 2 1

First Edition

This book is for Ava B.

CONTENTS

THE MOST FRIGHTENING STORY EVER TOLD

CHAPTER 1

BILLY'S LOVE OF BOOKS

Welcome to Hitchcock. It's an ordinary town of 250,000 people. When the town got started, in 1800, one of the first things its founders built was a beautiful public library so that people who couldn't afford to buy books could borrow them instead.

Let's go inside. Under a large onion-shaped roof is a big reading room, where Hitchcock's older citizens look at newspapers and fall asleep. And there are miles and miles of wooden shelves and on them lots and lots of books. The Hitchcock town library has over twenty thousand books, many of which have never been read by anyone.

One person who's read at least a hundred books in the library is the boy standing in Children's Literature. His name is Billy Shivers.

If Billy Shivers were able to talk, he would say "I'm very pleased to meet you," but this is a library, and if he did say anything, the librarian, Miss Junker, would make a cross, shushing noise, point at a large sign that reads SILENCE and very probably remind him that "there's no talking allowed in the library." So you'll forgive him if he just looks up from that book in his hands, smiles and nods back at you for now.

Still, silence is golden and, in this case, it's useful, too. It allows you a chance to look at Billy and see what kind of a boy he is. The first thing you'll notice is that he's tall, and kind of pale-looking—even a bit sickly, like he's been ill or something. But that's only to be expected of someone who was in a serious car accident.

Billy remembers very little about the accident, except that now he knows exactly what it feels like to be a thin layer of strawberry jam between two enormously thick slices of bread. Before the accident he was like any other boy his age, enjoying games and running around outside. But since the accident he doesn't do a lot of that. He gets tired very easily and doesn't care at all for loud noises. His eyes are more sensitive to sunlight, and he feels the cold more than he used to, so that he prefers being indoors to being outside. This probably helps to explain why Billy spends so much time in the Hitchcock Public Library. It's nice and warm there. That and the fact that he likes to read books. Lots of them.

Billy had always loved books. But after the accident his love of books grew stronger than ever. He just couldn't get enough of them. He loved the way a book could transport you to a different place in the space of just a few pages, like it was a kind of taxicab for the mind. Sometimes he would take a book and find a quiet corner to sit down, and the next time he looked up, several hours would have passed. Reading a book could make him forget who and what he was and that he had ever been in an accident at all.

Whatever subject you can choose, there's probably at least a hundred books that have been written about it. Billy could have remained in the library forever and he would never have run out of books to read, especially as the people of Hitchcock were always donating their books—most of them unread, of course.

At first Billy's favorite books were all about horses. Then his favorite books were all about space. When he'd read dozens of books about this, he went on to read several more dozens of books about detectives and murder. Next he decided his favorite books were about magicians and wizards. Billy wasn't much interested in books about sports. He much preferred watching sports to reading about them. In the same week that he grew tired of reading about wizards, he tried reading books about cooking, mountaineering, jungle exploration, spying, lions, Scotland and the history of music. But none of these books struck him as being particularly interesting. And then, quite by chance, he picked up and read a book about ghosts, then another, and another, and pretty soon Billy had come to the conclusion his favorite books were all about ghosts.

About the same time it happened that Billy became interested in reading about ghosts, his attention was drawn to a small, dog-eared poster on the library notice board. The poster had been on the notice board for a while and the event it advertised was long out of date, but it was only now that Billy paid any attention to it.

The poster read as follows:

> *You are invited to the Haunted House of Books on Hitchcock High Street, for a Halloween evening of chilling ghost stories and spooky tales. Not to Mention Our Newest Attraction: The Curse of the Pharaohs. Around midnight we will be joined by some creepy local authors who will be signing their Most Horrifying books . . . in blood. Free snacks and mulled wine, plus a ten percent discount on all cash purchases. For further details, telephone 555-6666, or email Rexford Rapscallion at s@tan.com, if you dare.*

Immediately Billy was fascinated. It didn't matter that Halloween had been over for several months and that none of the creepy local authors would be present to sign their horrifying books. What mattered most to Billy was the idea of a bookshop that was haunted. What could be more wonderful? What could be more exciting? What could be more fantastic?

It won't have escaped anyone's attention who has ever been in a bookshop that books cost money. Sometimes a great deal of money. The book you are reading now cost a small fortune and, frankly, you ought to be very grateful to whoever bought it for you. Unless of course you paid for it yourself, in which case you must be stinking rich. After all, why pay money for something that you are only going to use once? Unless of course you think you might want to read the book again. Or unless you want to put it on a shelf with a lot of other books to start a collection of house dust, or just to show people how clever you are. Which is fair enough. But these days, who's got money to waste on books? Or enough space in their houses to give it up to having bookshelves?

Billy's family didn't have money to waste on anything at all and nor indeed did Billy, which was why the boy went to the Hitchcock Public Library to read in the first place.

CHAPTER 2

THE HAUNTED HOUSE OF BOOKS

Billy left the library and walked around the corner onto Hitchcock High Street. As usual, High Street was busy with cars and pedestrians, and a large dog growled fiercely at him for no good reason, all of which made Billy feel very nervous. While Billy liked dogs, they just didn't seem to like him. Cats were even worse. So he quickened his step as best he could until he was standing outside the shop.

Billy didn't need to see the sign hanging from a gallows beside the front door to know that he was in the right place. The paint on the doors and the window frames was as black as a spider. The glass was covered with fake cobwebs of the kind that you can spray on your grandmother while she's asleep in a chair. In the window itself there was a sun-lounger, upon which lay an adult skeleton, dressed for the beach, who appeared to be reading a book called *Shadow of a Dead Man*. Beside the sun-lounger was a large heap of books that looked like they were waiting to be read by the skeleton. These included *The Phantom of Foggy Bottom, The Word of Death, Résumé for a Vampire, A Dark and Stormy Night, The Revenge of the House Wraith, A Cackle in the Dark* and *Creaking on My Stairs*. Immediately behind the skeleton's skull was a ghost—or at least a bedsheet that had been painted to look like a ghost. But the most exciting thing about the window display was a large mirror in which the face of a very frightening-looking witch appeared and then disappeared, every few seconds.

Billy thought it the most wonderful window display he had ever seen and clapped his hands and cried out with delight so that several other people who were passing the shop looked at him strangely, as if there was something wrong with him, and then moved swiftly away.

Grinning like a madman, Billy opened the shop door.

Now, some shop doors have a little bell that rings when you open them. The Haunted House of Books was a shop that had something very different—a hollow, wicked laugh, like something from an old horror movie. Not only that, but when you walked in the doorway, you stepped onto an old subway grating and a current of cold air came gusting up from below the floor. All of this was meant to give someone entering the bookshop a bit of a fright. And Billy was no exception. He yelled out loud and then he chuckled as he saw the funny side of what had happened.

The inside of the shop was no less interesting than the window.

Billy Shivers found himself standing in what looked like an

old mansion. There was a hall with a dusty chandelier, a grand piano, a big, curving wooden staircase and at the foot of the staircase, a polished wooden desk that was the shape of a coffin lid. On top of this sat a crank-operated steampunk cash register that was made of brass. Billy thought the cash register looked as if it belonged on an old submarine in a book by Jules Verne called *20,000 Leagues Under the Sea*.

The register seemed no less ancient than the extraordinary-looking man standing behind it. Indeed it seemed to Billy that the man was the most extraordinary-looking person he'd ever seen.

The man was a little stout but not stout enough to look fat.

His clothes were those of an old-fashioned undertaker: a long black tailcoat, black trousers, a white shirt and a black bootlace tie.

He was very old—almost sixty—and not very tall, but not very short either.

He had longish gray hair that he wore in a ponytail at the back of his head and a silvery beard and a mustache that matched the laugh lines on his face exactly, and framed his mouth like an extra set of jaws. And one of his eyebrows was arched like the Sydney Harbour Bridge.

On his stubby fingers were several skull-shaped silver rings and in his ear was a ring and on the ring was a tiny dagger and on the sharp tip of the dagger was a tiny spot of red paint as if the dagger had stabbed someone very small indeed.

He wore thick-framed glasses with peculiar yellowish glass that seemed to magnify the curious gleam that seemed to stay permanently in the white of his eyes. Billy was sure he had never seen eyes as gleaming as these. Nor indeed a smile that was quite so white, or wolfish. The man's smile was so white and wolfish that for a moment Billy wondered if he had fangs and if the man might be a vampire. And yet the smile was not unfriendly. Mischievous, yes, a little weary, maybe, but not at all hostile.

"Can I help you?" the man asked politely.

His voice was deep and resonant like a baritone in a coal mine.

Nervously, Billy approached the coffin-shaped counter. His mother had told him never to speak to strangers, but that just didn't seem to work when you were in a shop and someone who very likely worked there asked if they could help you.

"I was looking for a book about ghosts," he said.

The man sighed and pointed at a sign on the left side of the cash register. It read:

> *Valued customer: You are in the Haunted House of Books. This means haunted as in ghost, dummy. As in things that go bump in the night. That means we do not sell any books about computers, travel, music, theater, self-help, celebrities. If you just asked or were planning to ask for a book about any celebrity, get a life! Nor do we sell books about the Second World War, television, geography, religion, cooking or, God forbid, sports. If you just asked or were planning to ask for a book about sports, you must be a card-carrying moron. Go away and see if you can find your brain before it gets dark, you pathetic fool. We sell creepy books for people who want to get scared quick. That means books about ghosts, ghouls, wraiths, spirits,*

apparitions, vampires, werewolves, zombies, witches and hauntings. We also have a large selection for kids. Is that very clear?

"Er, yes," said Billy. "Very clear. Yes. Thanks. Er, what's a ghoul?"

"A grave-robber," said the man behind the coffin-shaped counter. "Someone who takes bodies from graves and sells them or eats them. For my money, eating them is harder to understand than selling them. Never did like the taste of human flesh all that much. Anyway, ghouls are up the wooden staircase, turn left, end room, last shelf."

"Who would want to buy a dead body?" said Billy.

"There used to be quite a trade in the sale of dead bodies, in a place called Edinburgh."

"Then I'm certainly never going to Edinburgh," said Billy.

"I'll be sure to write and tell them that before I do anything else today," said the man. "I assume they'll want to tell the bad news to the people of Scotland as soon as possible."

"Thank you," said Billy.

"Don't mention it."

Noticing a badge on the man's lapel, Billy leaned forward to read it. It read: REXFORD E. RAPSCALLION, PROPRIETOR.

"Proprietor," said Billy. "That means you're the owner, right?"

The man Billy now knew to be Rexford Rapscallion sighed and pointed to a sign on the right-hand side of the cash register. This one read as follows:

Valued customer. Congratulations! Pat yourself on the back because you're not nearly as dumb as you look. Yes, I'm the proprietor and that does mean that I'm the owner. And before you inquire, I started the shop myself, almost twenty years ago. Great idea, huh? And no, there didn't used to be a restaurant here. It was a coffeehouse but the coffee tasted like mud which is probably why they closed and sold the place to me for a lot of *money I wish I still had. And yes we have always specialized in selling books about ghosts etc. And, since you ask, the place really is haunted. By a ghost. I've not seen the ghost myself but people who have say you can sometimes see it in the voodoo section. But I wouldn't read anything into that. But it is supposed to be pretty scary so just remember. You've been warned. The management accepts no responsibility for anyone who dies of fright on these premises. If you are at all the nervous type about ghosts—what on earth are you doing in this shop anyway?!! Are you crazy? Thank you for your kind attention.*

Billy nodded. "Don't mention it," he said. "Why is the counter shaped like a coffin?"

Mr. Rapscallion flinched irritably. "It gives the place atmosphere, kid. It makes it feel haunted, you know? Like all the other stuff. The skeleton in the window. The laugh when you come through the door. And all the other stuff."

"What other stuff?" asked Billy.

Mr. Rapscallion smiled a particularly wolfish smile that Billy thought was just a bit frightening, raised the arch in his already arched eyebrow and said, with a really bright gleam in his eye,

"Now that would be telling, wouldn't it? You'll just have to find out for yourself, sonny. The hard way."

And then Mr. Rapscallion laughed. No ordinary laugh this. But a mad sort of laugh that just took flight out of nowhere, like a big flapping bird that a dog has scared out of a bush. A crazy, loud hyena laugh that kept rolling on and on, like a tire bouncing down a hill. A cackling, crying, out-of-control, never-ending sort of laugh that echoed all through the shop like a water faucet that couldn't be turned off.

It was a laugh like no other laugh Billy had ever heard. Nor ever imagined was humanly possible. It was a laugh that made Billy want to laugh himself and, at the same time, it was a laugh that made him want to run away.

"Which way to the Ghost Section?" Billy asked, bravely.

Mr. Rapscallion's peculiar couldn't-quite-help-it, loony laugh ended as abruptly as it had begun.

"The Children's Section is just around the corner," he said. "I think you'll find what you're looking for in there."

"I'm twelve," said Billy. "I'm a little old for a Children's Section, thank you."

"If you say so. But don't say you weren't warned, kid. The last thing I want is your mother in here later on threatening to sue me because I was cruel to her crybaby son."

"If you knew my mother, you'd know that just couldn't happen."

Mr. Rapscallion shrugged.

"The Ghost Section is up the wooden stairs, turn right. Through Vampires and Voodoo, up the shaky spiral staircase—don't worry, it's safer than it looks or feels—along the very long hotel hallway, beyond the Red Room—don't spend the night there unless you have to—and you'll see it right in front of you. Maybe."

Billy nodded and started to walk toward the main staircase.

"If you need any help," said Mr. Rapscallion, his eyes rolling wildly around his head like two marbles, and his voice dying to a whisper, "just scream."

And then he started to laugh once more.

CHAPTER 3

BILLY EXPLORES

The Haunted House of Books was much larger than Billy had expected. And much more fantastic than ever he had imagined. The floors creaked under his feet like the timbers on an old ship, and somewhere, from behind one of the walls, he was almost sure that he could hear the muffled sound of someone moaning or muttering or moaning *and* muttering—it was hard to tell one from the other.

Billy wasn't at all surprised to have learned from Mr. Rapscallion that there really was a ghost in the bookshop. A couple of times Billy thought he saw a ghost and he was more than a little relieved when these turned out to be other customers. One of these customers was a tall man in a black coat browsing in the Vampires and Voodoo Section. Billy was certain the tall man wasn't a ghost because while he was reading, he kept on scratching his head and, since Billy could hear the sound of the man's head being scratched and even see the dandruff flaking off his head, he thought it unlikely that the man could be anything other than solid. Anything solid seemed less than ghostly.

The other customer he saw was a thin woman with braided black hair and a dark green leather coat who Billy found staring uncertainly up the spiral staircase.

"Do you think it's safe?" she asked Billy. "To go up?"

Billy thought it wasn't very likely a real ghost would have been worried about going up a spiral staircase. A genuine ghost would surely have just floated up the stairs like a cloud without a care in the world.

"Yes," he said. "I think it's probably all right. At least, that's what Mr. Rapscallion told me just a few moments ago. He said it's safer than it looks or feels."

He started to climb the spiral staircase, watched by the woman in the green leather coat. It shifted a bit but no more than a tall ladder leaning against a building.

"Do be careful," she said, biting her fingernail anxiously.

Biting her fingernail was another thing Billy thought a ghost probably wouldn't have done.

"It's okay, really," he said. But a bit farther up, the staircase started to shift as if it wasn't secured properly to the walls and the floor, which was a little alarming, and, worried that the thing would collapse underneath him, Billy felt obliged to quicken his steps to reach the top.

"I think you must be braver than me," said the woman, and walked away.

"No," Billy called after her. "I'm not brave at all."

Turning around, Billy found himself at one end of a long carpeted hallway that seemed like a very ordinary hallway for a haunted house of books. A child—much younger than him—had left a tricycle in a corner and Billy thought this did nothing at all for the ghostly atmosphere that Mr. Rapscallion had talked about. Nor did the life-size waxwork of twin girls he found at the end of the hallway after he turned the next corner. Both the girls were about the same age as Billy. They were wearing pretty blue dresses and holding hands and looked very much as if butter wouldn't melt in their mouths.

That was just weird, thought Billy. And not at all frightening.

Pushing open the red door of the Red Room, he went inside and found it to be a much larger room than he had imagined. The Red Room was at least as big as a tennis court. There were many bookshelves containing thousands of books. To Billy's delight, all of the books were about ghosts. For several minutes he did nothing but look at the spines of the books. And almost half an hour had gone by before Billy noticed that there was nothing beyond the Red Room, as Mr. Rapscallion had said. Even more puzzling than this, however, was the discovery that the doorway by which he had entered the Red Room had disappeared. He was now enclosed on all four sides by bookshelves and nothing but bookshelves. Obviously there was a secret door in the shelves, but as to which wall of books this was in and how it was to be opened Billy hadn't the first clue. And for several minutes afterward, he just stood there in the center of the Red Room, looking in one direction and then another, and then another.

Billy supposed the Red Room was called the Red Room because the carpet and the ceiling and all of the bookshelves were the color red. About the only things that weren't red were the books and Billy himself. The room was lit by seven candles, which struck Billy as a little dangerous in a bookshop. But the candles created some strange shadows in the room and made it seem a bit more creepy.

Especially when one of the candles in a sconce on the wall blew out.

And then another.

Billy picked up one of the candles that were still lit and went to light the two candles that had gone out. But as he did so, two more candles went out, as if an invisible finger and thumb had nipped their wicks.

"That's a bit odd," Billy said to himself, turning to light these as well. Almost immediately the flames on another two candles were extinguished and the darkness seemed to take several large steps toward Billy himself.

The boy gulped loudly.

"What's going on?" he said, with a strange high note of panic entering into his already high voice. "I want these candles to stay lit." With a shaking hand, he leaped from one snuffed-out candle to another and, for a moment, he successfully managed to keep all seven lit.

But then four candles went out at once and Billy heard himself cry out with terror as the darkness seemed to gain on him. "Yikes. This is getting kind of creepy."

Worse was to follow. In his haste to reach one of the unlit candles, the flame upon the candle in his trembling fingers seemed to drag against the air, and then went out. Billy gulped again, dropped the dead candle onto the carpet and reached for one of the two that were still lit—even as this new candle flickered and died in a little wisp of wraith-like smoke.

Horrified, Billy bent down to pick up the candle from the

floor and turned to face the last remaining lit candle. Just as he raised it to the only candle that stood between him and complete and total darkness, this last candle went out as well.

Darkness surrounded the boy like a thick envelope. It was as if someone had picked him up and dropped him into a deep bag made of black velvet and then tied it tight before throwing the bag into a hole.

Then he heard the floorboards creak. He tried to tell himself that these were probably creaking under his own very nervous weight. But it was only too easy to imagine that he wasn't alone in the Red Room. That someone or something was in there with him. And trying to scare him, too.

"Is someone there?" he asked, hoping very much that someone or something didn't answer. "Because if there is, I think it's in very poor taste to frighten another person like this. Even if this is the Haunted House of Books."

The floorboards creaked again, in a sinister sort of way.

Somehow Billy managed not to lose control, hoping that as his eyes became accustomed to the darkness he might eventually see something. But the darkness remained as black as pitch. Indeed, the darkness seemed to intensify. It was almost as if the darkness surrounding him was becoming thick enough to feel. All he could hear was the sound of his own breathing and he could feel the hair lifting off his scalp and standing on end as if it had been trying to reach up and touch the ceiling.

Fear took hold of Billy like a clammy, cold hand.

And for no good reason he could think of, except that Mr. Rapscallion had suggested it in case he needed help, Billy began to scream.

CHAPTER 4

THE HOUSE REVEALS ITS SECRETS

Almost as soon as Billy started to scream, one of the red bookshelves swung open like a secret door to reveal the brightly lit hallway he'd walked along forty minutes earlier. The waxwork of the twin girls wearing the blue dresses was still there. The twins were holding hands sweetly, like before, but—and perhaps he imagined this—it seemed to Billy as he ran, still screaming, out of the Red Room that they were smiling now.

At the end of the hallway Billy kicked the tricycle out of his way and stepped, nervously, onto the spiral staircase. Trying his best to ignore the very definite swaying motion of the steps under his feet, he managed to descend safely to the floor below.

The tall man in the black coat was still browsing the Vampires and Voodoo Section, and now that Billy saw him again, he realized the man was wearing a priest's collar and had a cross on a chain around his neck.

Seeing Billy again, the priest smiled. "You've been up to the Red Room, I hear."

"Yes," said Billy.

"Your first time in there?"

"Yes." Billy tried to control the feeling of panic in his chest. And wiping the sweat from his forehead with his sleeve, gradually he recovered his breath and his nerve.

The man's smile widened. "I could tell. Maybe I should have said something before you went up there but I didn't want to spoil the fun for you."

Billy frowned. "You mean you knew what was going to happen?"

"Of course. This whole shop is rigged like a haunted train ride in an old carnival. A ghost train. Of the kind you might find in a theme park."

"You mean the Red Room—it's not haunted?"

"No, no, no," said the man. "Well, at least I don't think so. No, it's all a trick, my boy. A trick. For example, the door disappears when you step on a spring-loaded floorboard. And it only opens again when an electronic sensor detects the sound of someone, such as yourself, screaming. That is, provided you scream loud enough. The sound sensor is getting rather old and needs replacing, probably. You have to block the door with a heavy book if you don't want any of that to happen."

"I see."

The priest returned the book he was reading to the shelf and removed the pair of little gold-framed glasses he had been wearing on the end of his long nose. "I'm Father Merrin." He smiled and extended a long, thin hand to Billy.

Shaking the priest's hand, Billy said, "My name is Billy Shivers."

"Pleased to meet you, Billy," said Father Merrin. "I'm sure."

"What about the candles in the Red Room?" asked Billy. "How do they work?"

"Simple. After you've been in there awhile, the room switches on little currents of air that blow through tiny holes in the walls behind them."

"Oh."

Billy thought that Father Merrin was older than Mr. Rapscallion. He looked ill, too. And Billy wondered if Father Merrin might himself be a corpse, or something worse.

"Look here, you're not a real ghost, are you?" Billy asked the priest.

"No." Father Merrin smiled. "I'm flesh and blood."

Billy looked relieved. "A haunted train ride, eh?" Billy nodded. "That explains a lot."

"It explains everything," said Father Merrin. "Doesn't it?" He chuckled. "I mean, what else could the explanation be?"

"But it must have cost a great deal of money to build this place," said Billy. "Don't you think?"

"Oh, yes. A small fortune. I believe the man who helped Mr. Rapscallion to build this shop was a first-class professional magician. A stage conjurer all the way from Las Vegas, Nevada, who used to design and build tricks for some of the best cabaret acts in the world. For example, look here."

Father Merrin steered the boy gently toward a shelf at the back of the Vampires and Voodoo Section. In front of the shelf was a table. And on the table was a plastic voodoo doll with several pins stuck in its body.

"Now then," said the father. "The voodoo doll. Pick it up and see what happens."

Billy picked up the doll and stared at it expectantly. Nothing happened.

Father Merrin frowned. "Wait now. It's been a while since I played with this one. Ah yes, now I remember. You have to pull out one of the pins. That breaks an electronic circuit in the room, somewhere, but don't ask me to explain it exactly, I'm not very good with technical things." He nodded at Billy. "Well, go on, Billy. Do it."

Billy looked around nervously, as if wondering what would happen next, and then did as the priest had suggested. He pulled one of the long needles out of the plastic voodoo doll.

Immediately, a length of rug proceeded to remove itself from the floor, after which two of the floorboards slowly lifted up on hinges. Outside the window there was a flash of lightning and a clap of thunder and the electric lights on the ceiling flickered and then dimmed. A heavy kind of smoke started to billow from the open floorboards and creep across the room like something almost alive.

"Dry ice," murmured the father. "Atmospheric, don't you think?"

"That's the word Mr. Rapscallion used," said Billy. "'Atmosphere.'"

"Shh," said Father Merrin. "This is the best bit now."

Slowly, a man who seemed to have been buried under the floorboards sat up stiffly, as if coming to life after a very long time. His head was bald and his ears and nose were as pointed as the goblin's in a fairy tale. His eyebrows were joined in the middle like a horrible hairy handshake. His teeth were sharp, like a fierce animal's. And his fingernails were longer than the keys on an old piano and every bit as yellow. He wore a coat buttoned high up on the neck so that the strange-looking creature hardly seemed to have a neck at all.

Billy gasped and took several steps back onto the priest's big feet.

"Yikes," he said. "What is that?"

"It's all right, Billy. It's only a vampire. Well, a dummy that's supposed to be a vampire." Father Merrin bent forward and patted the dummy on its bald head. "See? But wait. We're not quite finished."

For a moment the lights went completely out, and when they came on again, the creature had disappeared and the floorboards and the rug had returned to their original positions.

"Wow," said Billy.

Father Merrin pointed at the doorway. "Watch over there."

Even as he spoke, Billy saw what looked to all the world like the creature's disembodied black shadow creeping out of the room. Billy ran to the door and watched the shadow slide as stealthy as a cat along the wall to the top of the curved staircase, where, finally, it disappeared.

"Wow," he said again, thoroughly impressed. "That was amazing. It really looked like that creature's shadow creeping out of the room all on its own."

"Didn't it?" said Father Merrin, happily. "Didn't it just?"

"Was that really supposed to be a vampire?" asked Billy.

"Yes. The shadow part is some kind of projection from a hidden camera. And the dummy is just a dummy. He looks hideous but that little bald fellow's always been one of my favorites in this bookshop."

"You mean you come here a lot?" asked Billy.

"Oh yes. Often enough to know that Mr. Rapscallion will be cross with me if I give any more of his shop's secrets away. I've said enough. But I didn't want you to be too scared, Billy. You see, there aren't many children who come into this bookshop. At least not anymore. Sometimes I forget that Mr. Rapscallion actually designed this shop for children."

"He did?"

"Yes. Years ago, this shop used to be full of children. Full of them. This was one of the most successful shops in Hitchcock. But as you can see, it's only grown-up children like me who come here now."

"This place is fantastic," said Billy. "Why don't the other kids come here?"

"I don't know."

"Maybe they got scared off," said Billy.

"I'm afraid it might have more to do with the fact that children these days don't seem to be in the least bit interested in books," said Father Merrin. "That includes Mr. Rapscallion's estranged daughter."

"How old is she?"

"Twelve, I think."

"Estranged, you say? That means they don't like each other, doesn't it?"

"I wouldn't like to say. Either way, she doesn't live with him. She lives with her mother, who's not much interested in books either."

"But I love books," insisted Billy. He looked up just in time to see some fantastic-looking rats scurrying across the ceiling, upside down. "I can't honestly imagine a life without books."

"Unfortunately, the majority of kids these days don't seem to share your opinion," said a voice.

Billy looked around to see Mr. Rapscallion standing in the door of the Vampires and Voodoo Section. He was looking tired and irritated. Just like before.

"They're too busy with their nerdy electronic games and their stupid televisions and their annoying cell phones and their geeky computers to think of reading books," said Mr. Rapscallion. "It makes you wonder why people even bother to teach reading in schools." Mr. Rapscallion sighed loudly. "It makes me worry for the future of the human race. Always supposing that I do actually care about something like that."

"Oh, come now, Mr. Rapscallion," said Father Merrin. "You don't mean that."

"Don't I?" Mr. Rapscallion grunted. "Don't I?"

"No," insisted Father Merrin. "I don't think you do."

"Maybe you're right." Mr. Rapscallion frowned. "Maybe."

"I know I'm right." He pointed at Billy. "This is young Billy Shivers."

Mr. Rapscallion grunted.

"How do you do, sir?" said Billy.

"You'll forgive me for being nosy, I hope," said Mr. Rapscallion. "But, this being a shop 'n' all, I have to ask. Is either of you two colorful characters actually planning to buy a book? Because otherwise we're closing up for the night."

Father Merrin handed Mr. Rapscallion the book he had been reading. It was titled *Résumé for a Vampire.*

"This one looks good," he said. "What do you think?"

Mr. Rapscallion looked at it and shrugged. "Could be." He looked at Billy. "What about you, sonny? Find anything you want to read?"

"Oh, there were plenty of books I wanted to read. And while I was in the Red Room, I actually read several chapters of a book before the candles started to go out, and I got scared." Billy looked awkward. "But to be honest, the plain fact of the matter is that I don't have any money."

"No money." Mr. Rapscallion sighed.

"No. None at all. I'm terribly sorry."

"Great," said Mr. Rapscallion. "Just what we need to have in a bookshop that's almost on its knees. A customer who doesn't have any money."

"Usually I go to the Hitchcock Public Library," explained Billy.

"Libraries." Mr. Rapscallion stared at Billy and pulled a face. "Libraries are full of people like you who borrow books instead of buying them. Cheapskates who seem to think that books just grow on trees. I ask you, what kind of world would we have if everyone just borrowed stuff? Just imagine if people borrowed cars or bicycles or chicken dinners or jewelry or cellular telephones instead of buying them. The world would be broke. That's the kind of world we'd have. But for some reason, people think it's okay to borrow a book. And then we wonder why booksellers are going bankrupt." He shook his head. "I hate libraries."

Father Merrin and Billy followed Mr. Rapscallion down the curved wooden staircase to the big brass cash register near the entrance.

"But what about poor people?" asked Billy.

"You're talking to poor people," said Mr. Rapscallion.

"Please don't make the mistake of thinking there's any money selling books, kid. Because there isn't. I'm the living proof of that." He smiled a slow, sly smile. "Well, almost living, anyway. You couldn't really call this a life."

"I might not have any money," said Billy. "Not a cent. But for what it's worth, I love your bookshop, Mr. Rapscallion. In fact, I think it's probably the most fantastic, the most wonderful, the best bookshop I've ever seen."

"Don't tell me, sonny," said Mr. Rapscallion. "Tell your friends."

CHAPTER 5

REXFORD RAPSCALLION SPRINGS SOME MORE SURPRISES

The next day Billy went back to the Haunted House of Books on Hitchcock High Street. And the day after that. And then the day after that. He turned up at opening time. And he was usually there until the shop closed. He read a lot of books about ghosts and ghouls. And quite a few about vampires and voodoo.

Mr. Rapscallion didn't seem to mind that Billy didn't buy a book. Or at least he didn't say so. Mr. Rapscallion wasn't exactly friendly to Billy. Then again, he didn't tell him to go away either. After a week or so, Mr. Rapscallion seemed to accept Billy being there, because one morning he nodded his head at the boy and mumbled something that sounded a little bit like a greeting. A bit like "Hello."

Later on that same morning, when Mr. Rapscallion was

going around the shop with a trolley, restocking the dusty bookshelves, he came across Billy in the Haunted Castles Section and forced a smile onto his whiskered face. And then he sort of grunted in Billy's direction.

"How are you today, Mr. Rapscallion?" Billy asked politely.

Mr. Rapscallion nodded and then shrugged and then sighed a bit and then inclined his head a little and then made a difficult face. "I dunno," he said. "Not too bad, I guess. I mean, I've had better, I guess. Like any other morning, you know? What can I tell you, kid? Life goes on, huh?"

"Yes," said Billy. "It does."

Mr. Rapscallion looked pained. "You know, you worry me, kid, do you know that? I mean, what are you doing in here? Every day. All day. Shouldn't you be in school right now?"

"It's the summer vacation," explained Billy. "The Hitchcock schools are off for three months. Until Labor Day."

"Three months?" Mr. Rapscallion grunted. "I didn't know that."

"Doesn't your daughter go to school?"

"Who told you I had a daughter?"

"Father Merrin. What's her name?"

"Altaira," said Mr. Rapscallion. "We got it from an old movie called *Forbidden Planet.* It means 'star.'"

"That's a lovely name," observed Billy.

Mr. Rapscallion sneered. "She hates it. Almost as much as she hates me. She calls herself something else just to bug me." He shrugged, sheepishly. "She and I don't exactly see eye to eye on a lot of things."

"So what does she call herself now?"

"None of your business." The bookseller shook his head.

"What I wouldn't give to be in school again. I can't even remember that far back. You know something? It's so far back I couldn't even tell you if I enjoyed school or not. I guess I must have, though, with a three-month vacation in the summer. What's not to enjoy about that?"

"Three months is too long for me," said Billy. "It's hard knowing what to do with yourself for that length of time."

"Well, if you're not at school, shouldn't you be outside in the fresh air?" asked Mr. Rapscallion. "Doing what other kids do during the summer vacation. Going to summer camp. Spraying tags on walls. Playing sports. Stealing cars. Things like that?" His eyes narrowed. "I mean, look at you. Painfully thin, pigeon-chested, pale-faced, undernourished, shadows under your eyes. Being in here all day can't be good for you. Frankly, you look like crap. You could use a little sun, kid."

"I'm afraid there's no money to spare in our home for things like summer camp," admitted Billy. He'd decided to ignore the remark about stealing things. Billy had never stolen anything in his life. "I have to make the best of things. Besides, I'm still recovering from a car accident."

"Is that a fact?"

"Yes it is." And Billy told Mr. Rapscallion all about his car accident. "Now I know what it feels like to be a thin layer of strawberry jam between two thick slices of bread," he joked.

"I'm sorry to hear that," said Mr. Rapscallion.

"Forget about it. I'm almost over it. Honest. And your shop has really cheered me up."

"That's good," said Mr. Rapscallion. "Nice to know that there's at least one kid who likes books in this miserable town."

At that very moment, the grandfather clock in the entrance

hall began to strike the hour and, from somewhere else in the house, the sound of a church organ was heard. It was a stirring sound but it was also a creepy one. "What's that?"

"Sounds to me like Bach's Toccata and Fugue in D Minor," said Mr. Rapscallion.

"But where's it coming from?"

"The organ music? Where else but the basement, of course."

"I didn't know there was one," admitted Billy. "A basement."

"The arrogance of it," said Mr. Rapscallion. "To think that you could know all the secrets of the Haunted House of Books in just the few days you've been coming here."

Fortunately, he was smiling as he said this and so Billy didn't think he was actually offended.

"And by the way," he said. "Try not to use too many numbers when you're talking to me. I have a thing about numbers. I mean, take my word for it. You wouldn't like to see me start counting."

Billy nodded. "Could we go and see?" he asked. "The organ."

"Why certainly," said Mr. Rapscallion, and led the way.

In the entrance hall, from behind the front sales desk, Mr. Rapscallion collected an enormous candelabra and lit the candles.

"Are those candles that blow out?" asked Billy.

"All candles blow out," said Mr. Rapscallion. "It's only scary when they keep on blowing out for no good reason and you end up thinking that someone or something is doing it deliberately. Right?"

"True enough," said Billy.

Mr. Rapscallion opened an ordinary door that looked like a

broom closet to reveal a set of descending stone steps. Their footsteps echoed as they went down into the basement. As well as the organ music, Billy could hear the sound of water.

"I keep all the antiquarian books down here," said Mr. Rapscallion. "A little bit of damp helps the books to look properly old. We've got books and old manuscripts in our basement that no one has ever read."

"Like what?"

"I dunno. I never read them. Some of the books contain things a lot of people shouldn't be allowed to know about, so I try to make it as difficult as I can for them down here. That way I can be sure that the customers who get as far as the books are really serious about the subject, you know?" He grinned. "I lay on a few extra surprises for them."

"Such as?" asked Billy.

"Now that would be telling, wouldn't it?"

At the bottom of the stairs they appeared to be in an old and forgotten windowless chamber, and in the farthest wall was a heavy wooden door. Still holding the candelabra aloft, Mr. Rapscallion turned a key in the lock and pulled open the creaking door.

Immediately a horrible smell filled the air.

"Ugh," said Billy, holding his nose. "What's that stink?"

"This is the oldest part of the house," explained Mr. Rapscallion. "Down here dates back to eighteen hundred. The town sewers run straight through the building's foundations."

He pointed at what looked like a small canal, which was overrun with rats.

"And the rats certainly don't make it smell any better."

They walked along a stone path at the side of the stinky

canal. The stone walls were covered with wet slime and a sign that read THIS WAY TO THE FORBIDDEN BOOKS ABOUT MAGIC AND SPELLS.

All the time the organ music grew louder.

At the end of the path there was an arched doorway, but just before they turned to go through, something vaguely human and as slimy as the walls came out of the black water of the canal and slapped a fishy-looking arm onto the path in front of Billy. Billy let out a yell as the creature burped loudly several times and made a grab for his ankle.

"Yikes," said Billy, jumping clear of the creature's scaly hand. "Is that one of the surprises?"

The creature grabbed at Billy again. Its eyes were huge and staring and its teeth as sharp as a shark's. Then, still burping loudly, the creature slid back into the water.

Mr. Rapscallion laughed and showed Billy how standing on one of the slabs of stone operated a pneumatic pump that pushed the creature, which was made of rubber, clear of the water and onto the path in front of them.

"Ingenious," said Billy.

"Come on, *Billy,*" said the shopkeeper, hurrying through the arched doorway. "Our resident Phantom only plays three organ pieces before he leaves, *Billy.*"

Billy smiled. This was the first time Mr. Rapscallion had used his name. Until now he had only ever called him "sonny" or "kid," which made Billy feel just a little like a goat. But the fact that Mr. Rapscallion had used his name was almost enough to make Billy believe he might actually have made a new friend.

Billy followed Mr. Rapscallion through the arched doorway

and found himself in a large subterranean library. There were ancient-looking globes, map tables, more candlesticks and tall shelves full of leather-bound books, some of which were as big as a car door. Everything was covered with yards of cobweb. In a huge fireplace an enormous log was burning. But dominating the room was a large church organ and playing it was a figure dressed in old-fashioned evening clothes.

That would have been remarkable enough in Billy's eyes. But there was much more to come.

As soon as Mr. Rapscallion and Billy entered the subterranean library, the figure playing the organ turned around abruptly and stopped playing. The room was not well lit and Billy found it hard to decide if the organist was wearing a mask or a hat. Billy had just decided that it must be a mask when the organist's head caught fire like an enormous candle and, cackling wildly, the figure jumped up and ran straight toward Billy and Mr. Rapscallion. If the bookseller had not been standing right next to him, Billy felt certain he would have turned and fled in terror.

As it was, Billy stepped quickly behind Mr. Rapscallion. The laughing organist sprinted past them, its black evening cape flying in the breeze of its own making, and the flame from its pointed head trailing like the tail of a blazing meteor.

"Yikes," said Billy.

For a moment, the organist paused in the arched doorway, pointed, it seemed, straight at Billy and said, in a loud, bass voice, "Beware, Billy. Beware!"

Then he disappeared around the corner, in a cloud of smoke and gasoline vapor.

Plucking up his courage, Billy chased after him.

He stopped in the doorway, peered carefully around the corner and was horrified to find the organist standing there. A split second later, the still-flaming head dipped down to Billy's level. It was close enough to singe the boy's eyebrows and for his flaring nostrils to detect a strong smell of lighter fluid.

The organist laughed a horrible, loud laugh that seemed to generate more heat and once again spoke to Billy. "Beware, Billy. Beware!"

Billy shrank back and then curled around the corner to shelter in the comparative safety of the other side of the wall.

"Yikes," he said.

"Yikes?" said Mr. Rapscallion. "Is that all you can say, kid? Yikes? Jeez, you can't just say 'yikes' and leave it there. That was one of my most expensive and hopefully frightening installations. Much too frightening I would suggest for as small a word as 'yikes.' 'Yikes' is just pathetic."

"But 'yikes' is what I say when I get scared."

"Yes, but you also said it when the creature from the black canal attempted to grab your ankle." Mr. Rapscallion shook his head. "It's a little disappointing, to say the least. I was expecting an ear-splitting scream of terror. Or that you might be reduced, as they say, to a gibbering wreck. But you're not gibbering. You're not even muttering."

"Perhaps it didn't seem quite as frightening because I was with you, Mr. Rapscallion," said Billy, by way of an apology. "All the same, it was pretty frightening. And impressive."

"All right, but we're certainly going to have to see what we can do about that 'yikes' of yours, Billy," he said ominously. "I'm sorry, but I simply can't have someone in the Haunted House of Books getting away with anything as lame as 'yikes.'

It's not good for my self-esteem. The fact is that now I'm going to have to render you a gibbering wreck before the day is out."

Billy thought he'd better add some more adjectives just to make Mr. Rapscallion feel better.

"No, really, it was horrifying. Terrifying. Ghastly. I'm sure I'll have a nightmare about that one, tonight. When I get to bed. I shouldn't be at all surprised if the sight of that flaming head haunts me forever. It was very frightening when the organist's head caught fire. And when the organist knew my name. By the way, how *did* he know my name? And what should I beware of, exactly? And how did his head catch fire? I mean, that was amazing. And how did you make a machine that could run so fast?"

Mr. Rapscallion grinned. "How did he know your name? Simple. Didn't you hear me say your name twice as I came through the doorway? That's how he knew. And it wasn't a machine you saw just now. That's Gary. Gary's the organist at St. Mary's Church, in Hitchcock. Father Merrin's church. He comes here once a week to wear that costume, play the organ and generally scare the heck out of anyone who's dumb enough to come down here."

"But the head?" said Billy. "Doesn't it hurt to set your head on fire?"

"Not if you're wearing a flame-retardant hood underneath a mask soaked with a little lighter fluid," explained Mr. Rapscallion. "That's *one* of the reasons Gary runs away from the organ while his head is on fire. If he runs fast enough, the wind puts the flames out. Eventually. Most of the time. Although twice he has had to dive into the canal to make sure."

"Ouch," said Billy.

"He's learned the hard way not to use too much lighter fluid. Gary used to have a full head of hair. Now he tends to keep it short. For obvious reasons."

Billy walked around the subterranean library, full of admiration for the effort Mr. Rapscallion had made to create his rather special bookshop.

"This is a wonderful place," he said. "Wonderful. I think it must be the best bookshop in all the world."

"Well, thank you, Billy. But like I said before, don't tell me, tell your friends."

"I don't really have any friends," said Billy. "There's you, of course. Would you mind it if I thought of you as my friend?"

"Next question," said Mr. Rapscallion.

"How did you get started?" Billy asked him. "What gave you the idea?"

"You really want to hear about that?"

"Of course."

"Well then, you'd better come over to the fireplace and sit yourself down."

Beside the fire they drew up two chairs as big as wooden thrones and sat down.

"Are you sitting comfortably?" Mr. Rapscallion asked Billy.

"Yes sir."

"Then I'll begin."

CHAPTER 6

A STORY BY THE FIRE

(Note: This chapter should be read out loud to your little brother or your small sister, immediately before bedtime.)

"This is a story that requires a pipe," said Mr. Rapscallion. "Perhaps two pipes." From the pocket of his coat he took out a strangely curving white pipe made of English clay and lit it with a taper from the fire.

"Years ago, when I was younger," he said, "I had a mind—well, half a mind, anyway—to see something of the world. The mountains. The seas. The jungles. And the deserts. I traveled far and wide in search of, what exactly? I don't know for sure. Perhaps an answer to the question of what I was going to do with my young life. You'll ask yourself a question like that one day. Anyway, when you're young you always make the mistake of believing that you have to go somewhere else to find yourself, when the plain and boring fact of the matter is that you need only stay at home and just take a look inside your own head."

"I don't understand," said Billy.

"One day you will," said Mr. Rapscallion. "Anyway, one of these travels in search of how I was going to live my life took me to a great, high, northern wilderness of endless, endless forest, high mountains and deep, deep snow. Somewhere along the way, I forget how exactly, I took up with *three* companions. They were all experienced, hairy woodsmen who knew how to survive in that desolate place. How to build a fire. How to put up a tent. How to fish and hunt. How to stay alive. How to avoid losing your mind in that empty wilderness. Which is easily done, let me tell you.

"I can still remember their names. These men were not made for towns or cities. Even their names had a strange touch of the wilderness about them. There was Jim Screech. Tom Lurker. And Bill Tremor. But of the three, Old Screech was the one who truly belonged to the forest. He didn't wash very much and was a terrifying sort of character, just to look at. Old Screech had never even slept in a bed. Always slept under the stars. Truly the wilderness was in his blood.

"For several days we walked north into the big forest, fishing in the river and hunting small game. We saw no other men. There were no other men. Not for hundreds of miles. All you could hear was the sound of the river, the occasional bird and the cold wind in the trees. And not just any wind. This was a wind that played tricks on a man's mind. A wind that sometimes, you fancied, could do more than just moan and groan. It seemed like a wind that might even speak to you. Whisper your fortune. Call your name. Tell you a story. Well, one night it did just that. Almost, anyway.

"We'd had a good day's fishing and were sitting around the blazing campfire, much as you and I are now. Smoking pipes.

Exchanging stories. Ghost stories. I always loved a ghost story. We each agreed to tell a story. And having done so, we'd all vote on who'd told the scariest one, and the winner would be excused from any camp duties the next day. I went first. Then Tom Lurker. Then Bill Tremor.

"Well, Bill Tremor told us a story that left us frozen with fear. Two of us, at least. And it's odd, but to this day I can't remember anything about it. Not one thing. And yet I agreed with Lurker that it was quite simply the most unnerving story we'd ever heard. Maybe it was what happened afterward that drove it from our minds. I don't think it had scared Screech very much. Because even while we were complimenting Tremor on scaring us half to death, Old Screech was gazing up at the stars like a timber wolf and shaking his head slowly. Then he stood up and raised one of his hairy ears into the air and seemed to be listening to something.

" 'Listen,' said Screech. 'Do you hear that?'

" 'What is it?' we asked Screech, looking around nervously. There was no moon. Beyond the flickering light of the fire there was only darkness and yet more darkness. 'What can you hear? A bear, perhaps?' (The bears in that part of the world are enormous. As big as a truck at the shoulder with teeth as long as a man's foot and claws like razors.)

"Screech kept listening for a moment, his dark, thin, weather-beaten face rigid with fear. Then he shook his head. 'Don't you fellows hear it?' he said. 'The wind. The wind is speaking to us. The wind was listening to your stories. But now the wind thinks it can do better. The wind wants to tell us a story, too.'

"The rest of us listened carefully and then looked at each

other, baffled. While we could hear the wind stirring the tops of the trees and see it fanning the flames of our campfire, it didn't seem to us that the wind was saying anything quite so specific as that.

"'Oh, come on, Screech,' said Tremor. 'If you want to tell us a story, then just go ahead and do it. But don't treat us like children. The wind wants to tell us a story. Really.' And he laughed. 'You must take us for the most absolute fools. It's clear to me that this is just a stunt to help you win the bet.'

"Screech kept on listening and then shook his head slowly, as if he'd just been told something important. 'You ask me, it would be extremely rude of us to refuse an offer like that,' he said gravely. 'It's not everyone the great north wind honors with a story. You wouldn't want to offend the wind, would you?'

"'Stop fooling around, Screech,' said Lurker. 'Can't you see we're spooked enough as it is without you trying to spook us some more?' He shivered and moved closer to the fire. 'I for one have had enough creepy stories for tonight.'

"Screech spat into the fire and looked at me. 'How about you, Rapscallion?' he asked me. '*Two* against the wind's story, and *two* in favor. It's your decision, sonny. The casting vote, so to speak. Only you'd better choose wisely.'

"'Wait a minute,' said Bill Tremor. 'Who are the *two* in favor? I only count *four* of us around this campfire.'

"'The wind is with us,' said Screech. 'Whether you like it or not.'

"And strange to say, at that very moment the wind seemed to gust and blow some smoke from the fire into our faces, as if to confirm what Screech had said. Screech kept on looking at me. 'Well? What do you say? Do we hear the wind's story or not?'

"'This is ridiculous,' insisted Tremor. 'He's just trying to frighten us. Can't you see it? In a minute he's going to laugh in your face that you were so easily fooled, sonny.'

"Smiling, I nodded at Tremor. He just had to be right: Screech was playing a practical joke on the rest of us. 'Come on, Screech,' I said. 'This is a hoax, right? The wind doesn't tell stories around a campfire.'

"'Is that your final word?' Screech's voice sounded ominous and full of foreboding.

"'Yes,' I said, and then bit my lip. It was just a feeling but almost immediately I regretted my decision.

"Screech was silent for a moment and, shaking his head, sat down. He looked very sad. 'The wind has spoken,' he said. 'The wind says we will have something more terrible than the story the wind was going to tell us. We will have the real thing.'

"'What do you mean?' asked Lurker.

"'Now we will have a visit from the spirit of the wilderness itself,' said Screech.

"He would say no more after this," Mr. Rapscallion told Billy. "And with all our former humor gone, we soon retired to our tents. Lurker to share with Screech. And me to share with Tremor. Despite our stories, I slept heavily. But it was a strange, dream-filled sleep that did not leave me feeling refreshed, and sometime before dawn, I awoke with the strong sensation that something was not right. My heart was beating wildly, and although it was cold, I was covered with sweat. In the pitch dark I heard Tremor stir beside me and sit up in his sleeping bag. And, certain that I had missed something in my sleep that might have explained the strange feeling of foreboding I had, I put my hand out and caught Tremor's hairy arm and asked him what it was that had disturbed him.

"'I heard someone calling my name,' he said. 'It was not Screech and it was not Lurker, I'm certain of it. The voice was not that of a man. And it wasn't the voice of a woman. What's more, it seemed to drift in here, as if from a very great distance. You'll think me crazy, Rapscallion, but I'm certain it was the wind, speaking to me.'

"'Nonsense,' I said. 'You were dreaming, obviously. Not that I'm in the least bit surprised after that silly story Screech told us.' I took hold of the man's hand and squeezed it. 'He's got us well and truly spooked. I just had the most peculiar dream myself. I was convinced that someone or some*thing* had come into this tent with us. It was quite real. My heart is still beating wildly.' I tried to laugh it off but my laughter had a very hollow tone, for there was no humor in it, only fear.

"'Perhaps it wasn't a dream at all,' said Tremor. 'Perhaps it was real.'

"And then we heard it. Quite distinctly. It was the sound of Tremor's name carried floating on the wind from a great long distance away, exactly as my now-trembling friend had described. A high-pitched whine of a voice that was neither a man's nor a woman's. Indeed, Tremor's own surname was the only thing human about it.

"'Trem-or,' it said. 'Trem-or.'

"'There,' he said. 'Do you hear it?'

"'Yes, I heard it.'

"And in the dark his strong, hairy hand gripped mine more tightly, as if he was suddenly very afraid. He had a heck of a grip, it seemed to me, but then fear makes a man appear stronger than he is, sometimes.

" 'Yes,' I told him again. 'I hear it. The voice seems to be coming from down by the river. Look here, it must be Screech, messing about. Trying to frighten us.'

" 'You're right,' said Tremor. There was a note of anger in his voice. 'Where's the flashlight? I'm going out there to speak to him. And if I find it is him fooling about, then I'm going to punch him on the nose. It's one thing to scare a man around the campfire. It's quite another to scare him half out of his wits while he's asleep. Now where did I leave the flashlight? Yes, it must be in my backpack. By the flap of the tent.'

"In the dark I heard Tremor get out of his sleeping bag and crawl toward the tent flap and the backpack. I heard him fumbling crossly for the flashlight. And it was then that I realized, to my mounting horror, what seemed to me at once a thing impossible: that I was still holding Bill Tremor's hairy hand in my own. And yet how could I be holding the hand of a man who even now was six or seven feet away, on the other side of the tent, fumbling inside his backpack? Whose bony, cold, half-human hand had I been holding for several minutes? Whose was the hairy hand that still held my own?

" 'Don't switch on that flashlight!' I yelled. 'Don't for pity's sake turn it on.'

" 'What are you talking about?' Tremor said angrily. 'I'm certainly not going out there without a flashlight. It's pitch-dark. There could be anything waiting for me in the forest. Some horrible creature. A monster of the night. A beast of the wilderness.'

"It was then that I noticed the smell. Something strong

and hardly human. The hand holding mine tightened so that I could feel the fingernails digging into my skin and flesh. Only these weren't fingernails. These were claws, surely. And yet the hand, strong as it was, had fingers. Long, thin, bony fingers.

"'Whatever it is,' I told Tremor, 'it's not out there. It's in here. It's in the tent and it has me by the hand. And if you switch on that flashlight, I know that I will see it and die of fright, do you hear?' All the time I heard my voice rising. 'Don't do it, Tremor. Please.'

"'What are you talking about?' demanded Tremor. He switched on the flashlight and pointed it my way and I turned to face the creature that was still sitting next to me and I heard myself . . . S-C-R-E-E-E-A-A-M-M!"

Mr. Rapscallion let out a terrible, animal-like scream. And the surprise of this sudden and unexpected end to Mr. Rapscallion's terrifying tale almost made Billy Shivers jump out of his skin. As it was, he jumped several feet out of the big wooden chair in front of the fire and landed on top of a tall pile of heavy leather books. At the very same instant he heard himself *S-C-R-E-E-A-M!* even more loudly than Mr. Rapscallion had done, although such a thing seemed hardly possible. And for several seconds afterward, the boy was the gibbering wreck Mr. Rapscallion had promised Billy he would become.

Mr. Rapscallion laughed and laughed as, piecing together his shredded nerves, and now only muttering with fright instead of gibbering, Billy climbed down off the tall pile of books.

"Well, that's more like it," observed Mr. Rapscallion. "That sounds a lot better than 'yikes,' let me tell you."

He started to laugh some more. It has been mentioned that

Mr. Rapscallion's laugh was no ordinary laugh, and it was clear to Billy that Mr. Rapscallion liked to laugh, and laugh a lot. As usual his laughter arrived like a clap of thunder and then kept on going long after most other people would have stopped. At this point it became something almost mechanical, like something battery-operated or one of the spring-loaded "surprises" that were in every room of the Haunted House of Books. And still the laughter persisted, like an echo.

Panting loudly, Billy Shivers sat down heavily on the stone floor and, pressing his hand against his chest, started to laugh himself. First he laughed with relief that the thing holding Mr. Rapscallion's hand was now gone from his vivid imagination; and then he laughed as he realized that he had been had.

"That was fantastic," said Billy, shaking his head. "Fantastic. I haven't had a fright like that, well, since the car accident."

"Good for you, Billy," said Mr. Rapscallion.

"But look," said Billy, "you still haven't answered my question: How did you start the Haunted House of Books?"

"That's really very, very simple," said Mr. Rapscallion. "And not much of a story at all. Not like the story you just heard, anyway. You see, when I was a boy, not much older than you, I loved *four* things. I loved doing magic tricks, I loved practical jokes, I loved old horror movies and I loved reading. And I couldn't make up my mind which of these *four* things I loved more, and to which of those four activities I wanted to devote my life when I was a grown-up. So I decided to do them all, and to combine professional magic and practical jokes with my enjoyment of books and horror movies. Hence this shop."

Mr. Rapscallion sighed and, for a moment, he continued to look happy.

"The definition of true happiness, Billy," he said, "is making your living from your hobby. It's getting paid for what you would do for nothing. Try to remember that."

CHAPTER 7

MR. HUGH CRANE OFFERS TO BUY THE SHOP

With Billy turning up at the Haunted House of Books every day, it wasn't long before he started to recognize the regular customers. Some of these were friendlier than others. Some weren't in the least bit friendly at all. But then, as Mr. Rapscallion had to remind Billy, it was a bookshop, and not a social club.

There was Father Merrin, of course.

And the lady with the black hair and the green leather coat who Billy now knew was called Miss Danvers. Weird.

There was Dr. Saki. Quite friendly.

There was Mr. Stoker. Friendly but a bit creepy.

There was Mr. Quiller-Couch. Not friendly.

There was Mr. Pu Sung Ling. Not friendly.

There was Miss Maupassant. Not friendly. Weird, too.

There was Mr. Montague James. Friendly. But weird.

And there was Hugh Crane. Who was not at all friendly.

Hugh Crane was a local lawyer and tycoon who wanted to buy the Haunted House of Books. Despite his interest in the shop, Crane was the only person who came in who wasn't in the least bit interested in books. In fact, Crane hated books. He hated books because Crane knew that it's easier to exploit and make money out of people who are ignorant. And of course no one who reads books—even books about ghosts and ghouls—can ever remain entirely ignorant.

The only things Crane ever read were his bank statement, law reports and the price of stocks and shares in the newspaper he owned, *The Hitchcock High Street Journal*. He wanted to buy the bookshop so that he could knock it down and build a different kind of shop. A shop to sell very expensive shampoo. Billy thought it odd that Mr. Crane wanted to sell shampoo, because he was as bald as an ostrich egg.

Once a week Mr. Crane would come into the shop with a large envelope full of cash and try to tempt Mr. Rapscallion into accepting his offer.

Mr. Rapscallion had once borrowed some money from Hugh Crane, to keep the shop going, but now he was unable to repay the loan. Mr. Crane wasn't pressing for the return of his money. Not yet. But it did mean that Mr. Rapscallion had to listen when, in order to get his greedy hands on the shop, Crane offered to wipe out the debt and give Mr. Rapscallion even more money.

Usually Mr. Rapscallion knew when Crane was coming and went into one of the rooms in the shop on purpose so that the tycoon would have to look for him. He always left a note on the counter to say in which of the many rooms he could probably be found. That way Mr. Rapscallion could be sure that Crane would encounter at least one of the shop's many surprises.

One day when this happened, Billy was with Mr. Rapscallion, in Monsters and Mad Scientists. This room was full of books like *Frankenstein, Dr. Jekyll and Mr. Hyde* and *Wagner the Werewolf.* Billy liked these books, especially *Dr. Jekyll.* The illustrated version seemed really fantastic. He also liked this room because there was a large table, and lying on it, underneath a sheet, was the figure of an enormous man, or, to be more accurate, a monster; and beside the monster stood a mad scientist in a white smock. The monster and the scientist looked all too real, as if at any moment both of them might come to life. And, of course, sometimes, they did just that.

"Are you up there, Mr. Rapscallion?" called Mr. Crane, coming halfway up the curved wooden stairs. "It's me. Your business partner. Hugh Crane."

"Yes, I'm here," Mr. Rapscallion shouted.

"Could you come down here, please?" shouted Crane. "I want to speak to you."

"I'm a little busy right now," Mr. Rapscallion shouted back to the tycoon. "Come along to Monsters and Mad Scientists."

"Oh, very well," Crane shouted crossly.

Mr. Rapscallion could hardly contain his mischievous excitement at what was about to happen. He grinned at Billy. "Wait until he gets a load of what's in this room," he said, chuckling happily.

Crane peered cautiously around the door, the lenses in his blue-tinted glasses shining like two tiny aquariums that were home to the two snakes that were his calculating eyes.

Crane had suffered several unpleasant surprises before in the Haunted House of Books and he was being careful not to encounter another. If there was one thing Crane hated more than books, it was surprises. Especially the kind of surprises that were to be found at the Haunted House of Books.

"Ah, Mr. Rapscallion, there you are." He smiled a wooden sort of smile. "Is this room safe? For me to come in?"

"Safe? Yes, it's safe," said Mr. Rapscallion. "Come ahead, sir. Come ahead. Only please, no large numbers. You know what I'm like with large numbers."

Crane stepped into Monsters and Mad Scientists and looked around nervously. "So here you are," he said, trying to sound pleasant.

"Yes, here I am." Mr. Rapscallion pointed at Billy. "Mr. Crane, this is my young friend, Billy Shivers."

Crane grunted. If there was one thing he disliked more than books and surprises, it was boys. Girls were bad enough, but boys did things he didn't like at all. They ran around in the street and played with balls, and shouted at each other, and didn't stand up straight; they laughed at stupid jokes and they kept their hands in their pockets, and they ate potato chips in shops, and they didn't blow their noses, and they mumbled when they were spoken to. But above all Crane hated boys because they disliked washing their hair. No boy likes washing his hair any more than he likes it being washed by his mother, and any boy worth his salt will usually find ways to avoid having his hair washed more than once a month. If at all. As a man who had made millions of dollars selling shampoo, Crane regarded any boy as nothing less than an alien species of life because boys dislike washing their hair.

"What can I do for you, Mr. Crane?" asked Mr. Rapscallion. "How about a book? This book, for instance. *The Lair of the White Worm,* by Bram Stoker. You might enjoy that."

"I'm not interested in worms," said Crane. "Of any color. Unless they're bookworms, of course. The quicker all these silly books are consumed by worms the better, in my opinion. It's a hard world we live in, Mr. Rapscallion. And books have no place in it."

Mr. Rapscallion nodded patiently. He'd heard all of this before.

"Besides," added Crane, "you know what you can do *for me,* Mr. Rapscallion. You can accept my very generous offer for this shop." He opened the envelope of cash and, bringing the wad of money up to Mr. Rapscallion's nose, proceeded to riffle the ends of the banknotes like someone about to deal from a pack of playing cards. "Do you smell that, Mr. Rapscallion? Do you smell that? It's hard cash, sir. Money. A generous cash offer considering the amount of money you already owe me."

"And please don't mention what that is," said Mr. Rapscallion.

"An offer that's more than enough for you to put an end to this madness and retire from business, sir. Frankly, sir, you are not cut out for business. Not cut out for it at all. Which is why this place is on its knees, sir."

"As you say, it's a very generous offer, Mr. Crane," said Mr. Rapscallion. "But this place is my living. It's my life. I wouldn't know what to do with myself if I didn't come here every day."

"Me neither," mumbled Billy.

"What's that you say, boy?" demanded Crane. "Stop mumbling. I can't tolerate a boy who mumbles."

"I said, me neither," said Billy.

"Me neither, what?"

"I mean I wouldn't know what to do with myself either," said Billy. "If I didn't come here every day."

"Of course you wouldn't," Crane said crossly. "You wouldn't know because you have no common sense. Because you're a dreamer, boy. All boys are silly dreamers. I can't tolerate a dreamer. Give me a man who has common sense. And I'll show you a man with a job, a mortgage, a car and a future. In short, I'll show you a man I can own."

"The answer is still no," said Mr. Rapscallion. "No, no, no."

"Then you're a fool, sir," said Crane. "You're a fool. All the same, I won't give up, sir. I won't give up. I'll be back. And one day you'll take my offer, sir. I can guarantee it. You'll have to accept my offer if only to repay the money you already owe me. You know it. And I know it. I always get what I want in business. Always. Not for nothing am I called Crane the Pain. One day this place will be mine, do you hear? Mine. MINE!"

Like any other tycoon, Hugh Crane was very fond of the sound of his voice. And listening to his own opinions had made him forget where he was. He started to walk around Monsters and Mad Scientists, oblivious to the possibility that a stray footstep might activate a hidden spring, or electronic sensor, and set something very monstrous in motion. And this is exactly what happened.

One moment everything was normal, and the next moment there was an enormous clap of thunder—frightening enough for anyone not expecting it. Then a bolt of lightning lit up the room and several electrical machines filled with a strange sparking blue light that seemed to transmit a deafening current into the body of the monster on the table. The monster's enormous hand lifted, at which point the mad scientist lurched toward it and began to shout hysterically.

"It's alive," he raved. "It's alive, it's alive, it's alive!!!"

Mr. Crane paled and took several steps back as the lights dimmed and the sheet covering the monster fell away onto the floor as it sat up on the table. As monsters went, this one was top-shelf; green, with a sort of crack in its square skull, and hooded eyes, the monster was only vaguely human. Frankly, this monster strongly resembled a *thing*. The monster growled unpleasantly, like a bad-tempered dog, and pointed straight at Hugh Crane.

"IT'S ALIVE!" screamed the scientist.

"Wow," said Billy. "Awesome."

Poor Mr. Crane had seen enough. He let out a howl that could have come whooping out of the monkey house in a zoo. The next second he turned and ran out of the room and down the curved staircase. Halfway down he slipped and descended the rest of the stairs on his behind, like someone sledding down a bumpy hill who has forgotten to bring a sled.

Mr. Rapscallion and Billy followed him out onto the gallery above the stairs just to see that he was all right.

At the bottom Hugh Crane picked himself up and, seeing Mr. Rapscallion laughing, shook his fist at him furiously. "I thought you said the room was safe, you madman," he yelled, crossly.

"The room *is* safe," said Mr. Rapscallion. "I didn't say it wasn't frightening."

He carried on laughing and chuckling and chortling and giggling for at least fifteen minutes after Hugh Crane had raced out of the door of the Haunted House of Books.

Finally Mr. Rapscallion sat down on the stairs, and when he had finished laughing, he let out a breath and sighed.

"Crane's right, though. One day this place probably will be his. I'll have no alternative but to sell. I already owe him money. And I just don't make enough money to keep the shop going, Billy. I have to pay the electricity bill, the telephone bill, the gas bill, insurance and taxes. I can't even afford to employ someone to help out around here. A book clerk. Every time I see that bundle of cash in Crane's hand and get the smell of money in my nostrils, I think that maybe he's talking sense. That maybe I should sell."

"No," said Billy. "You can't sell. I love this place."

"It's unfortunate that more people don't seem to agree with you," said Mr. Rapscallion. "But the figures don't lie. There just aren't enough people buying books to make this place break even. Let alone make a profit."

"But what about kids? Kids would love this place."

"Tell that to my daughter. Altaira hates this shop. Hates books. Not just books about ghosts and horror. I mean she hates *all* books. The only reading she does is when her dumb little friends text her with one of those messages that look like they were spelled by a moron from another planet."

"There are lots of other kids," said Billy. "Father Merrin said you started this place for kids. Where are they?"

"They used to come. But not anymore. Tastes change, I guess."

"Maybe you have to try to get them back in here. Have you tried?"

"Have I tried? Have I tried? Only all the time, Billy."

"What about Halloween? I saw your poster in the public

library. It's what persuaded me to come and check this place out. How did that go?"

"Halloween?" Mr. Rapscallion let out a sigh. "Last Halloween was the worst. That was nothing short of disastrous. Let me tell you what happened here last Halloween."

CHAPTER 8

HALLOWEEN

“Halloween used to be our best time of year to sell books,” Mr. Rapscallion told Billy. “It was like the Christmas holidays for a toy shop. Or Valentine’s Day for a florist’s. And each year I’d make a special effort to devise a new section in the bookshop and a new surprise to go in it.

“I’ve always loved Egyptology. And although I’ve never been there, Egypt’s a country to which I would dearly love to go. This year I decided I was going to do the next best thing and open a room of books dedicated to the Curse of the Pharaohs. Egyptian mummies coming back to life, living burials, flesh-eating scarabs and that kind of thing.

“So, I had a burial chamber built with golden bookshelves, a large stone idol of the Egyptian god Anubis—he’s the one with the head of a jackal, the Egyptian god of death—and, on its end, an open sarcophagus with a life-size mummy standing inside. It looked pretty good, if I do say so myself. The mummy was properly ancient and sinister. As if it really was an ancient Egyptian priest who had been buried alive for, well . . . many years. A man who had been wrapped in filthy gray bandages that were as old as the pyramids themselves.

"Of course, the best part was when the mummy came back to life. All you had to do was touch and read aloud the inscription written on the forbidden casket, activating the sound sensor and the touch sensor. This was in hieroglyphs, of course, but there was an English translation underneath for those who don't know ancient Egyptian. It read: DEATH. ETERNAL AND EVERLASTING PUNISHMENT FOR ANYONE WHO DARES TO OPEN THIS CASKET.

"The sensors would pass an electrical signal to the sarcophagus and, oh so silently, the mummy would start to reanimate. This would happen very slowly, too—the idea being that you might not even notice. That you might be too interested in the book you were reading to be paying attention to anything happening quietly behind you.

"First, the eyes of the mummy would open just a crack, like something that really had been sleeping for thousands of years. Then they would open just a little more and glitter with supernatural life. After a few more seconds, the bony, half-decayed hands, crossed over the mummy's chest, would shift underneath the dusty old bandages that wrapped him, and then drop slowly to his sides. Finally the horrible head would straighten on the mummy's shoulders and the thing would take a step out of the sarcophagus and then reach out and touch whatever was standing next to it. And, hopefully, give that person one heck of a fright.

"Believe me, Billy, when I tell you that it was impossible to see the poor creature and not think it stranger than Dracula, more fantastic than Frankenstein, more mysterious than the Invisible Man. Was it dead or alive? Was it human or inhuman? The first time I saw it working, I felt the awful creeping, crawling terror that stands your hair on end like sticks of raw spaghetti."

"Oh wow," said Billy. "It sounds awesome, Mr. Rapscallion. Really awesome. I love all that Egyptian stuff. Can we go and see the mummy right now?"

"That room is now locked." Mr. Rapscallion sounded grave.

"Why? Did something terrible happen in there on Halloween?"

Mr. Rapscallion looked pained. "Let me tell the story," he said. "I had put up several posters advertising our Halloween event in the Hitchcock Public Library, and in all the school libraries in and around the town. Several local authors had said they would come and sign copies of their books: Esteban Rex, the author of the Rigor Mortis books; Horace X. Horror, who wrote *Imagined Terrors,* of course; and the bestselling novelist Deacon Wordz, whose Elvis Weird books have been made into several successful and, it's fair to say, extremely scary movies. Victor Gespensterbruch, one of Hitchcock's leading ghost hunters, even agreed to give a short talk on the types of ghosts that there are.

"Everything had been prepared. There was bread and cheese. To drink there was Bull's Blood, which is a variety of Hungarian red wine, for the grown-ups. And for the kids there were Dracula Cocktails—just raspberry juice, but served in silver goblets to make it look more like something with lots of hemoglobin that a vampire would actually drink.

"On the night itself there were plenty of children. More than I've ever seen in here. They were mostly about twelve or thirteen years old. And many of them came from King Herod the Great Middle School, in Northwest Hitchcock."

"I know that school," said Billy. "It's a really tough school. And there are some really tough kids who go there."

"Don't I know it," Mr. Rapscallion said bitterly. "At first everything went well. The authors read and signed their books for customers. And Victor Gespensterbruch gave a fascinating talk. Everyone's heard of a poltergeist—a mischievous ghost. Well, he told us all about the *unterdembettgeist*—which is a recently discovered under-the-bed variety of ghost. We sold some books. Quite a few, actually. Everyone seemed to be having a good time. Some of the kids—especially the boys—were a little boisterous, but you expect that. Boys will be boys. Mostly they were showing off to the girls. The way boys do, right?"

Billy nodded, although he was certain that he had never in his life showed off to anyone, let alone a girl. Why would someone do that?

"I got an idea that things might be going wrong just before eleven o'clock," said Mr. Rapscallion. "Really, most of the children should have been at home by then. But their parents didn't seem to care. Then Deacon Wordz, the author, came and told me that there was trouble with the Curse of the Pharaohs. That something dreadful had happened. So I went along there and . . ." He shook his head. "It was truly horrifying."

"What was it?" Billy gasped. "Don't tell me that one of those boys had actually died of fright?"

Mr. Rapscallion could hardly speak, he was so upset.

"Would you care to see for yourself?" he asked Billy somberly.

"Why, yes, I would," answered Billy. "At least, I think so."

With a grave look, Mr. Rapscallion produced a key and led Billy to one of the upper floors and then along a low, dark corridor to the Curse of the Pharaohs room.

The heavy wooden door was painted gold and looked exactly like the door in an old Egyptian tomb. There were hieroglyphic symbols painted on it and the handle was shaped like an ankh, which is a sort of hieroglyph like a cross with a loop on the top: this symbol means "life."

Billy felt nervous as Mr. Rapscallion unlocked the door and turned the strange handle. He wondered what really terrible thing he was going to see in there. A dead body, perhaps? A large bloodstain on the floor? A severed head?

"I haven't been in here since the night it happened," explained Mr. Rapscallion. "I haven't felt strong enough to remind myself of the horror."

The door opened with a loud creak, as if it might actually have been closed for several thousand years. Mr. Rapscallion went in first, reached for the electric light switch and turned it on.

Gathering his courage, Billy followed.

He wasn't at all sure what he was going to see. Something that Mr. Rapscallion had described as horrifying could very probably have included just about anything. But certainly Billy had not expected to see anything like what he saw now.

It *was* horrifying, in a way. And, now that he thought about it, the sight that met his eyes was, perhaps, the most awful thing he had seen in the Haunted House of Books.

The mummy was standing in the sarcophagus. It still looked like a long-dead priest wrapped in bandages. Except for the fact that someone—presumably one of the wicked boys from King Herod the Great Middle School, in Northwest Hitchcock—had spray-painted the bandages completely pink, from head to toe. Which, of course, completely ruined the effect. After all, there is nothing terrifying about a mummy that is as pink as the icing on a birthday cake.

A pink mummy was bad enough. But there was worse. Much worse. A large pair of pink furry rabbit's ears had been stuck on the mummy's head and a big juicy red carrot had been placed in its moldering, wrapped hand so that the poor old thing now resembled a weird soft cuddly toy that had been abandoned by some careless child, instead of an Egyptian priest cursed for all eternity.

"There," said Mr. Rapscallion. The upset he felt was clearly written on his face. And in his voice. "Just look what they did to my mummy. Ruined. That's what it is. Ruined."

"Couldn't you just change the bandages?" suggested Billy.

"Bandages?" exclaimed Mr. Rapscallion.

"I mean, that's what they did to me in the hospital, after my accident, when my old bandages got dirty. So why not just take the pink ones off and put some dirty new ones on?"

"These weren't just any old bandages from a hospital, Billy," explained Mr. Rapscallion. "These were proper mummy wrappings from a genuine mummy of the New Kingdom of Egypt, nineteenth dynasty. They were covered with . . . years, many years of dust from the real Valley of the Kings."

"Yes, but would anyone know the difference?" asked Billy. "If you did just put ordinary hospital bandages on the mummy?"

"*I* would know the difference, Billy," Mr. Rapscallion said stiffly. "All of my sideshows in the Haunted House of Books—my little horrors, as I call them—they are all as close to the real thing as I can make them."

"Isn't that very expensive?" asked Billy.

"Of course it's expensive," said Mr. Rapscallion. "But I have my standards, Billy. I have my standards. This is what gives me pleasure. It's one of the reasons why this is no ordinary bookshop."

Billy nodded. He could not disagree with the argument that he was in no ordinary bookshop.

"Did you find out who did it?" asked Billy. "Who it was that spray-painted your mummy?"

"The culprits are known to me, yes, Billy," said Mr. Rapscallion. "Their ugly little juvenile-delinquent faces were recorded on closed-circuit television." His face wrinkled with distaste. "The police told me their names. Not that they did anything about it, of course. The police just bent their horrible little ears about damaging property and then let them go.

"Their names are Wilson Dirtbag, Simon Snotnose, Robbie Roach and Holly Hurl; Hugh Bicep, Brad Undershort and Lenore Gas; Michael Mucus, Kate Ramsbottom, Kevin Clipshear, Wilbur Dogbreath and Lloyd Sputum. And when I die you will find those names written on my heart, Billy."

Mr. Rapscallion ushered Billy out of the Curse of the Pharaohs room.

"Yes, the whole incident left me feeling quite depressed. I even saw a psychiatrist about it. The one who helped me with my number thing."

"And did it help?" asked Billy.

"Yes. It did. He advised me to write a song about it. That's what I do when I need to get something out of my system now. I write a song. Would you like to hear it, Billy?"

"I'd love to hear it."

They went down to the entrance hall, where Mr. Rapscallion sat down at the grand piano. To Billy's surprise, this was in tune.

Mr. Rapscallion composed himself and started to play.

Billy thought he played very well. And so, it seemed, did the other customers in the bookshop, because they came out of the various sections where they'd been book-browsing to listen.

Mr. Rapscallion played for several minutes. And then he began to sing.

"The Children of Today,"
a song by Rexford Rapscallion

VERSE 1
Wilson Dirtbag, Simon Snotnose,
Robbie Roach and Holly Hurl.
We've every little nasty habit
A boy or girl can exhibit.
Here you see, one group of us.
Yes there is a troop of us,
Nasty little brutes who must do bad.
We know we're pretty handy
When it comes to stealing candy;
But we'd much prefer to stay in bed all day.
Our mothers and fathers are encouraging,

When what we need's a walloping,
Or a clip around the ear.
Instead give each one of us the benefit of the doubt,
We loudly shout,
But getting it, we laugh and sneer.

CHORUS 1
The children of today
Are such a wicked streak.
They scrawl things on the wall
But think reading's for a geek.
Then there's the fact they swear so much,
Routinely call you such-and-such,
Have manners that belong in a hutch
To a horrible guinea pig,
A rabbit or a rat,
Or even worse than that.
They seldom do their homework,
Or help around the house.
If you ask them they'll just smirk
Or begin to loudly grouse.
And if someone else excuses them,
And argues it's all okay,
The rest of us will say—Baloney!
It's the children of today.

VERSE 2
Michael Mucus, Kate Ramsbottom,
Kevin Clipshear and Lloyd Sputum.
Here you see, just four of us.

Yet there are still more of us,
We're the kids who'll make you sick of us.
Since we're appallingly behaved
We watch TV all day and half the night
Or play computer games and fight
Whatever monster some nerd created
But our amusement's never sated
By destruction on a small square screen.
So we'd much prefer to have been
And smashed your window for the kick.
On cell phones we'll text illiterate tripe
To some poor bullied type
Even though it's rather sick.

CHORUS 2

The children of today
Are much nastier than of old
They don't get up in the morning,
Or go to bed when told.
There's the boy who threw his weight about.
His mother thought him such a lout
She bopped him on the snout,
And the boy let out such a wail,
That his mother's now in jail.
The girl who kicked her sister
Got taken off to court.
She called the judge a blister,
Then a blackhead and a wart
Not to mention a nasty smell.
The judge ordered her to a cell

In which she should be locked.
He was shocked
By the children of today.

VERSE 3

Wilbur Dogbreath, Hugh Bicep,
Brad Undershort and Lenore Gas.
We can't see the point of this or that,
We'd much prefer to set fire to a cat,
Or maybe an automobile,
But only after we've tried to steal
The contents of the trunk.
School we don't believe important
Which is why we're mostly playing truant.
We'd rather hang around the city streets,
Like a gang of idle deadbeats
Without a future or a purpose.
You'll find our expression is morose,
Each of us you'll probably think's a punk.
So don't be fooled we're actually quite vile
Given an inch we'll take a mile
And turn your property into junk.

CHORUS 3

The children of today
Have the chance to turn out well,
We've only ourselves to blame
If they make our lives a hell.
The court appoints them a defender
Who provides a story to embroider

And helps them get away with murder,
Or at least that's how it seems.
So to parents we would remind
Sometimes it's cruel to be kind.
You have to teach kids right from wrong,
And personal responsibility.
So that to something they'll belong
And contribute to society.
But if we don't, then we're in trouble
This song's incontrovertible,
Tomorrow's citizens we must develop
Or we'll simply end up
With the children of today.

When Mr. Rapscallion had finished singing his song, the customers on the gallery applauded enthusiastically. Billy had noticed some of them joining in the chorus, which made him think that they must have heard the song before. Mr. Rapscallion himself stood up and took several bows, as if he had been onstage in a concert hall.

Billy applauded as well, although he was just a little shocked by what he had heard. He was well aware that some children were naughty. And that some children from King Herod the Great Middle School could be very bad indeed. It could even be said that, sometimes, they were actually wicked. All over the walls and sidewalks of Hitchcock there was graffiti that had been put there by the KHG. And there was no doubt that much of this graffiti said some very wicked things indeed. Much of it about the KHG principal, Miss Dorkk.

Billy hoped Mr. Rapscallion didn't think he—Billy—was as

bad as some of those other children. So he decided to try to make up for their behavior with some exemplary behavior of his own. And remembering that Mr. Rapscallion couldn't even afford to take on a book clerk, he said, "Mr. Rapscallion, sir? I'd love to help out around here. And I wouldn't want any money for it. Helping out here would be a pleasure."

"Thanks, Billy, I appreciate the offer. But I couldn't let you work for nothing. I'd be taking advantage of your generosity."

"I could volunteer," insisted Billy. "Perhaps we could even call it an internship. And since I don't actually buy any of the books, it sounds to me like a fair exchange. Wouldn't you agree?"

Mr. Rapscallion nodded thoughtfully. "All right. It's a deal. When I need some help, I'll let you know. But I'd like to make one thing quite clear, Billy."

"What's that?" asked Billy.

"The only children I don't like are just a *dozen* or so nasty ones. The kind of children who could make an Egyptian mummy look like a giant pink rabbit. Most children I like. I only ever wanted to scare the kids because I thought they might appreciate it. Kids like a good scare, don't they?"

"Sometimes," said Billy. "Yes. A good scare is sometimes the best fun there is."

Mr. Rapscallion nodded again. "I just want you to know that, Billy, in case you think I'm a bad man."

"I know that," said Billy. "I wouldn't have volunteered to help if I thought any different."

CHAPTER 9

BILLY HELPS OUT

When Billy came into the shop the very next day, Mr. Rapscallion said, "Good morning to you, Billy."

"Good morning to you, Mr. Rapscallion."

"Billy, I wonder if I could impose on your kind offer of yesterday and ask you to mind the shop for half an hour while I go to the bank."

"Of course. I'd be delighted."

"There's just one thing I have to warn you about," said Mr. Rapscallion. "And it's this." He placed his hands on Billy's shoulders and steered him behind the metallic brown cash register.

"Is it a ghost?"

"No."

Up close Billy thought the cash register was the size of a Russian czar's throne and almost as shiny.

"Ever heard of Joe Louis?" Mr. Rapscallion asked him.

"No."

"Joe Louis was the greatest heavyweight boxing champion in history. His nickname was the Brown Bomber. I call this the Brown Bomber on account of the cash register's oxidized brown finish. And because it has a heck of a right hook. In other words, this register can hit you pretty good if you're not expecting it."

Mr. Rapscallion moved Billy to one side of the register. Then he reached out and carefully, as if he had been touching something very hot, pressed one of the keys. Immediately the heavy cash drawer shot out like something on the end of a powerful piston. At the same time a bell rang loudly like at the end of a round in a boxing match.

"I still forget sometimes," said Mr. Rapscallion. "And it catches me in the belly. Which is why I always remember that it's called the Brown Bomber."

He slammed the drawer shut.

Billy nodded.

"All right." And then Mr. Rapscallion went out of the shop.

Billy stood proudly behind the cash register. To the book-loving boy, this seemed like a dream come true: him, left in charge of a bookshop. And not just any bookshop—he was in charge of the Haunted House of Books.

The telephone rang. It was a company selling designer kitchens, and although Billy couldn't imagine Mr. Rapscallion being very interested in the company's half-price sale, he took a number anyway and told the salesman he'd pass on a message.

The next thing that happened was that the mailman turned up. The mailman wasn't a man at all, but a woman, and she seemed pleased to see Billy and talked to him for several minutes before handing the boy an important-looking envelope with the letters "IRS" on it.

As the mailwoman walked out of the door, a girl walked in and gave the place a dim once-over before approaching the cash register and Billy. Her face was pretty and round with big eyes, only she was dressed older than she looked. She was wearing jeans and a skirt, a hoodie and a pair of sneakers. Over her shoulder was a fisherman's bag and on her head was a green cap with a picture of Che Guevara.

"Hi," she said brightly. "Is my dad around?"

Billy shook his head.

"Good," she said.

"You must be Altaira," said Billy. "I've heard a lot about you."

The girl winced. "Nobody calls me that."

"What do they call you?" asked Billy.

"Redford," said the girl. "Like the famous movie star."

"Sounds a bit like your dad's name," said Billy. "Rexford?"

"That's not why I chose it," she said stiffly.

"But isn't that a man's name?" asked Billy.

"I don't think that sort of thing matters, do you?" She wasn't looking for an answer to the question. "Names aren't gender specific. Not anymore. There are models who call themselves Kelly, soccer players called Silvinho and basketball stars called Amar'e and LeBron."

"I guess you're right." Billy shrugged. "My name is Billy," he said. "It's short for William. Your dad stepped out for half an hour to go to the bank."

Redford pulled a face. "You look kind of young to be working in a place like this."

"I'm just helping him out. I'm a volunteer. An intern."

"That sounds just like my dad. Get someone to work for him without paying them any money. What a cheapskate. You're being taken advantage of, do you know that? In case you didn't notice, this place isn't a charity shop. They do expect to try and turn a profit, you know."

"Actually, it was my idea for me to work here," said Billy.

"I doubt that. You've no idea how devious he can be."

"No, really. In the beginning he was against the idea. He took quite a bit of persuading. And I'm the same age as you, Altaira. I mean, Redford. Besides, it's not a bar, it's a bookshop."

Redford gave the shop a withering look. "Really? You could have fooled me." She shook her head. "Who buys all this junk, anyway? No, wait, I'll tell you. No one. There's a layer of dust on some of these books that's as thick as an old encyclopedia."

"As a matter of fact, we have lots of regular customers. There's Father Merrin, of course. Miss Danvers. Dr. Saki. Mr. Stoker. Mr. Quiller-Couch. Mr. Pu Sung Ling. Miss Maupassant. Montague James."

Redford laughed scornfully. "I've seen them. Those aren't customers. They're just creeps and losers who come in here to get out of the rain, or because there's nowhere else for them to go in Hitchcock. Most of them are even too weird for the library, and that's saying something. Nobody ever actually buys a book in here. They sell more stuff in a funeral parlor."

"That's a little harsh," said Billy.

She turned and walked back to the door.

"Do you want to leave your dad a message?" said Billy.

"No," she said. "Why would I want to do that? Besides,

haven't you heard of texts? Email? If I wanted to send him a message, I certainly wouldn't trust a mere intern to do it."

"Then I don't understand. You said you were glad he wasn't around and you don't want to leave a message. So why did you come in here?"

"You ask a lot of questions for a volunteer, do you know that?"

"I don't mean to pry," said Billy. "You're right. It's none of my business."

Redford winced. "Sorry. I didn't mean to be rude. I guess I just wanted to know that he's still alive."

"You're very like him, you know," said Billy. "Tough on the outside. Not so tough on the inside, perhaps."

Redford Rapscallion rolled her eyes. "Now I really am going. Before I barf."

She went out of the shop even as two customers came toward Billy from opposite ends. One was Miss Danvers and the other was Mr. Stoker. Each of them was carrying a book and it seemed clear to Billy that he was about to make his first two sales.

Mr. Stoker, a tall man with a beard, arrived first. He wore a suit that seemed almost too large for him and a tie with little golden symbols on the dark silk. He was also very polite and insisted that Billy should serve the lady first, and Billy took this to mean Miss Danvers.

Miss Danvers was wearing the same dark green leather coat. Underneath it she wore a black dress with a little white collar that made her look a bit like a nun. She handed Billy a copy of *Rigor Mortis: 19* by Esteban Rex and a fifty-dollar bill to cover the $39.99 price.

Carefully, Billy pressed the fifty-dollar key on the register and narrowly missed being struck by the drawer. He put the fifty-dollar bill in the tray for large notes and took out the customer's change.

"Would you like a paper bag?" he asked her politely. "For your book?"

Miss Danvers let out a weary sigh. "Do I look like someone who would want a paper bag?" she asked Billy.

"I don't know," said Billy.

"The green coat should tell you something, boy," she said coldly. "I'm *green*."

"Oh," said Billy, still none the wiser.

"All bags and packaging in shops have a cost to the environment," she said. "Didn't you know that?"

"Er, yes," said Billy.

"Just think of all the trees we can save if we don't have paper bags," said Miss Danvers.

Billy nodded and then looked uncertainly at the book she had just bought. This was eight hundred pages long. A real blockbuster, thought Billy.

Mr. Stoker seemed to guess what Billy was thinking and said, "Ah yes, but think how many trees might be saved if Esteban Rex never wrote another book." He chuckled. "That really would save some trees. Not to mention one's arms. Esteban Rex must write the heaviest books in the world. Don't you think so, Billy?"

Without thinking, Billy agreed with Mr. Stoker, which seemed to make Miss Danvers very cross indeed because she snatched up her book and her ten dollars and one cent change and said, "Well, really. I can go somewhere else and be insulted, you know."

Billy had no idea what this meant and watched her leaving the shop with horror.

"What did I say?" he asked Mr. Stoker.

"Oh, forget about her," said Mr. Stoker. "She's always been a bit touchy."

He handed Billy his purchases: a copy of Deacon Wordz's book *Sick Schloss,* and *On Legs of Lightning* by Phyllis P. T. Barnum.

Billy didn't think much of either of them, but of course he was too polite to tell Mr. Stoker. Besides, that wouldn't have been good business. He'd noticed that whenever Mr. Rapscallion sold a book, he always said how good it was even when Billy knew Mr. Rapscallion thought that the book wasn't very good at all. In the beginning he thought that this was dishonest, until Mr. Rapscallion had told him that the first principle of running a shop was that "the customer is always right."

"What, even when he's wrong?"

Mr. Rapscallion had shaken his head. "The customer is never wrong," he said.

"Yes, but what if he is?" asked Billy.

But Mr. Rapscallion had just kept on shaking his head. "It's the trading policy of all good shops that they should always put the customer first in all situations. And that includes a situation when he's talking out of his hat."

"So what if the customer wanted *Sick Schloss* but insisted that it had been written by Esteban Rex?" Billy had asked Mr. Rapscallion. "Then what do you do?"

"You do what you can," said Mr. Rapscallion. "You do what you can without making the lunkheaded customer feel small or stupid."

"And if they are small or stupid?" Billy had asked him. "What then?"

Mr. Rapscallion started to shake his head again, and, inspired, Billy thought of an example of a customer Mr. Rapscallion could hardly disagree was small and stupid.

"What if the customer was Wilson Dirtbag?" he asked, giving the name of one of the bad children who had painted the mummy pink in the Curse of the Pharaohs room. And then some others: "Or Kate Ramsbottom? Or Lloyd Sputum? What if they were the customers? Are they always right?"

Mr. Rapscallion didn't have an answer for Billy.

"How much do I owe you?" asked Mr. Stoker.

"One hundred and twenty-one dollars," said Billy. The rest of the boy's mind was still occupied with the foolish notion that the customer is always right even when he's wrong. And that was probably why he was standing immediately behind the Brown Bomber when he hit the cash register's one-hundred-dollar key.

The drawer exploded out of the machine like a team of horses in a chariot race and almost took Billy's young head off.

"Yikes!" he said, finding himself on the floor. And, looking up, he saw Mr. Stoker peering over the counter to see if he was injured.

"Are you all right, young fellow me lad?" asked Mr. Stoker.

"Yes," said Billy, picking himself up. "I think so." He let out a nervous breath. "Phew! That was close."

"Close? Close? It looked like yon drawer went straight through you," said Mr. Stoker. "So it did."

"I guess I ducked just in time." Billy grinned sheepishly.

"It's a miracle, so it is. You ask me, you're very lucky to be alive."

"I don't think it was that bad."

"That fool Rapscallion needs to get a proper cash register. Sure, this one belongs in a police museum. Take my word. It could have killed you, son, and no mistake."

"Mr. Rapscallion did warn me," said Billy. "About the cash register."

"You might need this." Mr. Stoker handed Billy his business card. "In case you should wish to sue your employer. I'm a lawyer, you know."

"Sue?" Billy shrugged. "Why would I want to sue?"

"Nervous shock," suggested Mr. Stoker. "Or a possible whiplash injury from having to duck that drawer so quickly. My advice would be to see a doctor and have yourself checked out, as soon as possible. Just in case you sustained some kind of injury you don't yet know about."

"I've seen enough doctors to last me a lifetime," said Billy. "Besides, Mr. Rapscallion's not my employer. He's my friend."

Mr. Stoker nodded. "Well then, we'll say no more about it, eh?"

"Yes, that would be best," said Billy. "Honestly, I'm fine."

And when the sale was concluded, Mr. Stoker left the shop.

Ten minutes later Mr. Rapscallion returned from the bank.

"Sell any books?"

"Yes, I sold . . . a few," said Billy, and recited the three titles that had been sold to Miss Danvers and Mr. Stoker.

"Excellent," said Mr. Rapscallion.

"Your daughter dropped by," added Billy.

"Oh yeah?" Mr. Rapscallion tried to look indifferent. "What did she want? Money, I guess. It certainly couldn't have been that she came in here because she wanted to buy a book."

"She didn't say what she wanted," said Billy.

"That figures."

"I liked her. She was . . . pretty."

"You think?"

"Definitely."

"Did anything else happen while I was out?"

"No." Billy grinned. "Nothing at all."

CHAPTER 10

THE INVITATION

Before very long, Mr. Rapscallion was frequently relying on Billy to mind the store while he went to the bank or to get a latte from the coffee shop. Sometimes he got one for Billy, too.

One day, the mailwoman, whose name was Janine Delafons, delivered a rather formal-looking envelope on which, in very fine handwriting of the kind for which you really need a good fountain pen, was Mr. Rapscallion's full name and address:

REXFORD ERASMUS RAPSCALLION THE THIRD

C/O THE HAUNTED HOUSE OF BOOKS

65 HIGH STREET, HITCHCOCK, MA 01779

"I wouldn't have ever guessed that Erasmus was his middle name," admitted Janine.

A little later on, Billy watched Mr. Rapscallion come behind the cash register and open the envelope.

"What is it?" he asked.

Mr. Rapscallion showed him a letter and a large square of stiff card with a lot of embossed writing and a golden edge.

"It's an invitation," said Mr. Rapscallion. "To the B.A.B. dinner. They want me to make a speech about independent bookselling."

"What's the B.A.B.?" asked Billy.

"It stands for Bankrupt American Booksellers," said Mr. Rapscallion.

Billy frowned. "You're not bankrupt," he said. "At least not yet. So why have you been invited?"

"Good question," said Mr. Rapscallion. "And thanks, by the way."

"For what?"

"For sounding like you were surprised I should get myself invited to such an event. Except, of course, that I was joking. It's actually called the Board of American Booksellers. Not the Bankrupt American Booksellers, although I sometimes think it should be. Every time I go to the dinner, I think that everyone there is on the edge of going out of business."

Mr. Rapscallion looked thoughtful for a moment, which meant he kept on gathering his ponytail and drawing its length through one of his heavily ringed hands.

"You know, that gives me an idea," he said. "This is a ticket for two people. Me and a guest. And I don't have anyone else to take. Last year I hardly wanted to go myself. But I guess I'll have to go because they seem to want me to make a speech. And, well, since you've been working here, you do kind of qualify as an American bookseller. So how would you like to go along with me, Billy?"

"Me?"

"Well, why not?"

"Wouldn't you prefer to take your own daughter? Altaira?"

"Are you kidding? She'd hate it. It was Altaira who first started calling the B.A.B. the Bankrupt American Booksellers in the first place. She thinks the whole business is on the edge of going belly-up."

"Or a lady? Miss Danvers, for instance?"

"Miss Danvers?" Mr. Rapscallion nearly choked. "That nutcase? I'd rather ask a skunk to tea than take her along."

"Then what about Janine, the mailwoman? She's attractive."

"True." Mr. Rapscallion looked embarrassed. "But if I was going to ask her, then it's plain I'd actually have *to ask her,* if you know what I mean. And the fact of the matter is that I just don't have the nerve to ask her anything except what kind of day she's had. Besides, she's not even a bookseller, so I don't know why we're even having this conversation. Do you want to come to the stupid dinner, or not?"

"Yes, all right," said Billy.

"Of course, as a minor you'll have to get permission from your parents," said Mr. Rapscallion.

"I'll get my dad to write you a letter," said Billy. "Will that do?"

Mr. Rapscallion nodded. "Good, well, that's settled. Now all I have to do is think what the heck I'm going to talk about. In my speech." He shrugged. "To that extent, it's like real life, I guess."

"Can I see the invitation?" asked Billy.

"Sure." Mr. Rapscallion handed it over.

"Oh my god," said Billy. "You didn't tell me that it's in Kansas City. This is so great."

"It's always in Kansas City. At the public library."

"You don't understand. I've never been out of Hitchcock in my life. I've never even been to Boston, and that's just nineteen miles away. This is so fantastic."

Mr. Rapscallion winced. "No more numbers, please. I told you. I've always had a thing about numbers."

But Billy was so excited about the idea of going to Kansas City he had quite forgotten Mr. Rapscallion's fear of numbers. Besides, he didn't really understand how anyone could ever be nervous of numbers. Especially in the Haunted House of Books.

"How far away is Kansas City?" he asked unwittingly. "Exactly."

Mr. Rapscallion closed his eyes and looked weary. "Now you've done it, Billy."

"Done what? All I asked was the distance between Hitchcock and Kansas City."

"Let me see now." Mr. Rapscallion started counting on his fingers. "Boston is one hour ahead of Kansas City. One thousand and eighty-nine nautical miles. Except of course that we can't go there by ship. On account of how there's no water between here and Kansas City. Not enough to put a ship in, anyway. So we'll be going west. By plane."

"We're actually going on a plane?" Billy gasped.

"We're certainly not going by covered wagon," said Mr. Rapscallion.

"I've never been on a plane," said Billy. "I'd better get myself some ID."

Mr. Rapscallion was still counting, madly. "That means we'll have to take account of the curvature of the earth. And using the great circle formula to compute the air travel mileage, as the crow flies, so to speak, I should say the distance is exactly one thousand two hundred and fifty-three miles. Which will take us three hours and twenty-seven minutes. That's aboard a Boeing 707, which normally seats one hundred and fifty passengers. But only one hundred and thirty-nine on a Boeing 757-400."

"It's okay," said Billy. "It's okay. I just wanted to know how far it was. You can stop now."

"Shh, let me finish," said Mr. Rapscallion. "Now then. The total carbon footprint for a flight on the 707 from Boston to Kansas City is seven hundred and two pounds of CO_2. That will give us each a carbon footprint of around four and a half pounds of CO_2, so call it nine, there and back. That's assuming the plane is full, mind. So it could be more."

"Thanks," said Billy. "I think you've answered my question. Really."

"*You asked me this, Billy. This is your fault.* Of course, the flight time ought to be less than that. I mean, if you were to assume a flight speed of five hundred miles an hour—not unreasonable on a 757—it ought to be just two and a half hours. But they fly slow to save on fuel. So you can't make that assumption."

"Hello-oh," said Billy. "Mr. Rapscallion, sir. You can shut up now."

Mr. Rapscallion was starting to look desperate. He nodded at the Brown Bomber. *"Hit the key, Billy."* He said this even as he started off on yet another calculation. "Incidentally, Kansas produced a record 492.2 million bushels of wheat last year and that's enough to make 35.9 billion loaves of bread. Of course if we drove there it would take us twenty-two hours and forty-seven minutes," added Mr. Rapscallion. "Assuming an average driving speed of fifty-five miles per hour. *Hit the key on the Brown Bomber, Billy.* At six dollars a gallon for gas, that means—"

"But the drawer will hit you," protested Billy.

"—in a car like mine, that gets twenty-five miles to the gallon, at a steady fifty-five, we'll use approximately fifty gallons of gas, which means that we'll spend around three hundred dollars in gas to get to Kansas City. And three hundred back again, which is six hundred dollars; and we would spend forty-five and one-half hours driving, in total, spending thirteen dollars an hour on fuel. . . . *For Pete's sake, hit the key, Billy!*"

Billy hit the key on the Brown Bomber. The drawer came flying out of the cash register like an express train and struck Mr. Rapscallion square in the tummy like a car trapped on a level crossing. The impact carried him halfway across the shop and dumped him on his behind at the front door, where he sat like a pile of junk mail.

"For every locked mind there's a key to find," said Mr. Rapscallion, rubbing his stomach in pain.

Billy rushed to Mr. Rapscallion's side. "Are you okay?"

"Yes, I think I'll live," said Mr. Rapscallion, standing up. "Thanks for helping me out there, kid. Once I get started on those numbers, it's like I get trapped inside an electronic calculator and I have to keep doing the math on things. Stupid things. Once I get going, I have to see the process right through to the end. Until I can't think of any other numbers to calculate. Sometimes that can take days. So it's quicker if something hits me. That breaks the chain of concentration, see?"

"There was a boy in my class at school who was a bit like that," said Billy. "People used to say he had an allergy to asparagus. But if you ask me, that guy would eat anything."

Mr. Rapscallion smiled. "Sounds to me like what he actually had was Asperger's syndrome."

"Oh, I see. Yes, that makes more sense, doesn't it? Dumb of me."

"Forget about it. Anyway, that's what I have. A mild form of A.S. It just means that sometimes I appear to be a little eccentric."

"If you ask me, the world would be a pretty boring place if everyone was the same. So three cheers for eccentricity. That's what I say."

"You're right," said Mr. Rapscallion. "If it wasn't for eccentricity, we'd have to light the streets with gas."

CHAPTER 11

REDFORD'S CONFESSION AND AN ANONYMOUS STORY

The next day Mr. Rapscallion left Billy in charge of the shop for a whole morning while he went to the dentist. When, an hour later, the front door opened, it was to admit neither a customer nor Mr. Rapscallion but his daughter, Altaira, who preferred to be called Redford.

"You seem to have a knack for coming in here when your father is out," Billy told her. "He's gone to the dentist and won't be back until lunchtime."

"That's all right," said Redford. "As a matter of fact, it was you I came to see, not my dad."

Which was true, only she hadn't actually realized this until she said it. There was something about Billy she liked a lot. He wasn't the same as other boys she had met. She thought that most of them were dorks, always fooling around and saying stupid things. But Billy was more thoughtful than them. Sensitive, too. She appreciated that.

"Oh?" Billy blushed and nervously smiled a little ghost of a smile. "That's nice. Er, what can I do for you, Altaira? I mean Redford."

"Nothing." Redford bridled a little with embarrassment. "Do I need a reason for wanting to talk to you?"

"No, of course not."

"I was passing, okay? I thought I could just hang out here awhile with you."

"Okay." Billy shrugged. "That'd be great."

"Only don't make the mistake of thinking I have nothing else to do with my time. I do. I'm actually a very busy person. In that respect I'm quite like my dad. At least that's what my mother tells me."

"Right."

"As a matter of fact, I knew he wouldn't be here," said Redford. "You see, my mom is also my dad's dentist. I know that sounds weird, given that they're not actually married anymore. But this is a small town and good dentists are kind of few and far between. Personally, I wouldn't care for the idea of having my ex-wife in charge of my dental procedures. I would be too worried that she might take the opportunity of inflicting some extra pain on me. Then again, if I was my mom I might find that idea just too tempting to resist."

Billy smiled. "You've got such a lot of imagination it makes me wonder that you don't like reading."

"Did he tell you that?"

"Yes."

"Yes, but did he tell you why?"

"No. But he kind of implied that it's because you hate him."

"That is so not true. And typical of my dad to believe he's the reason. He's not. You want to know the truth?"

"Sure." Billy shrugged. "If you want to tell me."

"The fact is, it was one particular book in this shop that put me off reading, *forever,*" explained Redford.

"Gee, that must have been a really bad book."

"On the contrary," said Redford. "It was a really good book." She paused. "But there was something about it I didn't like."

"That sounds like a book I want to read," said Billy.

"To be more accurate," said Redford, "it was an anonymous story in a book called *Juvenile Tales of Mystery and Imagination*. My dad thinks it might actually have been written by the young Edgar Allan Poe. But he doesn't know for sure. Nobody does. He's shown it to all kinds of experts who can't say for sure if it is or if it isn't."

"Scary, huh?"

"I don't know that 'scary' is the right word," said Redford. "It's not the kind of story that makes you look over your shoulder or keeps you awake or anything. It's more subtle than that. And it still haunts me, to this day. Like the memory of a terrible accident."

"I know what that's like," said Billy, and told her about his own car accident.

"Hey, I'm sorry," said Redford when Billy was finished. "If I'd known that you'd been in a car accident, I wouldn't have used that as an example to explain how the Poe story stays with me."

"It's no problem," said Billy. "I'm over it. Honest."

He smiled at her to make her feel comfortable again, and she found herself smiling back at him. Fondly.

"But I'd still like to read that story," he added.

Redford grinned. "You sure about that?"

"I like scary stories."

"Why?" Redford shook her head. "Why do people like being scared so much?"

Billy thought for a moment before answering. "I think we've just evolved that way," he said. "Somehow it's tied in to our survival. We like to test ourselves. See if it's still there. Maybe if we hadn't had it, we'd have died out long ago."

Redford nodded. "I guess that makes sense."

"What is it called, anyway?" Billy asked her. "This story?"

"The Pocket Handkerchief," said Redford.

"And where can I find a copy?"

"Fortunately, there's only one," said Redford, pointing at a little revolving bookcase beside the sales desk. "I'm pretty sure he keeps it in there with all his other rare books and first editions." She knelt down and quickly found the book she was looking for. "Yes, here it is. But do me a favor, okay? When we see each other again, don't tell me your opinion about it. It gives me the creeps just to think of anyone reading it."

"Sure," said Billy. "Don't worry. I won't ever mention it."

"And don't tell my dad I was here. I don't like him knowing what I've been doing."

"All right. If you insist."

"I do insist. It'll be our secret."

Billy loved the two of them having a secret. No girl had ever asked him to keep a secret before. It was like they now had a bond between them. He was already looking forward to the next time Redford came into the shop. At the same time, he could hardly wait for her to leave so that he could find the story; and as soon as she was gone, he opened the slim volume and started to read.

"THE POCKET HANDKERCHIEF"
by Anonymous

PART I

I cannot remember precisely when I met Scipio for the first time but I have the strong sense that he knew me before I ever came to live in the house of his master, Mr. A——, in Richmond, Virginia, during the year of our Lord 18—.

I was aged only two when that happened, my own father having died of the consumption, and my mother married Mr. A—— with a haste that bordered on the indecent. For myself I do not remember my own father at all but, if the reader will permit the apparent contradiction, I have never forgotten him. He was buried in the churchyard of St. John's Episcopal Church, where, it is said, General Benedict Arnold, the traitor, quartered his troops and their horses during the War of Independence.

Another six years passed before my beloved mother, Elizabeth, also succumbed to the same malady as my father, leaving me and my brother, William Henry, alone with our stepfather. She was just aged twenty-nine. I was myself but eight years old at the time, yet not a day has passed since then when I have not thought of her.

Scipio, who was one of my adoptive father Mr. A——'s three house slaves, and very well educated—it was he, not Mr. A——, who usually helped me with my Latin homework—told me that on several occasions he saw my mother on the stage in Richmond, for she was an actress, and thought she was one of the handsomest ladies he ever saw. This is also my own opinion.

Memories grow dim, however, and the one portrait I have of her is I think a porcelain miniature which makes her look like a child's doll and, at the very least, something not alive; that is its greatest failing. Would that were all. But I am also reminded of my mother as something not alive whenever I look at the only other thing of hers I now possess, which is a white pocket handkerchief with her initials stitched upon its corner. This is to hardly state the truth of the matter, however, which is that whenever I contemplate this handkerchief—as, from time to time, my strange nature compels me so to do—I am obliged to think of her as something dead and in awful torment. I confess I have often thought of burning the handkerchief; and yet cannot by reason of the fact that it serves to remind me that my living suffering is deservedly shared with her eternal one.

I am now aged twelve and while I am eternally grateful to Mr. A—— for taking my brother and me into his home, the want of true affection has been the heaviest of my trials. Indeed, my sense of grief and loss is sometimes so heavy that it might reasonably be supposed that I had been bereaved but recently. Especially since it is my habit to go walking through cemeteries and I confess I can no more pass a newly filled grave without stopping to consider the fate of the poor wretch who lies beneath the soil than another boy of my age can ignore the sight in a grocery store of a jar full of candy.

My stepfather says I have a morbid disposition, and I must admit that as long as I can remember I have been fascinated by death, and rare is the night that I do not stare into the too solid darkness of my room and imagine death's hard unseen face staring coldly back at me.

Scipio said that it was perfectly natural that any child alive should be interested in death, for you couldn't have one without the other, and that back in Africa, where he came from originally, a boy such as myself who demonstrated such an interest in the afterlife would have marked himself out as a future houngan, which is a kind of priest or witch doctor. Scipio also told me that his own grandfather Msizi had been a great houngan and knew better than anyone how to connect the world of spirits and ancestors with the living world of human beings.

"All the same, young Master Edgar," said Scipio, "it seems to me that you got all of eternity to find out the answers to these questions. So maybe it's best you don't go rushing that particular inquiry."

I persisted, however, with the result that Scipio and I often talked about what might lie on the other side of death's mildewed curtain, although the poor man might easily have felt by reason of his station that he was obliged to indulge my youthful questions about the matter upon which I most earnestly wished to know more, and that was this: What is it really like to be dead?

Persistence paid off with the discovery that Scipio himself was in possession of a houngan's secrets and knew very well how the world of the living might become better acquainted with the world of the dead; and I must confess that I took unfair advantage of our relationship, constantly badgering that unhappy African to give me a clearer account of exactly how such a closer acquaintance might be achieved.

Finally, and with great reluctance, he told me something of what I wanted to know.

"Anybody who wants to find out what it's really like to be dead," he explained, "has no choice but to go and visit with the folks in the underworld. That ain't easy. And it ain't for the faint-hearted, boy. If you is going to visit the underworld, you needs to find yourself a door. Ain't but one place in Richmond to find a door like that. The cemetery. And don't think I'm talking about a stroll around them headstones like you is partial to. I'm talking about something much more profound, in the true Latin sense of that word.

"The plain fact is, Master Edgar, you needs to get yourself buried

alive. Just like one of them vestal virgins from Roman times, when they was accused of violating their vows. They got sealed up in a cave with a small amount of bread and water, so that the goddess Vesta might save them, supposing they was innocent, of course. Or like Saint Castulus, who was chamberlain to the emperor Diocletian. You remember what happened to him? They buried him alive in a sand pit on the Via Labicana."

I knew the story well, of course, and I was hardly as horrified at the idea of premature burial as perhaps Scipio had hoped I might be.

"It's not just that," continued Scipio. "It's the way you is buried, too. You got to be buried alive with the lid of the coffin facing down. Now, most folks who get themselves buried do it the other way, of course. With the coffin lid facing up. On account of that's the general direction they want their souls to travel in. But if you is going calling on the underworld, you got to be going the other way. You got to head down."

"That's it?"

Scipio laughed. "'That's it,' he says. Listen to yourself, boy." Scipio laughed some more. "Being buried alive even for a short while ain't no Sunday school picnic, boy. For one thing, you got to last from dusk until dawn without going plumb crazy. Why, one solitary hour of buried alive would be enough to drive most folks mad. Let alone one whole night."

"If I am going to visit the underworld, then, strictly speaking, I can hardly be buried alive for the whole night, can I?" I said, with precocious logic. "The coffin lid has to open like a door, you said. In those circumstances it doesn't make any sense for me to be afraid."

"Land sakes, I do believe you're not," he said, with some admi-

ration. "Very well, Master Edgar. You figure out a way to get yourself buried alive and Scipio promises he'll have a quiet word with his granddaddy to come and fetch you out of the coffin to give you the five-cent tour of the underworld."

"Very well. I will."

And, sooner than either of us expected, I did exactly that, albeit in circumstances that, perhaps, did not reflect well on me.

When a boy in my class at Richmond Academy called Wilson began regularly to bait me for being an orphan and Mr. A——'s adopted son, he made himself my enemy and I was soon plotting how I might humiliate him in return. One day, when he started to make light of my poor mother's death, I called him a coward and when he denied this I challenged him to swim the span of the Mayo Bridge, which is some four hundred and fifty yards, and Wilson accepted.

I have always been a good swimmer. At the age of eleven I could swim the James River from Shockoe Bottom to Rocky Ridge. The distance of our swim was not so great for me but when the river is in flood as it was then, the current is strong and even a good swimmer risks being swept away. Which is what happened to poor Wilson; and when eventually his drowned body was recovered from the water at Hampton Roads several miles downstream, they buried the boy in Shockoe Hill Cemetery.

Almost as soon as Wilson was in the ground I was pestering the understandably reluctant Scipio to help me put my plan into nocturnal action. No, that is incorrect. I plagued him, like he was that hard-hearted pharaoh of Egypt and I was the prophet Moses.

"Wilson's grave is just soft earth," I told Scipio, "so his coffin should be easy enough to dig up. We can disinter the body tonight and I will take his place in the coffin until morning."

"You're serious, aren't you?"

I nodded. "Scipio, please try to understand that it's something I feel compelled to do."

"Ain't you afeard, Master Edgar?"

"Yes, of course I am," I confessed. "But I still want to do it."

"Very well. I'll help you. But listen here, you can't never talk about this. Not never. Not to nobody. If'n we get caught or anyone ever finds out what we done, they'll hang old Scipio for sure. You hear?"

"Yes," I said. "So long as you are alive, Scipio, I won't ever peach."

By which you may reasonably deduce, gentle reader, that poor Scipio is dead. But more of that anon.

St. John's Churchyard was largely full by 18—, which is why the city of Richmond established Shockoe Hill Cemetery. It was outside of the city and to the northwest of the river and, as cemeteries go, rather a pleasant place where I had sometimes walked, being full of trees such as Virginia elm, pin oak, silver maple, locust, Kentucky coffee, eastern red cedar and yew, and all enclosed by a high brick wall that Scipio and I were obliged to scale after dark, for the cemetery has a gate that is locked every night at eight o'clock. This was to our advantage, however, as the locked gate and the high wall of Shockoe Hill made it seem unlikely that we would be disturbed. It was also fortunate that my stepfather was away at the time and there were only the other house slaves, Mammy and Thomas, to notice that we were not at home and neither of them would ever have informed on us.

In the lowering darkness we set to our nefarious work with pick and shovel excavating the unfortunate Wilson's coffin. It was a hard task for a man and a boy and took the best part of an hour. By the time we had hauled the simple pine box out of the grave I was exhausted and almost looking forward to resting in peace awhile. But I was certainly not looking forward to seeing the dead face of my enemy, Wilson. Perhaps it was guilt, but I had half an idea that he still might awaken and accuse me of getting him drowned. This apprehension was hardly diminished by the sight of the dead boy's face, for he hardly looked dead at all and, indeed, so lifelike did Wilson appear to me that I felt compelled to offer him a double apology—once for bringing about his untimely death and again for disturbing his eternal rest.

Gently, Scipio collected the body from the coffin and carried it to the shadow of the brick wall that enclosed the cemetery, and there he laid him down and covered him with some sacking that the sextons had used to line the edge of another open grave that was to be filled the following day.

Then, equipped with a burning tallow candle and a few provisions, I lay down in the coffin on my front. Before Scipio closed the lid on me for the night, however, I sought some assurance from him that all would be well.

"You did remember to speak to your granddaddy, the houngan, Scipio, and tell him to expect me tonight?" I said.

"I can't say for sure that Msizi will be there," said Scipio. "But I told him, all right. The man knows you're coming to visit awhile. Reckon it'd be rude not to show up and say hello, given all the trouble you and I have been to here."

"You won't leave the cemetery either," I said. "Not to go and get a drink from that still in Rocky Ridge like you did last Saturday when you didn't come home until late. I sure wouldn't want you to forget to come back here and dig me up again in the morning, Scipio."

"I'll be here all night. Like we agreed."

"Because I think it would be a terrible way to die. Inhumation, they call it—being buried alive."

"Don't worry, Master Edgar," said Scipio. "I wouldn't do that to my worst enemy. 'Sides, I got to come and get you or else there is nowhere to put your friend Wilson."

All the same, as Scipio put the lid on the coffin and hammered in a few small nails so that I might more easily be lowered into the grave, I wished that I had thought to bring a Bible with me so that I might have made the slave swear a solemn oath not to leave me buried alive, forever. But were there not many other things that might go wrong with my plan? What if my air ran out? What if Scipio had a heart attack and died before he could dig me up again? What if he was apprehended before he could tell his story? And what if having been apprehended he did tell his story and no one believed him, as well they might not? After all, I knew from my own experience that few if any twelve-year-old boys were as strange as me. Had my own stepfather, Mr. A——, not said so? My imagination generated a hundred different anxieties that crowded in upon my mind as I felt the coffin containing my living body descend into Wilson's grave.

Billy stopped reading and shivered, not sure that he had the nerve to read the rest of the story; and yet he knew he would.

"I couldn't ever do something like that," he said. "Not in a million years."

CHAPTER 12

THE GHOST HUNTER

Billy and Mr. Rapscallion stayed at the Savoy Hotel in Kansas City. It was a nice old redbrick hotel—perhaps the oldest in the city—with stained glass windows and high, beamed ceilings. It was even said that Harry Houdini had once stayed at the Kansas City Savoy.

Billy liked it a lot. At least he did until Mr. Rapscallion said he had chosen that particular hotel because it was supposed to be haunted. Billy was a little unnerved by this news and wondered what his father would have made of it. Not much, probably. It had been hard enough for Billy to persuade him to write the letter to Mr. Rapscallion granting permission for the boy to travel with the Hitchcock bookseller.

"Why on earth would you do something like that?" Billy asked him.

"Well, I've always wanted to see a ghost," explained Mr. Rapscallion. "And I never have. Between you and me? I think I probably never will. But I'd sure like to. You see, it's kind of embarrassing that Rexford Rapscallion, the owner of the Haunted House of Books, has never seen a real ghost. Not ever. That's right, Billy. Not so much as an apparition. It's bad for business. Back at the shop I even have a stuffed raven with a message capsule on its leg where a ghost who was minded to do so might leave me a message. So far I've had nothing. But I haven't given up. So, whenever I visit a different city, I always try to stay somewhere that's supposed to be haunted. And this hotel is haunted. That's what *Shudders*—the haunted hotel guidebook—says, anyway."

"I see. So, er, which part of the hotel is the ghost supposed to haunt? The cellars? The kitchen? Where?"

"This part," Mr. Rapscallion said calmly. "Right here. In fact, this very bedroom. Or, to be more accurate, the bathroom of our bedroom suite."

Billy gulped loudly. "But what if we do see him?" he asked nervously.

"Actually, our ghost is a she. Her name is Betsy Ward. And if we do see her, that'd be just great. But previous experience teaches me that we won't actually see anything."

Billy was about to breathe a sigh of relief when Mr. Rapscallion added, "Which is why I've invited along a professional ghost hunter to give us some extra help."

Even as he spoke, there was a knock at the door.

"That's probably her now." Mr. Rapscallion grinned. "That, or Betsy Ward was just eavesdropping on our conversation."

Mr. Rapscallion opened the door to reveal a girl about fifteen years old. She had several heavy-looking bags on her slim shoulders. She had long blond hair and retainers on her teeth. In spite of that, Billy thought she was very pretty.

"Mr. Rapscallion?" said the girl.

"Yes." Mr. Rapscallion nodded uncertainly.

"I'm Mercedes McBatty."

"You are? Gee, I was expecting someone older," confessed Mr. Rapscallion.

"Everyone says that," said Miss McBatty. She pushed her way past Mr. Rapscallion and into the room. "But it's a proven fact that ghosts like to scare children. That's half the reason why kids are scared of the dark. And since I am technically a child, and not at all easily scared, this gives me a unique advantage over other ghost hunters. Most of whom are rather old and, despite their profession, very easily frightened. Think about it. At my age I'm hardly likely to check out on you if we do see something. Which might take some explaining to the hotel's management, right?"

"Check out?"

"Have a heart attack."

"You have a point there," admitted Mr. Rapscallion. "I never thought of that."

"Well, maybe you should. If someone died while they were trying to raise a ghost, the hotel would be within its rights to sue you. I know that because I spoke to a lawyer about it. Plus I'm fully insured against any mishap. To me or you."

"I suppose that's reassuring," said Mr. Rapscallion.

Miss McBatty dumped her bags and glanced around the room. "This is the haunted room, huh?"

"Actually, it's the bathroom that's haunted," said Mr. Rapscallion.

"A clean ghost, huh? I like that."

Billy and Mr. Rapscallion followed Miss McBatty into a room with the largest bathtub the boy had ever seen. Billy turned the hot water faucet experimentally.

"Some woman called Betsy Ward is supposed to have died in the bathtub sometime during the eighteen hundreds," explained Mr. Rapscallion. "According to the rumors, her ghost turns the faucets on and off during the night."

"Just as long as she doesn't do it when I'm in there," said Billy. "The water's very hot."

"I must say I can't feel any indication that this is a haunted bathroom." Miss McBatty frowned. "No, wait just a minute. What's that rising from the bath?"

"Steam," said Billy.

Miss McBatty relaxed a little, looked crossly at Billy and then said to Mr. Rapscallion, "Who's the kid?"

"This is Billy Shivers," said Mr. Rapscallion. "He's my intern at the bookstore."

Miss McBatty said, "Hmm," and turned away. "He looks kind of young to be an intern at anything."

Billy ignored that. "Have you ever seen a ghost?" he asked the apparently fearless girl.

"That all depends on what you mean by 'seen,'" said Miss McBatty. "I've filmed something on a thermal imaging camera. That's a special camera you use to film things in the dark."

"What did it look like?" asked Billy.

"The camera? It's just a black box, with a bit of glass on the end."

"The *ghost,*" said Billy.

"I know what I'm doing, okay?" Miss McBatty sounded defensive. "At the age of twelve I was the Grand Cerveau

Smart Kid Scholar of the Decade at Georgetown University. And at the age of fourteen I was nominated as a junior Nobel Prize Laureate for my work on psychic penomn—phemon—menoffandon—"

"Phenomenon," said Billy. "Phenomena."

"That's right." Miss McBatty pulled a face. "For me that's a *reisedewortes.* That means it's a word I have trouble with. Everybody has one."

"Interesting," said Mr. Rapscallion. "With me it's numbers."

"A word I have trouble with," confessed Billy, "is 'ghost.' I sincerely hope we don't see one."

"We'll never see a ghost if you think like that, mister," said Miss McBatty. "Too many negative waves."

"Don't worry about him," said Mr. Rapscallion. "He's just the nervous type, that's all."

"Just what we need for a ghost hunt," she sneered.

"I can't help it," said Billy. "I only like ghosts in books."

"And I can't work around a scared kid," said Miss McBatty. "Fear has a very definite electrical vibration that affects my ghost-detecting machines." She shook her head. "Maybe we should forget the whole thing."

"Nonsense," said Mr. Rapscallion. "Look, Miss McBatty, you're here now, so let's just see what happens, eh? You go ahead and set up all your gear in the bathroom. Meanwhile, Billy and I will go off to the B.A.B. dinner in the Kansas City Public Library. We'll spend the evening there. I'll make my speech. And when we get back here, at around midnight, we'll see if you've found any ghosts or apparitions. And then take it from there. All right?"

"All right," agreed Miss McBatty. "You're paying."

"If necessary we'll stay up all night and then wait for someone to run a bath."

Miss McBatty relaxed. "Yes. Good idea." She even managed a rueful smile at Billy. "Sorry, Billy. I shouldn't have been so rude to you."

"Forget it," said the boy.

"You're making a speech, Mr. Rapscallion? Sounds like it will be quite an evening."

"I hope so," said Mr. Rapscallion. "I'm beginning to wish I'd remembered to bring a camera."

"Here." She handed him a disposable camera. "You can have this one. I keep it just in case the digital ones pack up. Which they have a habit of doing when there are ghosts around. Film seems more sensitive than pixels."

They had an hour or two before leaving the hotel to go to the dinner, and while Mr. Rapscallion got ready, Billy read the second part of "The Pocket Handkerchief" by Anonymous.

PART II

There was no room for a lamp inside the coffin. Only a candle. Scipio had made a small hole in the wood of the coffin and covered this with a piece of metal gauze so that the flame from my candle would not cause the coffin to catch fire, but before I dared to place the candle under this spot I waited until I had felt myself settle on the floor of the grave for fear that the candle might be overturned and my light lost, and waited again until I heard the explosive sound of earth being shoveled back onto the coffin, which was sufficient confirmation that I would not move again.

It is the most wretched, ghastly sound—perhaps the most ghastly thing I have ever heard—and would surely have terrified someone who did not have the hope of escape from burial that I myself did.

Fearing discovery, Scipio worked quickly and, gradually, the noise of earth and stones crashing onto the wooden box I was in diminished as the layer covering me grew thicker, until I could hardly hear anything but the unnervingly close sound of my own breathing. Perhaps it was the slight smell of damp and decay, or a little dust that might have been clinging to the wooden interior, but something caught my throat and, for a moment, I was convulsed by a violent fit of coughing and found my head turning one way and then the other as I tried to clear my lungs of irritation. But I was not yet worried that the air inside the casket was about to run out, having been assured by Scipio that a whole day might pass before that finally happened: and hence I did not panic—at least not until the expulsion of air from my mouth blew out the candle that was my only source of light.

Immediately I forgot about my coughing and reached for the little tinderbox containing flint, fire steel and char cloth that was in my breast pocket to relight the candle. I was horrified to discover that it was not there, and my fingers scrambled like a spider over my chest and body, searching the other pockets of my clothes, only the tinderbox was not there. And in my mind's eye I suddenly saw it quite clearly on the table in my room at home where foolishly I had left it.

If I had not panicked before, I started to panic a little now, for there is something about the darkness inside a coffin that is so palpable and close that a person might actually bite it. But equally there exists the very strong and alarming sensation that something might reach out of the darkness and bite you.

I shouted for Scipio and kicked the toes of my boots on the coffin, but to no avail. He was surely gone by now, cowering by poor Wilson's pale corpse in the shelter of the Shockoe Hill Cemetery wall, and wouldn't be back at my graveside until dawn the following morning. Half stifled by the intensity of the darkness, I stared hard into the black air above my head and willed my mind to detach itself from my nerves, to pretend that I was back in my own bed at home and that I was half-asleep and dreaming, beset by the usual tricks of my own nocturnal imagination.

I do not know for certain how long I lay there like this, for although I had a pocket watch with me, I had not the means to see even the hand that might have held it, let alone the watch face. Perhaps I may even have dozed a little, for I was tired after the exertions of the exhumation. But gradually I became aware of a muffled sound beneath the coffin and, thinking at last that this might be Scipio's grandfather the houngan called Msizi come to play Virgil to my Dante, I cried out to hurry up and open the coffin, for I had no light.

At this, my cry for help, the sound stopped altogether and, thinking that someone or something might be there—wherever "there" was—I shouted out my name and announced that I was a friend of Scipio's, which was something of an exaggeration given the fact that Scipio was a slave owned by my stepfather. Indeed it was the nature of my relationship with Scipio that now gave me some pause for thought, concerning how, in similar circumstances, I should have reacted to meeting a person who was master to my own brother. And I decided it was unlikely that I should have been at all well disposed to such a creature. Why had I never considered this matter before? Was it not the height of arrogance to assume that I would be greeted with warmth and hospitality? I was about to loudly declare my apologies for Scipio's unfortunate station in life and my own unhappy relationship with his owner, the cold Mr. A——, when the coffin opened—not from below as I had expected, but from above, which seemed impossible, but there it is. And if I now hesitated to climb out of my wooden berth it was not because the sight that greeted me was too awful to contemplate but because there was nothing at all to be seen—so much nothing that I was reminded of the second verse of the Book of Genesis, where it says that "the earth was without form and void; and darkness was upon the face of the deep."

I was not buried in the ground, of that much I was certain. The coffin was not six feet deep in anything very much. I could raise both my arms into the air—for I was breathing—and after a while I stood up, as if in an Indian canoe, and since evidently the coffin was supported by something, although it was in no way apparent what this was, I stepped out onto what felt like solid ground.

It might reasonably be asked how I could see any of this, since, as I have already said, "darkness was upon the face of the deep." There was no source of light that I could see; and yet my own person and the coffin were as clear to me as if I had been standing in the drawing room at home. With eyes straining from their sockets to see more than my own poor self, and hands outstretched in front of me lest I come upon some wall or door, I looked one way and the other, but there was only darkness visible.

Plucking up what remained of my sorely tested courage, I called out. "Hallo," I said. "Is there anyone there?"

A loud bang was my answer, which made my heart leap in my chest like a dog storming a gate. Still shaking a little, I turned around to discover, with some relief, only that the lid on the coffin had fallen shut. So it was all the more surprising when, looking up again, I saw that I was no longer alone, but accompanied not by an African but by an Oriental-looking man wearing a black frock coat. I say a man but the truth is more macabre, for this was a man with two heads, four arms, one body and one pair of legs, which is to say that they were conjoined twins. One twin had his right arm around the other's shoulder while the other kept his arm around his twin brother's waist, which lent him an amiable aspect, although this was not apparent in their greeting to me.

"What do you want here?" said one.

"You don't belong in this place," said the other.

"This is most irregular."

"Nevertheless, I think I was expected, sir," I said, as politely as I could. "Msizi was informed that I would be visiting for a short while, by his grandson Scipio."

"Scipio?" said one.

"That is not his real name," said the other.

"His real name is Bhekisisa," said the one.

"I'm sorry," I said. "I didn't know that."

"It's him you should apologize to," said the one.

"Not us," said the other. "Well, now that you are here—"

"What do you want to see?" asked the other.

I opened my mouth to speak and found myself short of an answer. It was an obvious question and yet it was one I had not really considered; but now that I did I realized there was only one thing I wanted to see, had ever wanted to see, which was the whole reason I had wanted to come in the first place.

"Sir," I said. "I should like to see my mother again. Her name is Elizabeth P—— and she died in Richmond, Virginia, during the month of November 18—."

"Your mother," said the one. "Well, that changes everything."

"You should have mentioned it before," said the other. "It might

have speeded things up a little. She could have been here to greet you."

"I'm sorry, sir," I said. "I didn't mean to inconvenience you."

"No matter," said the one. He turned to face his other head. "It's a reasonable request, don't you think?"

"Reasonable, and not uncommon given the young woman's premature demise," said the other.

They both nodded. "Lots of boys and girls your age come down here looking for their mothers," said the one.

"Elizabeth P——? She was an actress, was she not? From England?"

"That's quite correct, sir. I believe she lived there until the age of nine."

The two strange men smiled. "Where someone lived and for how long is hardly relevant down here. Life, any amount of it, is of no consequence at all when measured next to all of eternity. Life is but a dream. What goes before and what comes afterwards are true reality."

"But you shall see your mother, boy," said the one.

"It will be our pleasure," said the other, and waved his hand at the coffin, which opened magically, as if he had uttered the word "sesame." "If you will walk this way."

He stepped into the coffin and began to descend a staircase that had not been there before, and I followed without demur.

We walked down an invisible black staircase in silence for several minutes and only gradually did I perceive that the staircase was spiral in its design and that we appeared to be going down into a very deep pit. Minutes more elapsed. Perhaps as long as half an hour before finally the floor leveled out and I found myself in a dim, circular room furnished only with a black longcase clock in which *a brass pendulum dully marked time with mechanical indifference. The face of the clock was like none I had ever seen, for it appeared to me to be that of my own mother, or at least the same indifferently painted portrait miniature I had of her at home.*

I stopped and stared at it for a full minute before the case opened and my mother stepped out of it.

"Five minutes," said my guide. "Agreed?"

"Agreed," I said vaguely.

She was delicate and pretty with large, dark eyes, curly brown hair, a slender neck and a small nose. She wore a pearl earring on her right ear, a low-cut dress and a large bonnet with a bow upon it. She stared blankly at me for several seconds and it was a moment or two before I realized that I had grown a great deal since last she had seen me and she almost certainly did not recognize me.

"Mother," I said. "It's me, Edgar."

"Edgar who?" She glanced nervously at the conjoined twins. "Who are you and why am I here?" Her accent was English, with just a touch of Boston in it.

"Don't you recognize me, Momma?" I asked. "I'm your son."

She looked at me with barely disguised contempt. "I've never seen you before."

I shook my head. "Surely you remember me," I insisted. "Your son Edgar? I have a brother called Henry, who's two years older than me. You were married to my father, David. And then to Mr. A——, my stepfather. We lived in Richmond, Virginia. Surely you remember us, Momma?"

I felt a sharp pain in my heart as my mother continued to stare at me with a look of cold incomprehension.

"I remember nothing, boy," she said. "Nothing at all. Not who I was, not who I am. Why have you come here? Is this a joke? Some new torment that you have devised for me?"

"No, Momma, no. I'm telling you the truth. I really am your son. I just wanted to see you again because . . . I miss you so much. More than words can say. That's why I'm here. To tell you that I love you and I miss you and that I've never forgotten you."

Her dark brown eyes narrowed and she let out a little sigh that drew her hand to her mouth.

"Oh," she said, as if something had been awoken in her mind. "Yes. I do begin to remember something. From long ago. Before I came here. Yes. It's been so long, I had quite forgotten, yes. Forgive me, Edgar, yes. I remember now."

I moved to embrace her but found my guide interposing his twin selves between my mother and myself.

"Time's up," he said.

"What?"

"Five minutes," said the one.

"You agreed," said the other.

A curious thing now happened. The twins separated at the hip. One took hold of my mother around the waist and the other took firm hold of my arm and began to lead me away from her, back to the stairs.

"Please," I said. "Give us two more minutes, I beg of you."

"He begs," said the man holding my mother. "Here, of all places. He begs and expects us to listen. Can you credit it?"

"Please," wailed my mother. "Don't go."

The man holding me laughed and led me to the stairs, for he was much too strong to resist. "Is it possible that you still do not understand where you are, boy?"

"Edgar, my son."

My mother's little hand reached out for mine and our fingers touched fleetingly.

"Edgar, my boy. Don't leave me here. Forgive me, son. Yes, it's

true, I had forgotten. But I remember now. I remember everything. You, Henry, your father. Our house in Richmond. When we were a family. Everything. Please, don't abandon me here. Please."

This last word was not spoken so much as screamed in anguish, cutting through my chest like a huge, sharp blade.

"Please," she screamed again. "Don't leave me, Edgar. Please!"

"Momma, I'm right here. I'm here."

And then she was gone, although that terrible scream stayed ringing in my ears for several hours after I saw her no more. No more!

Suddenly it was horribly plain to me the awful truth of what I had done. Until she had seen me again, my mother had been reconciled to our being parted by the grave; but now, as a result of my stupid underworld tourism, she would have to endure the awful torment of our being parted once again, only this time until I myself was dead.

Why had I never perceived any of this before? Why had I not recognized where I was and the true identity of my smiling Oriental guide?

"What have I done?" I whispered as he led me back upstairs. "What have I done?"

"Done?" He grinned a sulfurous, evil grin that was part man and part wolf. "Why, you've done my job for me, old fellow. You've done my job for me."

I heard a hum of voices, only some of which belonged to him.

"Normally we try to discourage contact between the living and the dead. But, all things considered, your visit has been a great success. It's always a challenge devising new torments for our guests. And I don't mind confessing that I thought I had seen every torture known to man or imp. But this was something special. I congratu-

late you, old fellow. And offer my humble thanks. For this was the first time that a torment worked in this world and yours. As I know you will soon discover."

And then I must have fainted.

When I opened my eyes again, I was in my own bed at home and sick with a fever. Mammy was there with a cold cloth to mop my brow. I have no idea how I got there. Had the whole thing been a dreadful nightmare? Or had I really visited the underworld like Orpheus? I cannot say for certain, because by the time I was well enough to speak to Scipio again, he himself was sick of the same fever and, very soon afterwards, was dead by it, for which I was extremely sorry.

But a strange thing happened while I was helping to nurse poor Scipio. When I took out my own handkerchief to mop his brow, as Mammy had mopped mine, a second handkerchief fell out of my pocket. But it was not one of mine. It was made of lace.

Mammy picked it up. "What's this, Master Edgar?" she said. "You got yourself a lady friend?" She was about to hand it back to me when she noted the initials "E.P." on the corner. She lifted the little handkerchief to her nose and then sniffed it. Her eyes widened like she had seen a ghost. "Where'd you get this handkerchief?"

"I don't know," I said, looking at it.

"Don't lie to me, Master Edgar," she said.

"Really, I don't. I've never seen it before."

"Your momma, Elizabeth, she been dead these four years but her perfume is mighty powerful on the material," said Mammy. "Extract of jasmine and violet. Like she just got done holding it."

"E.P.," I said, looking at the initials. "Was it my mother's?" I asked.

"Ain't possible that it is," she said fearfully. "And yet that's what it looks and smells like."

"It's just a handkerchief." I shrugged. "I really don't see why you're looking so alarmed about it."

"I knew your momma's linen, Master Edgar. That woman owned but six handkerchiefs with her initials on them and every one had blood on it on account of the fact that she had the consumption. Like this."

And she showed me a spot of blood on the handkerchief. The blood hardly looked old. Surely this was fresh blood. As she spoke I felt a chill come over me. Was it possible that she was right?

"Which is why I burned them all when she died," said Mammy. "So you go ahead and tell me, boy. Where'd you get this? 'Cos it seems to me that it couldn't ever have been got in this world. Not ever."

Now, when I am asked why in my life I have more often thought upon certain apprehensions and unendurable tortures than upon the free air of heaven, by way of an answer, I recount this story. It is, I do solemnly declare, no bugaboo, no mere fanciful tale, and I can honestly state that there are indeed moments when, even to a skeptical scientific eye, this living world and the sepulchral realm of terror appear as one, and man and a grim-faced demon do indeed walk, hand in hand, along the banks of the river Styx.

Billy closed the book and shook his head. "Wow," he said.

"So what did you think of it?" asked Mr. Rapscallion as he tied his curious-looking tie. It had a picture of a woman screaming on it that was a copy of a famous painting by a Norwegian artist called Edvard Munch.

"Awesome," said Billy.

"What made you want to read it, anyway?"

"I dunno. It looked like an interesting book, I guess. And it was on your special shelf so I figured it might be, er . . . special." Billy tried to change the subject so as to avoid talking about Redford. "You really think it's by the young Edgar Allan Poe?"

"This side of a séance, I don't suppose we'll ever know for sure," said Mr. Rapscallion. "But I kind of think it might be."

"If it was true, it would certainly explain a lot about Poe," observed Billy.

"How do you mean?"

"The kid in the story is only twelve, right?" Billy shrugged.

"As far as I can remember, yes."

"If you really did visit the underworld at that age, then it would kind of affect your whole outlook on life. I think it would make you kind of morbid. So perhaps it's no wonder that he wrote all those creepy stories like 'The Masque of the Red Death' and 'The Pit and the Pendulum.' I mean, if that had happened to me, it would totally freak me out."

Mr. Rapscallion smiled.

"What did I say?" asked Billy.

"Nothing. It's just nice to talk to a kid who's interested in books, that's all. Makes a pleasant change from being told what was on the idiot box last night."

Billy looked at Mr. Rapscallion blankly.

"Television," said Mr. Rapscallion by way of explanation.

"We don't watch much TV in our family," confessed Billy.

"Now that you've read 'The Pocket Handkerchief,' I'll be interested to see what you make of *Uplifting Stories for Boys.*"

Billy repeated the title with some suspicion. "It doesn't sound like my kind of book," he said.

"On the contrary," said Mr. Rapscallion. "It's exactly your kind of book. One of the scariest things I've ever read."

"Yeah, sure." Billy smiled wryly.

"No, really," said Mr. Rapscallion. "When we get back to Hitchcock, I'll lend you a copy. It's kind of old. Published in the nineteen-sixties. But it still has the power to shock."

"Just like that tie," said Billy.

"Isn't it a doozy?" Mr. Rapscallion straightened his *Scream* tie and slipped on his jacket. "Come on," he said. "Let's go to this stupid dinner."

CHAPTER 13

THE B.A.B.

The Kansas City Public Library, located on Tenth Street, in the center of Kansas City, is opposite the largest bookshelf in the world. Or so it appears. Because opposite the actual library is a large parking garage with an exterior that has been designed to look like a row of book spines that is twenty-five feet high. These books include *Invisible Man, A Tale of Two Cities, To Kill a Mockingbird, The Lord of the Rings, Charlotte's Web, Catch-22, The Adventures of Huckleberry Finn* and several others.

Billy and Mr. Rapscallion were outside the library. Before the B.A.B. dinner, the bookseller had insisted on taking the boy's picture in front of the titles on the side of the garage, with the camera Miss McBatty had given him back at the hotel.

"It'll be a nice souvenir of our evening." Optimistically, he added: "We can put it in the album alongside the one

Mercedes takes of the ghost." He grinned. "Wouldn't that be something?"

"You bet," said Billy, who was none too sure about this.

Meanwhile, he was ashamed to discover that the only one of these books on the giant shelf he had read was *Invisible Man*.

"Actually, you haven't even read that one," announced Mr. Rapscallion.

"Yes, I have," protested Billy. "It's by H. G. Wells. And I thought it was pretty good."

"Yes, but look again," said Mr. Rapscallion. "This book on the garage here's not *The Invisible Man,* but another book altogether. This one's just *Invisible Man*. And it's by a completely different author. Someone called Ralph Ellison."

"So who ripped off who?" asked Billy.

"Wells came first," said Mr. Rapscallion. "He's the more famous writer, of course. But as to which is the better book, I couldn't say, since I've only read one."

Billy kept looking for a moment. "About how thick would you say these books are?" he asked Mr. Rapscallion.

"Nine or ten feet wide," said Mr. Rapscallion.

Billy nodded. "That's what I thought. Which makes you kind of wonder that there's nothing by Esteban Rex up there. If anyone really had written a book that's ten feet thick, it would probably have to be him."

"Good point." Mr. Rapscallion chuckled. "Good point. We'll make a critic out of you yet, Billy."

They went into the library, where lots of other men and women were arriving. As they arrived they left their coats in the cloakroom and then lined up to be greeted by a very large lady wearing a long purple dress and a knitted brown shawl, and next to her a very stout man with a red face wearing a dark brown suit that smelled strongly of mothballs.

"That's Miss Bertolucci," said Mr. Rapscallion. "She's the chairperson of the B.A.B. And next to her is Mr. Brando, the vice chairperson."

Miss Bertolucci greeted Mr. Rapscallion and then Billy warmly.

"And who is your young friend, Rexford?" she asked in a squeaky little voice that sounded like someone polishing a windshield.

"This is Billy Shivers."

Miss Bertolucci took Billy's hand and introduced herself, and, trying to make polite conversation, Billy asked her if she was from Kansas City.

"As a matter of fact, I'm not," she said. "I'm from Detroit. And so is Mr. Brando." She turned to Mr. Rapscallion. "We're so looking forward to your speech tonight. Aren't we?"

Mr. Brando nodded enthusiastically. "Can't wait." He grinned a big grin. "Hey, Rexford, what did you think of the new Esteban Rex?"

"I hated it," said Mr. Rapscallion. "But don't quote me on that. Especially to him. He's the kind of author you don't cross if you can help it."

While Mr. Rapscallion talked about books with some of the other booksellers, Billy went to explore the library. This was much bigger and better than the one in Hitchcock. From the outside it had looked like a Greek temple. And it was a little like a Greek temple on the inside, too, with marble columns and polished floors. It was full of books, of course. But it was also full of people. And none of them seemed to be paying any attention to the large sign above the main desk that read SILENCE AT ALL TIMES.

Billy was shocked.

Mr. Rapscallion came and found Billy in front of an enormous Leaning Tower of Pisa–pile of books that looked like it was about to topple over.

"That could injure someone if it falls," whispered Billy.

"It's a sculpture," said Mr. Rapscallion. "It's designed to look like it's about to topple over. But it won't."

"They should ask for their money back."

"I agree."

"Are all these people booksellers?" whispered the boy.

"All people who are involved in the business of selling books," said Mr. Rapscallion. "Publishers, booksellers, agents, even a few writers. See that skinny guy, by the far pillar? That's Jonathan Graft. He writes crime and mystery. Thinks he's the greatest writer since Herman Melville. Only he's not. And the rather muscular lady he's talking to? With the short hair and the motorcycle jacket. That's Gill Razoredsky. She writes books about murder."

"Why are they talking?" said Billy. "You're not supposed to talk in a library."

"Ordinarily, I'd agree with you," explained Mr. Rapscallion. "But the library is now closed to the public for the evening. So it's all right to talk normally." He smiled and lowered his voice. "Not that there are many normal people here. Did you ever see such a crowd of deadbeats? Booksellers. A lot of these people couldn't sell a glass of water to a man dying of thirst."

Soon afterward a man wearing a tailcoat announced very loudly that dinner was served.

It was chicken. Mr. Rapscallion didn't eat his. He said he was too nervous about making a speech to have an appetite. "Besides, normally you don't get chicken like this below thirty thousand feet."

Billy didn't eat his chicken either. He wasn't sure if it had ever flown as high as thirty thousand feet but it looked like it was made of rubber.

Finally, the moment arrived when Miss Bertolucci stood up and introduced Mr. Rapscallion to all the guests. She said he needed no introduction, which Billy thought was a bit confusing given that she was supposed to be introducing him. Then everyone clapped as Mr. Rapscallion rose in his place.

Billy thought there must have been at least five hundred people waiting to hear what Mr. Rapscallion would say.

"Thank you, Madam Chairperson," he said, nodding at Miss Bertolucci.

Then he looked at the audience.

"My fellow American booksellers. Agents. Publishers. Writers." He grinned nervously. "If I'd known the chicken was going be as tough as that, I'd have brought a dog to chew it for me." He swallowed nervously as no one laughed at his joke. "Now, as some of you know, I run an independent bookshop called the Haunted House of Books. We specialize in books about ghosts and horror, and vampires. The trouble is that people aren't buying as many books as they used to. Especially kids. They used to buy a lot more than they do now. I think it's because there's so much for them to do these days. Television. Internet. Cellular telephones. Computer games. Grand Theft Auto. Graffiti.

"Tell me something I don't know, I hear you say. But it

used to be that the one thing we knew they *were* reading was books about witches and wizards and ghosts and vampires and monsters. The trouble is, they're not reading any of those books very much either. Not anymore. And I ask myself why? Why?

"The answer is, I think, that kids just don't get scared like they used to. Not like when I was a kid. When I was a kid, I stood outside a movie theater where *Frankenstein* was on the bill and, looking at the poster, I thought it was the most frightening thing I'd ever seen. *Dracula,* too. And that was just the poster. I didn't even have the nerve to go through the door. Not that I'd have been allowed, of course. I was too young. But these days, heck, the kids just laugh at something like that.

"Nothing like that *scares* them today because they've all seen much worse on the televisions in their bedrooms. Or on their laptops. And that's another thing. Kids don't sleep in the dark. They sleep with the TV on, or the computer. Or even the light. And the lighting is electric, so it's more efficient than a candle, or firelight. That means there are no shadows. It means that there are no dark places where their imaginations can run away with them. What's more, our houses are efficiently heated. So children just don't tremble and shiver like they used to. And if there are no creepy shadows, and no shivering, how can we ever be properly afraid?

"The fact is that these days, scaring the kids is so much harder to do. The only thing that seems to really scare them is their friends laughing at them for being fat, or stupid, or listening to the wrong music.

"I don't have an answer to this. But I just wish that one of the writers here would write a book that is really scary and that maybe one of you publishers will want to publish it. So that we can scare the pants off kids again like *we* were scared. Because if we don't learn how to scare our kids again—and here's the important thing—we won't be able to control them. They'll just do what the heck they want, when they want. And that'll be a bad, bad thing.

"You see, if our kids aren't afraid of the bogeyman, or ghosts, or vampires—if kids aren't even afraid of the dark, then there's going to be no way of making any of the little rats toe the line. We will be powerless to stop them answering the teacher back in class, or being rude to their parents, or trying to write their names on the wall.

"Not only that, but the kids themselves will be missing out. Because you know something? It's fun getting scared. Frightening yourself can be a blast. My fellow American booksellers, a healthy amount of *fear* is the key to everything. We have nothing to fear except the lack of fear itself. The fact is, I wouldn't be the man I am today if I hadn't been terrified of the dark. If I hadn't believed that there was some foul fiend lurking underneath my bed. If I hadn't believed there was a ghost in my attic or a wolf-man in the forest. In other words, if I hadn't believed all that childish nonsense, I wouldn't ever have developed an imagination. And where would any of us be without one of those?

"Remember. We use it or we lose it. Thank you."

Mr. Rapscallion sat down. Most people clapped politely. But one woman was standing up and clapping with great enthusiasm.

Billy thought she was beautiful but also kind of weird. Her dark hair looked like she'd stuck her finger in a light socket and there were shadows under her big gray eyes. Her thin face was as pale as milk. He'd seen healthier-looking vampires.

"Bravo!" she shouted. "Bravo!"

Mr. Rapscallion leaned toward Billy. "Come on," he growled. "Let's get the heck out of here before I say something really tactless."

CHAPTER 14

THE BATHROOM BETSY

A taxi took Billy and Mr. Rapscallion back to the Savoy Hotel.

They found Miss McBatty in the bathroom with all her camera and recording equipment set up to monitor if the ghost of Betsy Ward put in an appearance. But she reported that so far there had been no sign of any ghostly activity.

"Not a squeak, not even a faucet turning," she said. "Of course, it's not midnight yet, so there's still plenty of time for her to make an appearance."

"According to the *Shudders* guide," said Mr. Rapscallion, "her appearances are usually accompanied by a strong smell of soap and then a woman's voice asking where the light is."

"It's common for a ghost to want to know where the light is," explained Miss McBatty. "Most ghosts are just lost spirits, looking for the light. They're confused. Lost. They don't know where to go. Or if they do, they're afraid to go there. Most ghosts are probably more fearful than we are."

Mr. Rapscallion closed the lid on the toilet and sat down. "I think you're right, Miss McBatty. We'll have to be patient if we're going to see anything."

"Talking of lights," said Miss McBatty. "It might help if you were to put all the lights out. In here, and in the bedroom next door. Ghost hunting is usually conducted in the dark."

"Yes, yes of course," said Mr. Rapscallion. "Billy. Do you think you could turn the lights off for Miss McBatty?"

"Sure."

Billy got up and shut off the lights. Then he groped his way back along the wall to the corner of the bathroom and sat down beside Mercedes McBatty and Mr. Rapscallion on the tiled floor to help them keep watch.

"Mercedes is an interesting name," he whispered.

"My dad was into cars," she said, and then shushed him loudly. "I'm sorry, Billy, but we need silence as well as darkness. Just about anything tends to spook a . . . a ghost."

"She was going to say 'spook a spook,'" said Mr. Rapscallion, "but she thought it sounded less than scientific."

Outside the window the street grew quieter as Kansas City people went home to their beds. Mr. Rapscallion coughed a couple of times, and once, Billy sneezed. The only light was a low infrared glow from the screen of one of Miss McBatty's spook monitors. After a while the girl whispered, "By the way, how did your speech go?"

Mr. Rapscallion whispered, "Very well, I think."

"Oh. Good."

After that they were all silent for a long time, and it seemed to Billy he must have fallen asleep for a while because he had the strangest dream. In fact, it was worse than a strange dream; it was a frightening one. So frightening and real and vivid, in fact, that inside that haunted bathroom he wondered if it was a dream at all.

Billy saw a woman standing at the end of a long, dim corridor waving to Billy as if she wanted the boy to go with her somewhere.

"Billy," said the woman. "Come with me. Come with me now. You don't belong here. This isn't right. You shouldn't be doing this."

Billy was certain that the woman was dead, which made Billy quite sure he didn't want to go anywhere with her. He was also certain that what he saw had something to do with the haunted bathroom they were in. He blinked against the darkness and rubbed his eyes until the woman had disappeared. Then he said, "This room is haunted. I'm certain of it."

"How?" asked Miss McBatty.

"Just now, there was a woman here who wanted me to go with her somewhere," said the boy.

"I didn't see or hear anything," said Miss McBatty.

"Me neither," said Mr. Rapscallion.

"You were dreaming," said Miss McBatty.

"I don't think so," said Billy.

"If it wasn't a dream," said Mr. Rapscallion, "then maybe she'll come again. The woman you saw."

Suddenly all of the monitors turned off.

"What happened?" asked Billy.

"Some sort of power outage," said Miss McBatty, flicking some switches but with no result.

"Odd," said Mr. Rapscallion. "Don't you think?"

"Perhaps you overloaded the circuit," said Billy.

"Shh," said Miss McBatty. "I heard something. In the bedroom."

Billy froze. It was true. There was something moving around in the bedroom next door.

"Where am I? Where's the light?" The voice—a woman's voice—was muffled.

And then they heard a sort of dreadful groan. "Can someone help me, please?" said the voice.

"Did you hear that?" asked Mr. Rapscallion.

"Of course I heard it," said Miss McBatty. "Quiet. You'll scare it away."

"Is there someone there who can help me?" said the woman's voice. "I don't know where I am. Please help me, if you can. It's very dark and I'm lost."

Mr. Rapscallion gasped. And so did Billy.

The door of the darkened bathroom opened slowly with a loud and sinister creak. And there appeared the shadow of a figure. A woman's figure. She had a large head of mad-looking hair and was accompanied by a strong smell of soap. "I can't see a thing in this darkness," whispered the woman.

"Betsy," said Miss McBatty. "Is that you?"

The woman gasped in the dark. "Who's there? And how do you know that name?"

"We've been expecting you, Betsy," said Mr. Rapscallion firmly.

"Mr. Rapscallion? Is that you?"

"Yes," said Mr. Rapscallion bravely.

And then the woman said: "Thank goodness for that. Just as I came along the hallway and was about to knock on your bedroom door, there was a power outage and all the lights went off. I hope I'm not disturbing you but I really didn't have any choice but to come in here and look for you. I've been fumbling around in the dark for several minutes."

Billy thought that the woman sounded English. And not really very much like a ghost at all.

"You're not a ghost, are you?" he asked.

"I sincerely hope not," said the woman. "Although after the dinner I ate tonight, I wouldn't be surprised if I ended up dying. I was at the B.A.B. dinner. I looked everywhere for you afterwards but you'd gone, so I decided to come and speak to you here."

"Wait a moment," said Miss McBatty. "I've got a flashlight in one of my bags, somewhere."

A second or two later, they had some light in the bathroom. And it revealed a person Billy recognized as the vampire-like woman who had applauded Mr. Rapscallion's speech so enthusiastically at the Kansas City Public Library.

"But why did you say your name was Betsy?" asked Miss McBatty.

"Because it is," said the woman. "Elizabeth Wollstonecraft-Godwin. Some of the girls used to call me Betsy when I was at school. I must say you gave me quite a turn when I heard it just now. What are you all doing huddled in here, anyway?"

"Ghost hunting," said Mr. Rapscallion. "There's a ghost of a woman called Betsy who haunts this bathroom. We were kind of hoping to see her."

"And then you turned up and ruined everything," complained Miss McBatty.

"She can hardly ruin anything when there's no power to work your machines," objected Billy.

"Thank you—Billy, isn't it?"

"Yes."

"Miss Bertolucci told me your name. And that you were both staying here at the Savoy."

A second or two later, Miss McBatty's monitors flickered back into life and Billy got up off the floor and switched on the electric light.

"That's better," said Mr. Rapscallion. "Thank you, Billy."

"Don't mention it."

"So, Miss Wollstonecraft-Godwin," said Mr. Rapscallion.

"Please, call me Elizabeth. Or Betsy, if you must."

"Very well, Elizabeth," said Mr. Rapscallion. "This is Miss McBatty. She's a ghost hunter."

"Jolly good," said Miss Wollstonecraft-Godwin. "Any luck?"

"Not so far." Miss McBatty spoke coolly. Then she switched off her monitors.

"Perhaps we'd be more comfortable in the bedroom," said Mr. Rapscallion.

They all went out of the bathroom and sat around the edge of the bed.

"So, what can I do for you, Elizabeth?" asked Mr. Rapscallion.

"Well, I was very impressed by your speech, Mr. Rapscallion. Marvelous stuff."

Mr. Rapscallion smiled modestly. "You're just saying that."

"Oh no, it was marvelous. Jolly interesting. Top-hole stuff. And very much related to my own field of inquiry. You see . . ." Miss Wollstonecraft-Godwin paused and looked around the room. "I say, is someone running a bath?"

Straightaway Billy, Mr. Rapscallion and Miss McBatty

leaped up from the bed and dashed into the bathroom to find that both the faucets in the bath were now running.

Miss Wollstonecraft-Godwin followed, nervously. "Did I say something rude?"

Mr. Rapscallion sighed. "No, not at all. It's just that . . ." He shrugged.

"She was here," said Miss McBatty. "The ghost of Betsy Ward. She was here. She came in here and turned on the faucets and we missed her. Can you believe it? We missed her."

CHAPTER 15

AN ARISTOCRAT OF HORROR

The disappointment they felt at not seeing the ghost of Betsy Ward turning on the faucets in the bathroom soon gave way—at least as far as Mr. Rapscallion was concerned—to a fascination with Miss Wollstonecraft-Godwin.

"That's an interesting name you have there," he said after he had turned off the faucets.

"Elizabeth?" Miss Wollstonecraft-Godwin pulled a face. "Actually, I don't much like it. My mother named me after Her Majesty the Queen. It suits her better than it does me, I think."

"No, I meant your surname," said Mr. Rapscallion. "Wollstonecraft-Godwin."

"With a hyphen," said Miss Wollstonecraft-Godwin.

"What's a hyphen?" asked Billy.

"It's the little dash that connects two parts of someone's

surname," said Miss Wollstonecraft-Godwin. "Silly, really. And rather old-fashioned, but there it is."

"I never met anyone with a hyphen before," said Billy.

"Actually, we used to have two," admitted Miss Wollstonecraft-Godwin. "Two hyphens, that is. My father shortened our name for the sake of convenience. It saves time when you have to write it out."

"If that's the shortened name," said Miss McBatty, "I can't imagine what the longer one must be like."

"It was Wollstonecraft-Godwin-Shelley."

"Yikes," said Billy. "What a mouthful."

Mr. Rapscallion looked flabbergasted. "But that means you must be descended from the person who wrote the very first creepy story. Mary Shelley, who wrote *Frankenstein*."

"I am," said Miss Wollstonecraft-Godwin. "Quite a name, isn't it?"

"Quite a name?" said Mr. Rapscallion. "I call it living history. I call it the Holy Grail. I call it the mother lode. The Klondike. I call it living history. I call it aristocracy. Forget Her Majesty Queen Elizabeth. For me, meeting you, Miss Wollstonecraft-Godwin—that's like meeting the queen. The queen of the creepy story, that is."

And so saying, he went down on one knee and kissed Miss Wollstonecraft-Godwin's little gloved hand, as if she really had been the queen. Either way, it was love at first sight for Mr. Rapscallion.

"Oh, I say," said Miss Wollstonecraft-Godwin. "How utterly romantic. And I insist, do please call me Elizabeth. You can't go on calling me Miss Wollstonecraft-Godwin. We'll be here all night."

"Amen," said Miss McBatty. "You mentioned your own field of inquiry, Elizabeth. What exactly is that? If you don't mind me asking."

"I'm a child psychologist," said Elizabeth.

"A shrink," said Miss McBatty. "I might have guessed."

"I've been making a special study of fear in children, so that I can write a book about it."

"We like books, don't we, Billy?" said Mr. Rapscallion.

"Sure do," said Billy.

"I've often thought of writing a book myself," said Miss McBatty. "But so far I just haven't had the time. I expect I will one day. When I'm not so busy with much more important stuff."

Elizabeth didn't seem to notice Miss McBatty's apparent jealousy. "I found what you said at the B.A.B. dinner quite inspiring," she told Mr. Rapscallion.

"You flatter me, Elizabeth," said Mr. Rapscallion.

"Nevertheless, that is what happened," said Elizabeth. "I was inspired. Listening to your fabulous speech, I suddenly had the most fantastic idea for an experiment. An experiment involving children."

"Yes," said Miss McBatty, "perhaps you could get hold of a lot of dead kids and chop them up, to make a living one. Like Frankenstein."

"Well, as a matter of fact, it does involve a lot of dead children," said Elizabeth.

"You intrigue me," said Mr. Rapscallion.

"Me too," admitted Billy.

"You probably know the story of how Mary Shelley, my ancestor, came to write the story of Frankenstein," said Elizabeth.

"Yes," said Mr. Rapscallion, "but maybe Billy doesn't."

Billy shook his head.

"She and her husband, Percy," explained Elizabeth, "went on holiday to Italy with Lord Byron, the poet, in 1816. Byron took along his doctor, John Polidori, my other ancestor."

"How very convenient," said Miss McBatty. "To take your own doctor. Me, I have a problem just remembering to get some travel insurance."

"Anyway, the weather was terrible and they were all cooped up in this villa Lord Byron had rented on the shores of Lake Geneva, called the Villa Diodati. And this being 1816, of course, there was absolutely nothing to do. No television. No Internet. No Scrabble. They couldn't even use the swimming pool. So, anyway, they all dared each other to write and read out the scariest story they could think of."

"It must have been some holiday," murmured Miss McBatty.

"Shh," said Mr. Rapscallion. "This is fascinating."

"Doctor Polidori read out the first ever story about a vampire. But it was Mary who won, of course, because that particular night, everyone thought that her story, *Frankenstein,* was quite simply the scariest story of all. But what most people don't know is that the weather really didn't get any better for the rest of the week and that Mary Shelley and John Polidori wrote another story *together.* A story they judged to be the scariest story ever written and much too frightening ever to be read to anyone. Including Lord Byron and Percy Shelley."

"Cool," said Billy.

"Isn't it? Well. After this holiday, Polidori's interest as a doctor in the subject of fear grew more intense. At the same time he probably went a little bit mad. People did go a little bit mad in those days. Which perhaps explains the peculiar events that subsequently took place at the workhouse in the London parish of All Hallows Barking by the Tower, in 1820. This workhouse had some one hundred inmates, of whom more than a dozen were boys aged between five and sixteen—just like those poor boys in Charles Dickens's great book *Oliver Twist*.

"The churchwarden of the parish workhouse was, like Polidori himself, of Italian origin. His name was Victor Creap. Creap had made a very bad job of running the All Hallows workhouse, which is probably why the poor lads had revolted against his authority. And, hoping to terrify these rebellious boys into behaving themselves again, Victor Creap persuaded his friend Polidori to come to the workhouse and—under the guise of giving them the very unusual treat of a bedtime story—to read to the boys the very story that Mary Shelley had deemed too terrifying ever to be read aloud.

"According to a London newspaper report of the time, the effect on the boys of Polidori reading the story to them was simply earth-shattering. Most merely fainted with fear. Several ran screaming from the workhouse, their hair turning white, even as they were running out the door. Three went to the madhouse and were confined there for the rest of their lives. One boy actually died of fright. It caused a sensational scandal. Victor Creap was dismissed from his position by officials of the parish while John Polidori found himself shunned by polite society. So much so that, weighed down by depression, not to mention some substantial gambling debts, poor old Polidori poisoned himself.

"Following his death, it was thought that the manuscript of the story read by Polidori to the naughty boys of All Hallows Barking by the Tower had been destroyed by John's sister Charlotte. In fact, a copy of this, the scariest story ever written, survives to this day and is in my possession."

"Yikes!" said Billy.

"Yikes indeed, Billy," seconded Mr. Rapscallion.

"As I listened to your wonderful speech," said Elizabeth, "about how nothing much seems to scare the kids of today, I wondered what they would make of the story read all those years ago by John Polidori to the boys of the All Hallows Barking by the Tower workhouse. And when you said that you wished someone would write a book that is *really* scary so that it might scare kids again like *we* were scared, I thought to myself—gosh, someone already did, back in 1816: Mary Shelley and John Polidori.

"And I was thinking," continued Elizabeth Wollstonecraft-Godwin, "that it might be excellent publicity for your bookshop if you yourself were to read the story to a group of modern children. Good publicity for you and an excellent case study for me to write about in my book."

"Not a bad idea at that," admitted Miss McBatty.

"I dunno," said Billy. "It sounds kind of cruel."

"Billy's right," said Mr. Rapscallion. "I'd have to read the story myself to make sure that modern kids could actually stand to hear it."

"Of course," said Elizabeth.

"After all," said Mr. Rapscallion, "I wouldn't want anything bad to happen to anyone."

"Not even some really naughty children?" said Elizabeth Wollstonecraft-Godwin. She chuckled. "Oh, come on, Mr. Rapscallion. Surely you'd like to scare the wits out of a few of *them*?"

"The idea does have its upside, I'll admit," said Mr. Rapscallion.

"For example, the kids who painted your mummy pink."

She nodded. "Miss Bertolucci told me all about it after your speech. Scaring some of them just a bit would only seem like payback, right?"

"Now you're talking," said Mr. Rapscallion.

"If they came," said Billy.

"Besides, only volunteers would be allowed to hear the story," said Elizabeth. "And only provided their parents let them."

"But why would anyone volunteer to hear a really scary story?" asked Billy.

"For the honor of being declared the child not scared by anything," said Mr. Rapscallion. "Any kid would love to have that badge of honor, don't you think?"

"Honor?" Miss McBatty shrugged. "Are kids interested in that?"

"She's right. There's only one reason to do something that I know of that always works in all circumstances in this country," said Elizabeth.

Mr. Rapscallion nodded. "Yes, of course. Some sort of financial reward. I know. I could offer a prize to the boy or girl who is the *least* scared by the story. Say a thousand dollars' worth of books." He flinched as he used the number.

Miss McBatty laughed. "I can see you know absolutely nothing about modern children, Mr. Rapscallion. I think you'd get a much better result if you just offered a prize of a thousand dollars. What do you say, Billy? Am I right? Or am I right?"

Billy nodded. "She's right. There's not much most kids today won't do for a thousand dollars."

"That's enough numbers, I think," muttered Mr. Rapscallion.

"In cash," said Miss McBatty.

"But how will we be able to measure who is scared by the story and who isn't?" Mr. Rapscallion asked Elizabeth.

She looked blank. "Hmm. That's a point."

"Obviously the ones who actually die of fright won't be eligible for the prize," said Billy. "And anyone whose hair turns white or faints or runs away or ends up in the loony bin like those other kids from the All Hallows Barking by the Tower workhouse will also be disqualified."

"Yes, that's right, Billy," said Mr. Rapscallion, his face bright with excitement. "Go on, go on."

"If more than one kid manages to stick it out, then you could have some sort of a tiebreaker," said Billy. "Like an ordeal. You could send them up to the Red Room and see which of them screams the loudest."

"Either that or I could devise a new horror," said Mr. Rapscallion. "A new room, with a new theme. Just in case any of the little brutes who come and hear the story are familiar with what's already in the Haunted House of Books."

"That's a great idea," said Billy.

"Very well, I'll do it," said Mr. Rapscallion. "The minute we get back to Hitchcock, I'll call the local newspapers and television and tell them all about the scary story and the contest and the prize."

"Brilliant," said Elizabeth. "It'll be a bit like the cash reward that Madame Tussauds in London used to offer anyone who would dare to spend the night in their Chamber of Horrors."

"Yikes," said Billy. "You mean people used to do that?"

"That's what I've always been led to believe," said Elizabeth.

"Where's the story now?" asked Mr. Rapscallion.

"In my handbag," said Elizabeth.

"In your *handbag*?" exclaimed Mr. Rapscallion. "You mean it's with us? Here? Now? In this room?"

"I always take it with me wherever I go," explained Elizabeth. "There's a copy at home, of course, in London, but I couldn't ever bear to be parted from the original."

"Could we see it?" asked Mr. Rapscallion.

"Of course," said Elizabeth, and, opening a satchel as big as a pillow, she took out a book and laid it carefully on the bed.

With Billy looking over his shoulder, Mr. Rapscallion picked the book up like it was something really valuable.

Which it was.

Really valuable.

CHAPTER 16

THE CREEPY OLD BOOK

It was an old book, of course. Any book privately printed in 1816 would have looked old. And it was a slim volume, as might have been expected of a book that contained just one short story. The binding was polished dark green morocco leather decorated with the intertwined initials of the authors, M.S. and J.P., in gold. Around these four initials were other inlaid and gilt figures of skeletons and gravestones and the faces of two very frightened-looking people—a man and a woman. Billy could tell that they were very frightened because their eyes were wide open and their hair was standing on end.

"Gilt titles," said Mr. Rapscallion. "Marbled endpapers, some skillful repairs to the joints, but still a very fine copy."

Mr. Rapscallion opened the cover, which creaked loudly like an ancient wooden door in a remote Romanian castle, and a rather damp musty smell filled the air, as if a coffin had been opened.

"That's unusual," said Miss McBatty.

"Yikes," said Billy.

Mr. Rapscallion grinned. "It sounds and smells as scary as it looks, right?"

And then he said, "I don't believe it." He shook his head in apparent wonder. "It's signed, by both of the authors. Mary Shelley and John Polidori. I can't believe you're carrying this around with you, Elizabeth. *In a handbag.* This book must be worth tens of thousands of dollars. Probably more."

"As a matter of fact, I had it valued in New York just a few weeks ago," she said. "An antiquarian bookseller estimated it's worth at least five hundred thousand dollars. Not that I could ever sell it, of course. It's been in the family for so long it feels like some aged great-aunt or -uncle."

"Wow," said Billy. Which Mr. Rapscallion thought made a very welcome change from "yikes." "Five hundred thousand bucks."

"Anyway," she added. "As a child I was always told that some terrible disaster would befall us all if ever this book went out of our immediate family. Which, given the book's curious history, does seem like a rather dreadful possibility."

This prompted Miss McBatty to go and fetch one of her ghost-hunting devices and to point it at the old leather book in Mr. Rapscallion's hands.

"I don't think the book is actually cursed or haunted," said Elizabeth.

"I've seen stranger things than an old book that had a peculiar effect on my equipment," murmured Miss McBatty. "Such as a cigar box, a doll's house, a rabbit's foot on a key ring, a pennywhistle, a teddy bear."

"A teddy bear?" said Billy. "You're joking."

Miss McBatty shook her head. "Sometimes it's the smallest or least likely objects that end up producing the creepiest results."

"The book does do one rather peculiar thing," admitted the Englishwoman. "Not including that rather frightening creaking sound you heard a minute ago. It happens as soon as you read the book's title aloud. So, do be warned, Mr. Rapscallion. This book is not to be read lightly or without careful consideration of the possible consequences."

Mr. Rapscallion read the title aloud he found on the first page: "*The Modern Pandora,* or *The Most Frightening Story Ever Told.* By Mary Shelley and John Polidori."

The second that Mr. Rapscallion finished reading out the title and before he could read any more of what was printed there, a very peculiar thing happened. The book seemed to produce a knocking, hollow sound, like someone banging the tip of a walking stick on the bare wooden floor of an empty old house.

At the same time the nameless electronic device in Miss McBatty's hand lit up like a lightbulb.

Mr. Rapscallion shivered and almost dropped the book in surprise. "Ooooer," he said, and immediately put it down on the bed. Then he rubbed his fingers nervously on his body. "Weird, or what? I actually felt the vibration of that sound in my hands. Which are now quite cold. Here." He held out his hands to Miss McBatty. "Feel them."

Miss McBatty touched them for a moment and nodded. "Gosh, they're freezing."

"Yes, I forgot about that part," admitted Elizabeth. "I should have warned you to wear gloves."

Miss McBatty let go of Mr. Rapscallion's hands and then looked at her ghost meter. "Interesting. That's the most powerful reading I've seen in a long time."

"What *was* that banging sound?" Billy asked Elizabeth.

"I don't know. But it always happens after anyone reads the title out loud. No one has ever explained how that happens. Creepy, isn't it?"

"It certainly is," admitted Mr. Rapscallion. Nervously he picked the book up once again and opened it.

"There's something written in what looks like Mary Shelley's handwriting," he said. "Underneath the two signatures." He read it aloud:

> *Let the reader beware. The story contained in these pages is not to be trifled with. Frightful it is. And supremely frightful is the effect of that which lies herein. Under no circumstances should this story ever be read alone, or on a dark and stormy night. No more should this story ever be read aloud to children, to the mentally infirm, or to those of a nervous disposition. You have been warned. M.S. Villa Diodati. Italy. 1816.*

"Caveat reader," said Elizabeth.

"Is that supposed to be a joke?" said Miss McBatty.

"If it is, I don't get it," admitted Billy.

"From the Latin *caveat emptor,*" said Mr. Rapscallion. "Which means 'let the buyer beware.' "

"Oh," said Billy. "I see. It's not meant to be a *funny* joke." He smiled all the same, just to be polite. "What's the story about, anyway?" he asked Elizabeth.

"I don't know," she confessed. "I haven't ever dared to read it myself. I know that sounds awfully wet of me, but you see, on the very night that my father first read the story, *he died.*"

"Are you serious?" Mercedes McBatty looked and sounded disbelieving.

"I'm deadly serious," insisted Elizabeth.

"What happened?" Billy asked her.

"Daddy had been jolly keen to read it all his life, only my grandfather had made him promise that he never would. But finally curiosity overcame him, I suppose, and so one night, he did read it. I don't think Daddy could have taken the warning contained on the book's title page very seriously, because he read it alone, and what's more, he read it on a dark, stormy night. None of us knew he was reading it, of course; otherwise we'd probably have tried to talk him out of doing it at all. The next morning we came downstairs and found him sitting in his favorite chair beside the dying embers of the fire, with the book still open on his lap at the last page. He was quite dead and as cold as ice. So, as you can imagine, when I inherited the book, I wasn't in a hurry to read it. I thought that maybe I'd wait until I was really, really old before I tried to read it myself."

"At least fifty, yeah," said Billy. "Good idea."

"No one else has read it since," added Elizabeth. "So when you do read the story aloud, in your shop, Mr. Rapscallion, it will be the first time that I've heard it myself."

CHAPTER 17

THE TEDDY BEAR'S PICNIC

When, the next day, Billy and Mr. Rapscallion returned from Kansas City to Hitchcock, Elizabeth Wollstonecraft-Godwin and Mercedes McBatty decided to go with them.

Elizabeth had to go to Hitchcock with them because she couldn't ever allow herself to be parted from *The Modern Pandora,* or *The Most Frightening Story Ever Told* in case something terrible happened to her. And of course to see for herself what happened at the reading so that she might write a book about it.

Mercedes McBatty decided to come to Hitchcock because she was keen to hunt for the ghost in Mr. Rapscallion's shop. And, of course, to see what happened at the reading.

And Mr. Rapscallion was pleased to see her setting up her ghost-detecting equipment, because he said it was good publicity for the shop ahead of his announcement to the local media of the reading of the story.

While Miss McBatty was setting up her camera monitors, Billy kept her company, bringing her snacks and cold drinks from the ancient refrigerator in Mr. Rapscallion's kitchen. All of this was a good excuse for him to ask lots of questions about being a ghost hunter.

One of the questions Billy asked Miss McBatty was this:

"When we were in Kansas City, and we were staying in that hotel, you said that sometimes it's the least likely objects that end up producing the creepiest results on your equipment. And one of the objects you mentioned was a teddy bear."

"That's right," said Miss McBatty. "In fact, that was the creepiest case I was ever on. I suppose you want to hear the story."

"Yes, please," said Billy.

They went and sat in the Reading Room, in some of the tatty old leather library chairs that Mr. Rapscallion had bought from the Edgar Allan Poe Club in Boston because it was rumored that Poe—himself a writer of extremely creepy stories, of course—had once sat in one of the chairs. Just above the door was the bust of Pallas, a Greek god, and sitting on top of the bust was a large stuffed raven, in honor—said Mr. Rapscallion—of Poe's greatest story-poem, *The Raven*.

Attached to the raven's leg was a message capsule for any ghost that was so minded to leave a message for Mr. Rapscallion—like the message capsules that are attached to the legs of carrier pigeons.

Mr. Rapscallion checked the message capsule every day and, when he was near the raven, as he was now, so did Billy. But there was never anything there.

"I'm no Mary Shelley or John Polidori," said Miss McBatty, naming the two long-dead authors of *The Modern Pandora*. "I don't know that you could call it a ghost story, exactly. But this is the scariest story that *I* know.

"Before I went to live in Kansas City, I lived in Chicago. The city's biggest and most expensive houses are located on the shores of Lake Michigan. And in one of the largest of these lived the billionaire Dearborn Dublin and his young son, Kildare. Despite the family's massive wealth, they were not a happy family. And I was to learn why this was on the day that Mr. Dublin asked me to come and see him. He was a very tall man with a gray beard and tinted glasses. He wore a green blazer and a darker green tie.

" 'You come highly recommended, Miss McBatty,' he said. 'To be honest, I'm not sure that you can help, but the fact of the matter is that you're my last resort. Believe me, I've tried everyone and everything else. I won't bore you by telling you about all that. Instead, I'll just tell you the story and let you make up your own mind.

" 'What I'm going to tell you is certainly strange. Possibly it's not the strangest story you've ever heard. But it's true. Every word of it, I promise you. My son, Kildare Dublin, is a spoiled child, Miss McBatty. All his life he's had exactly what he wanted. My only excuse is that his mother died when he was still a small boy and I tried to make up for her absence by indulging his every wish. Too late I've learned the importance of giving a child discipline as well as love. Well, there it is. You can't turn back history. I only wish you could.

" 'I mentioned the boy's mother. She died giving birth to Kildare's little sister, Liffey. It was the saddest day of my life. Kildare was about five at the time, and in a pathetic attempt to try to make it up to the boy, I took him to Grabber's, Chicago's largest toy shop, and offered to buy the boy any teddy bear in the store. Well, of course, choosing a teddy bear is no simple task for a boy or a girl. It's like choosing a puppy or a kitten and there has to be something about its face that appeals. To cut a long story a bit shorter, none of the hundreds of teddies in Grabber's appealed to my son. Not one. I tried to get him to choose a teddy but he simply wouldn't, and so we left empty-handed.

"'Our way back to the car took us down an old alley, where we passed an antiques shop. In the window of the shop was a largish teddy bear, about eighteen inches high. But this was no ordinary teddy bear. This was an extremely valuable teddy bear made by the German toy firm Steiff. Old Steiff teddy bears are extremely rare and expensive. And this one was no exception.

"'As soon as little Kildare saw the bear in the shop window, he wanted it. And, foolishly, I promised young Kildare that I would buy it for him. Although in truth, Miss McBatty, it was not an attractive-looking teddy bear. In fact, I would go so far as to say it was the least attractive-looking teddy bear I've ever seen. There was something nasty about its face that reminded me of a wicked goblin. Its eyes seemed rather too narrow. Its nose was rather long and hooked. And the way its mouth had been stitched made you think of a sneer instead of a smile. Also, the ears were not round but pointy. But we went into the shop and I told the man who owned the shop that I wished to buy the bear in his window for my son.

"'The man shook his head and told me the bear was not a toy. That it was a Steiff and this one was perhaps the rarest of the rare, in that there was a little brass tag on the bear's ear with a number six-six-six on it and therefore this particular bear was one of the first six hundred and sixty-six ever made by that company. Consequently, the bear's price was two hundred and fifty thousand dollars. Moreover, the man told me that he would not sell the bear to me, as he thought it would be a kind of crime to give a child a teddy bear that was a rare and valuable antique.

"'Hearing this, my son let out such a wail that, against my better judgment, I insisted that the shop owner sell me the bear. But still he refused.

"'It is not a toy, he said firmly. The man who sold it to me told me in no uncertain terms that this teddy bear was under no circumstances ever to be given to a child. That it could never be treated as a toy. And that it would be a dreadful crime if this bear was ever allowed in a nursery. And he made me take a solemn oath that I never would allow that to happen.

"'At this my son began to wail even louder, and it was at this point I think I told the shop owner who I was and offered a higher price than he was asking. Three hundred thousand dollars. A strange look now came into the shop owner's eye. "You wouldn't be the Mr. Dearborn Dublin who owns the lease on all these properties in Central Chicago?" he said. "The famously fabulously wealthy Mr. Dearborn Dublin who's planning to tear down all these properties and build a skyscraper." "Yes, I think that must be right," I admitted. At which point he seemed to change his mind about selling me that bear, which, in retrospect, I now know was suspicious in itself.

"'But I thought no more of it, and left the shop with a three-hundred-thousand-dollar teddy bear and a very happy son. We took the bear home and I left my son in his nursery playing happily with his new teddy.

"'Weeks passed. I forgot how much I'd paid for the bear. I suppose I even forgot the thing existed. Then one day my sister and her family came to stay with us. Her own two small children played in the nursery with Kildare and his toys. They brought a hamster with them. I think it may have been called Lucky. But when the time came for my sister to leave, we couldn't find it and presumed it must have escaped from its cage. We looked everywhere but with no result and my niece and nephew had to leave without poor Lucky, which upset them greatly, of course.

"'While I'd been looking for the hamster I came across the teddy bear, and perhaps my imagination was playing tricks on me, but it seemed to me that it was slightly larger than I remembered. Fatter somehow. And with a slightly different expression on its face from the one I remembered. It looked sort of smug. Like it was pleased with itself in some horrible way.

"'Weeks passed. And we forgot the missing hamster. We went to visit my brother and his family to see their new puppy. Kildare took the bear with him and left it on the sofa beside the puppy while we ate some lunch. When we returned the puppy had disappeared. And once again the teddy bear looked fat and horribly pleased with itself. The poor puppy was never seen again. And I told myself that I was imagining things. That teddy bears, even ones that cost three hundred thousand dollars, can't eat pets. I told myself I'd been working too hard, that I was imagining things, and decided to see a doctor. The doctor told me it was only to be expected that I should feel under strain following the death of my wife, and he gave me some pills.

"'Several more weeks passed. And for a while everything seemed normal. As normal as things can be after someone's wife has died. One morning I came into my daughter Liffey's room and found the teddy bear in her cot. I assumed my son had put it there for entirely innocent reasons. All the same, a chill came over me, and you can call it fanciful but I took the bear out of her cot and put it back in my son's room.

"'A little later on, Kildare went off to school, so imagine my surprise when around lunchtime I came across the teddy bear lying on the floor of the hallway that connects my son's room with my daughter's. How had the bear gotten there? I called my butler to question the servants but not one of them was prepared to admit having taken the bear from my son's room. They must have thought I was mad.

"'I had to fly to New York on business the next day, but before I Ieft, I took the seemingly absurd precaution of locking the teddy bear in my study.'

"Mr. Dublin let out a big sigh and wiped a tear from his eye," said Miss McBatty. "'Go on,' I said. 'What happened next?'

"'I am not sure,' he said. 'That night I received an urgent telephone call to tell me that my infant daughter had gone missing. And, fearing the worst, I flew back home immediately. The police were there and told me they thought Liffey had been kidnapped. Ignoring them, I went straight to my daughter's cot and breathed a sigh of relief to find that the bear was not there. Nor was it in my son's room. It was in my study and everything seemed just as I had left it except for one thing. And of this there could be no doubt: the teddy bear's stomach was larger. Much larger. And when I squeezed the thing it seemed to me that I could feel something hard inside its stomach. Not only that, but on the teddy bear's face there was a look of dreadful gluttony, as if the bear had eaten a very large meal. And, in short, I supposed that the thing had indeed eaten my baby daughter, who, like the hamster and the puppy before her, has never been seen to this day. But I could hardly bring my suspicions to the police. Not without them thinking me a lunatic. Or, worse, that I had done away with my daughter myself. So I kept silent. But not before placing the teddy bear in the safe, which is where it remains even now.'

"'So what would you like me to do?' I asked Mr. Dublin.

"'To be honest with you, Miss McBatty? I was hoping that you might examine the thing so that I might know for sure if I'm mad or not. That you might use your electronic ghost-hunting equipment to keep a watch on the bear and see if I'm right. To see if it's alive.'

"I asked to see the teddy bear and found that it was indeed kept inside Mr. Dublin's safe as he had said. Looking at the thing, it was hard to accept what Mr. Dublin had told me beyond the fact that it was an old and rather ugly Steiff bear. The face was much as he had described and reminded me of an old man who had stuffed himself at the dinner table. All the same, I pressed its stomach and found it quite soft to the touch. It was difficult to imagine, as Mr. Dublin believed, that this teddy bear had eaten a hamster, a puppy and a human baby girl.

"I was allowed the use of a room to set up my cameras and monitors and, having placed the bear in their middle, I went to work. Hours went by and I soon thought I must be mad. As mad as Mr. Dublin, I concluded.

"Day turned to night. And I grew tired. Yawning, I took my eye off the thing. And then, just for a second, I imagined that I had seen the bear move—as if, in the blink of an eye, it had glanced at me before looking away once again.

"Horrified, I went to the recording equipment and played the tape back in slow motion. And I saw that I had not been mistaken. The teddy bear had moved, if only for the tiniest fraction of a second.

"Nervously I picked the bear up and looked at it more closely. Still it seemed normal to me. And yet the more I looked at it the more I was sure its expression had changed, but so subtly it was hardly noticeable. The mouth was different, wider, thicker. It was as if there were more of the stitches that made the mouth than before. And fetching a penknife from my bag, I started to unpick them, one at a time. None of the stitches were tight, as stitches ought to have been, but loose, hardly stitched at all, in fact. And it wasn't long before my efforts with the penknife revealed a tiny mouth full of very sharp-looking teeth.

"This discovery shocked me, I don't mind telling you. A teddy bear with teeth was not at all what I had been expecting. Whoever expects a teddy bear to have any teeth? Let alone a mouth like a tiny shark. At this stage I ought to have left well enough alone. Called the police, or perhaps the zoo. I don't know. But scientific fascination overtook me, I suppose, and, putting aside my penknife, I pulled the threads of stitching aside with my fingers' ends."

Miss McBatty stopped speaking for a moment. For several moments.

"What happened?" gasped Billy. "What happened next?"

Her face looked grave, as if the memory of what had happened was all too painful. Which it was.

Silently she held up one of her hands. And it was clear to Billy that Miss McBatty was missing the tip of a forefinger.

As if something had bitten it off.

Billy felt his jaw drop like a dead man's hand. He let out a gasp.

"Yikes," he said. "Did it—the teddy bear—did it—?"

"Yes, Billy," said Miss McBatty. "It bit off the end of my finger. By the time I had picked myself off the floor and bandaged my finger with a handkerchief, the teddy bear had run out into the street and was never seen again.

"I am not permitted to say very much more by the Chicago police, as the case is still open and under investigation. What I can say is that the investigation revealed that Mr. Dublin's baby daughter, Liffey, was not the first family pet or little sister that had been eaten by that teddy bear."

CHAPTER 18

BEATEN-UP MERCEDES

"Wow, that is such a creepy story," exclaimed Billy. "I don't know, but that might just be the creepiest story I've ever heard. I don't think I'll sleep tonight thinking about it. And if I do manage to sleep, I bet I have the worst nightmare anyone has ever had." He shook his head. "The kind of nightmare where you think you're falling from a great height. Or the kind of nightmare where you're dead. I have that one a lot."

"Everyone has nightmares like that, Billy," said Miss McBatty.

"But that story is so creepy. Gives me goose bumps just thinking about it."

"Creepy, yes," said Miss McBatty. "But unfortunately for me, it wasn't supernatural. After all, it was only a teddy bear, not a ghost."

Billy shrugged. "So what's the problem?"

"Bil-ly," said Miss McBatty. "I'm a ghost hunter. I'm supposed to hunt ghosts and find them and stuff. A teddy bear just doesn't qualify, on account of the fact that it wasn't a ghost, but something very much alive." Miss McBatty sighed and looked sad for a moment. "Can I tell you a secret, Billy?"

"Of course you can," said Billy, leaning forward on Edgar Allan Poe's armchair.

"It's this." Miss McBatty sighed again. "Back in Kansas City I may have given you the impression that I might have actually seen a ghost. But the honest truth is, I haven't. Not ever. Not once. Those bath faucets turning on in that Kansas City hotel were about the nearest I've ever come to a genuine ghostly experience."

"I see," said Billy, trying to hide his disappointment.

Only he didn't do it very well, because Miss McBatty said, "You're quite right to be disappointed, Billy. I wouldn't blame you if you thought I was a total fake."

"I don't think that at all," insisted Billy. "In fact, I think you're kind of wonderful."

But Miss McBatty wasn't really listening. She was too busy listening to the sound of the disappointment in her own self that she was failing to hear what Billy had to say.

"I mean, I've got all this expensive equipment for detecting ghosts, but the fact is that I never have actually detected a ghost. Let alone seen one. What kind of ghost hunter does that make me?"

"An unlucky one?" Billy suggested. And when Miss McBatty didn't look convinced, he added, "You've only just started, Mercedes. May I call you Mercedes?"

Mercedes McBatty nodded. "I wish you would, Billy. I can't ever get used to the idea of people calling me Miss. It makes me sound like a sort of target."

Billy nodded. "What I mean is this: you're just fifteen years old, Mercedes. You ask me, you've got plenty of time to see a ghost before you can start calling yourself a fake and a failure. I think you're brave and wonderful. I know I wouldn't have had the courage to pick up a teddy bear I suspected of having eaten someone's baby. And certainly I couldn't ever have put my finger near its mouth."

"Thank you, Billy," said Mercedes. "I think you're one of the kindest people I ever met. And I think it's really great, the way Mr. Rapscallion trusts you to look after the shop when he's not around. He must think a lot of you."

Billy shook his head. "I'm just an ordinary kid who likes books, that's all."

"Believe me, Billy, that makes you someone worth trusting."

Billy shrugged modestly. And then he smiled. A compliment from Mercedes McBatty felt like something important.

"Tell me about your accident, Billy."

Billy shrugged again. "Not much to tell. We were all of us in the car, my parents and me, when it happened. A truck on Hitchcock High Street came from nowhere and hit us from behind. I really don't remember very much about it at all. Anyway, the next thing I knew, I was in the hospital. For months, I guess."

"Is that when you got interested in books?"

"Oh no," said Billy. "I was a keen reader long before that. As far back as I can remember, I've always loved books. Our family never had money for much, but there were always plenty of books around. And when I'd finished reading those, I went to the library. The great thing about books? It's the way they take you out of yourself. The way they make all your troubles seem so small. I couldn't live without books. It beats me how anyone can live without reading books."

CHAPTER 19

THE CREEPY CONTEST IS ANNOUNCED

A few days later, Mr. Rapscallion took Billy outside the Haunted House of Books to ask his opinion of the sign he had posted on the shop window. The sign said:

TO ALL THE KIDS IN HITCHCOCK

Scare yourself silly and win a thousand bucks.

Just five enormously brave kids will have the chance to hear a unique in-store midnight reading of the scariest story ever written in the whole history of the world.

But only the kid who isn't scared totally witless by hearing it will win the grand prize of a thousand dollars in cash. (Yes, we do mean American dollars, and yes, we do mean green stuff in your hand.)

In other words, absolutely no chickens need apply. We mean it, folks. If you're frightened of the dark, or your own shadow, or you think that maybe there's a bogeyman underneath your bed, then you'd probably better think again.

Take it from us, this story isn't for the faint of heart. Seriously. The last time it was read aloud, in 1820, there were actual casualties.

So if any of you kids think you've got the guts, then come in today, buy a book and enter your name and address for the draw. You could be one of the lucky five who are chosen to hear the story, one of whom will end up a thousand dollars better off.

ALL TERMS AND CONDITIONS APPLY:

1. The five "lucky" kids will be chosen by means of a daily draw. There will be five daily draws in total. Each day the name of one lucky child will be drawn. The organizer reserves the right to increase or decrease the number of "lucky" children and to increase or decrease the number of daily draws. The in-store event will take place at midnight on the night of the day following the final draw.
2. To enter the draw, you must buy a book in

this bookstore, write your name and address on your proof of purchase and place it in the shoebox provided by the cash register. (Just so you dummies know, a book is a collection of sheets of paper containing continuous printing, or writing. Luckily for you, you don't have to prove that you've actually read the book that you buy.)

3. The contest is open to all children between the ages of 10 and 15, but on the night of the reading a parent will be required in person to give written permission to the effect that their child is allowed to hear the scariest story ever written.
4. All participating children will have to provide evidence of age and a medical certificate that they are physically and mentally healthy. (Physically healthy, anyway. Let's face it, some of the loons in this town probably couldn't even tie their own shoelaces without help.)
5. Parents will also be obliged to sign a waiver absolving the Haunted House of Books and its proprietor from any legal responsibility should the child suffer nervous, emotional or physical damage as a result of hearing the scariest story ever written read in the store. (That just means you agree not to sue.)
6. Parents will NOT be allowed to accompany the child to the actual reading of the scariest story ever written, because any kid can feel

brave when Mom or Dad is there to hold your hand. Come on!

7. The decision of the judges as to the winner of the thousand-dollar cash prize is final. But frankly, it'll be obvious to the organizers who's scared and who isn't. (So don't even think of arguing about it. Parents will be obliged to sign yet another form agreeing to the terms and conditions of the contest. If you don't like that, then you'd better not even show up.)
8. Anyone who leaves the store during the reading will be deemed to have left because they are scared and will forfeit the contest. Anyone who screams during the reading will be deemed to have screamed because they are scared and will forfeit the contest. Anyone who faints or whose hair turns white during the reading, or who loses their mind, or who dies of heart failure, will be deemed to be scared and will forfeit the contest. Anyone who falls asleep will be disqualified. (Is that clear enough?)
9. In the event of a tie, then the remaining contestants will be asked to spend ten minutes proving that they're really not scared by entering the Haunted Cellar. No entry to the Haunted Cellar is permitted prior to the reading. That would be cheating.
10. No recording equipment is permitted. Anyone caught recording the story will be

ejected from the reading. Questions are not permitted during the reading. Translators will not be permitted. If you can't understand English, then tough luck, because the story was written in English. Anyone who fools around will be deemed to be fooling around because they are scared and will forfeit the contest. Cellular telephones are strictly prohibited at the in-store event.

11. The contest is not open to the employees of the Haunted House of Books or their relations. Just in case any of you get the idea that it's fixed. "Employee" means someone who gets paid to work here, okay?

    Books from the subterranean library may not be purchased as a qualification for this contest. Many of those books are unsuitable for children and probably quite a few adults. Besides, they're antiquarian books and I'd rather you didn't go in there.

12. Anything else you might mistakenly think we haven't thought of is contained in the very small print underneath. That's right. This is just the small print. Our lawyers can get much smaller than this, believe me.

The Very Small Print: All rights reserved, whatever the heck that means. We wouldn't have to print this kind of almost invisible and meaningless rubbish if people weren't such greedy morons, always trying to make a quick buck from other people who are just trying to scrape out an honest living. Or if there weren't so many greedy, grasping lawyers. Which reminds me, if you're a lawyer and you try to sue me or persuade other people to sue me, I shall take great pleasure in pointing out that everything is covered in the small print, or the very small print. So there. Now you know what it feels like. Get yourself a better pair of glasses and a decent job. I've got more respect for vampires than I do for lawyers: vampires have to suck blood to stay alive; lawyers do it because they like it. The organizer's decision is final. Blah blah blah. Blah blah blah. Mary had a little lamb, its fleece was white as snow. And everywhere that Mary went she was too dumb to take a book with her. But I bet she took an iPong or an iDork or an iDumb or an iThick or an iMoron or whatever they call one of those portable devices that are an excuse not to use your brain on a plane or a bus. Get a life, you dork. Haven't you figured it out yet? This is why bookshops are closing all over the world. Because people are too stupid to read books. In case you're interested, that's why we're running this contest. To try to get people through the door. Because if you mugs stop buying books there won't be any bookshops. And this town will look as ignorant as the others in this state. Use it or lose it. That's what I say.

Billy read it all carefully—even the very small print—and then nodded with approval.

But even before he'd finished reading, the sign in the window had attracted a large crowd of local people who started to discuss the contest with excitement.

"It looks like it's working already," Billy told Mr. Rapscallion.

"Good, because I told Mr. Johnson Hildebrand from the local newspaper all about it and he agreed to come over here with a photographer and to interview me. Aha." Mr. Rapscallion pointed at two men walking across the street toward the shop. One of them was carrying several pounds of cameras around his neck. The other had a pencil behind his ear and a notebook in his hand.

"This might be them now," said Mr. Rapscallion.

They were both fat and smelled strongly of beer.

"In fact, I'm sure of it."

"Hildebrand," said the man with the notebook. "From the *Hitchcock Hard News*? And this is Bill Snapz, our photographer."

"Hey," said Snapz. "How're you doing?"

"And you must be Mr. Rapscallion," said Mr. Hildebrand.

"How did you know?" asked Mr. Rapscallion.

"I'm a journalist," said Mr. Hildebrand. "It's my job to know things and find out stuff that sometimes people would prefer to remain hush-hush and covered up. Besides, there's a tag on your shirt with your name on it."

Mr. Rapscallion took Mr. Hildebrand into the shop to answer some questions for an article on the contest in the newspaper. Meanwhile, the photographer stayed outside taking pictures of the growing crowd. And Billy stayed to listen to what local people were saying about the contest.

"The scariest story in the world?" A tall man shook his

head. “Ain’t no such thing. It’s just an obvious gimmick. To get people through the door.”

“Once upon a time, I met my wife,” said the man standing next to him. “That’s about the scariest story I know.”

Both men seemed to think that was pretty funny.

“I think it’s a fantastic idea,” said another man. “I must say my eldest son, Grub, could do with a good fright. He’s too cocky by far. You ask me, a scary story’s just what he needs to wipe the smug smile off that kid’s ugly face.”

“It’s the same with my daughter, Loopy,” said a woman. “It might be easier to get her home on time if she was a bit more frightened of the dark. I think it’s a great idea, too.”

“Nuts,” said someone else. “The guy’s crazy. Nothing scares kids these days. I caught my five-year-old watching a horror movie. And he was laughing. *Laughing.* I saw the same film when I was eighteen and I had nightmares about it for weeks afterward.”

“It’s just an easy way to throw away a thousand dollars.”

“You’re missing the point, mister,” said a clever little girl called Gnomi, who was about nine or ten years old. “Do you really not get it? This might be an easy way *to pick up* a thousand bucks.”

“She’s right,” said another kid. “What couldn’t I do with a thousand bucks?”

“Come to think of it,” said a policeman who had stopped to see what all the fuss was about, “there ain’t much that scares my boy, Wham, either. And our family could sure use a thousand dollars. We could buy a wide-screen TV. Or use the money to take a vacation.”

People were already starting to go inside the shop. And

immediately several bought the cheapest book they could find—a very thin paperback by the Canadian horror writer F. Chankly Bore entitled *Newfoundland Nocturnal*—so that they could enter themselves or their child in the contest without any further delay.

And pretty soon the shoebox beside the cash register had several dozen names inside it.

CHAPTER 20

LUCKY NUMBERS ONE AND TWO

The very next day, the front page of the *Hitchcock Hard News* carried a picture of the first child who would get to hear the scariest story ever written, and have a chance to win the thousand-dollar prize.

His name was Wilson Dirtbag and he was fifteen years old.

The picture in the newspaper showed a boy standing in front of the Haunted House of Books. He had short straw-colored hair and a pointed, nasty little pixie nose that looked like someone had been at it with a pencil sharpener. But what was really noticeable about Wilson Dirtbag's face was the number of spots on it. There were so many angry-looking zits on his face it looked like some classroom comedian had dotted them on the photograph with a red pen.

Wilson Dirtbag was smiling in the picture but it was not a

pleasant smile. For one thing, he was the kind of boy who only smiled when something nasty happened—like someone slipping on a banana peel, or falling down a flight of stairs—and so he was out of practice doing it just to seem agreeable, even if it was for the front page of the local newspaper. Also, he hadn't cleaned his teeth in a long time, and as a result, these were a milky coffee color, with bits of food stuck between them.

"Like, I'm not scared of anything, you know?" he had told Mr. Hildebrand, the reporter. "I watch horror movies all the time when I'm at home but none of them frighten me in the least. You know? Not only that, but I don't believe in ghosts or any of that junk, so the chances of some stupid story in an old book scaring me are, like, zero. Those historical kids in that old workhouse, in London? They must have been pretty dumb, if you ask me. 'Sides, kids then would have been scared by pretty much anything we take for granted, you know? Television. Telephones. Chances are they'd have run away if they'd seen an automobile."

The boy's mother, Fedora Dirtbag, was pictured in front of her trailer home in South Hitchcock with a cigarette in her lipsticked mouth and curlers in her bottle-blond hair.

"We've raised our son not to be scared of anything or anyone," she had informed the newspaper reporter. "Least of all his teachers, or the police. When he was nine, a judge tried to scare him with some talk of prison but Wilson just laughed in his face. In my opinion? That thousand bucks is as good as ours already."

"If you win the contest, what will you spend the money on?" Mr. Hildebrand had asked Wilson and his mother.

"There are some unpaid fines I suppose I'd better clear,"

the boy had explained. "If there's any dough left after that, I'll probably get myself a decent air pistol. A Delinkwen one seventy-seven, or a Hoolihan magnum with a six-inch barrel."

Elizabeth Wollstonecraft-Godwin shook her head and handed Mr. Rapscallion the newspaper.

"That is the most ghastly, horrible boy I think I have ever seen," she said. "A rabid chimpanzee would have more appeal."

"It's even worse than that," said Mr. Rapscallion. "This juvenile horror was most probably the ringleader of the so-called children who painted my mummy pink in the Curse of the Pharaohs room last Halloween. At least that's what the police seemed to think."

"It looks like you're going to get your revenge," said Billy. "On him, at least. When you read him the story."

"That would be more than I could hope for," admitted Mr. Rapscallion. He clenched his fists and his teeth and his toes at the same time. "I'd love to scare this little swine out of his spotty little skin," he said.

The story in the *Hitchcock Hard News* had two immediate effects.

The first effect was that it brought hundreds more children and/or their parents into the store to buy a book so that they could enter the contest. (This ended up having the effect that F. Chankly Bore's book became a bestseller.)

The second effect was that it brought several more local newspapers and television crews into the Haunted House of Books to interview Mr. Rapscallion. This in turn drew the attention of the whole country to what was happening in Hitchcock. And it wasn't long before important and clever people were going on national television to talk about the scary story contest.

A professor of child psychology, Loren Gytis, went on *The Johnny Gross Show* to say that what Mr. Rapscallion was planning to do was criminally irresponsible and that he should be arrested before he could read the story and "damage young, impressionable minds." Unfortunately for Professor Gytis, she herself was arrested after driving her Maserati car past an elementary school in Burpbank, California, at ninety miles per hour and crashing it into the back of a school bus. Fortunately, there were no children injured. But the accident left the professor looking like someone who was herself criminally irresponsible. Which was good for Mr. Rapscallion.

The very next day a top scientist, Doctor Werner Voercrime, who worked for the U.S. Army Research Institute of Fantastic New Weapons, suggested that if the scary story did prove to be lethal, as it had done in 1820, it should be treated like any dangerous virus and contained in a special vault at Fort Detrick, in Maryland, until such time as a possible military use for a scary story presented itself. When it was revealed by a leading Washington newspaper that the USARIFNW had been secretly and illegally developing a scary story of its own against the direct orders of the U.N. and the U.S. president, the research institute was closed and Dr. Voercrime was sacked.

Then an entirely hairless man living in London called Colin Careless claimed to a newspaper that he was descended from one of the boys from the workhouse at All Hallows Barking by the Tower who had heard the story in 1820, and subsequently tried to sue Miss Elizabeth Wollstonecraft-Godwin on the grounds that her ancestor had given his ancestor such a scare that he and his descendants had lost all of their hair in perpetuity—which is a legal word meaning forever and ever. An English judge dismissed Mr. Careless's claim when it turned out that he had just been released from an insane asylum, where he had spent the last five years claiming he was actually the famously bald actor Yul Brynner.

By the time that Mr. Rapscallion drew the second child's name from the box by the cash register, the story of the forthcoming contest had gripped the entire country and the English-speaking world, which is another way of saying that the French weren't much interested in it.

The second name to come out of the shoebox was that of a rather beefy, muscular boy called Hugh Bicep, and very soon he and his even more muscular, beefy father and mother and his two brothers appeared on local television to talk about themselves. Hugh's father, Arnold Bicep, wore a blue sweater, and his mother, Olympia Bicep, wore a red one. Hugh's two brothers, Harry and Adolf, wore a yellow sweater and a green sweater. Hugh sat between his brothers and wore a black sweater that barely contained his bulk. The Bicep family was so muscular and colorful they looked like the five Olympic rings.

"I've always liked books," said Hugh. "My room at home is full of them. I like the leather ones with the gold titles on their spines the best. They look really old and important. And when people see them on your shelves, they think you're really clever. Of course, you couldn't actually read any of them, I don't think. I mean, they're much too boring. Mostly I prefer to listen to music when I'm working out. But, you know, I did read a book once. It was about how to build a real washboard stomach. Which really worked, as these days my abs are like a brick wall." And, so saying, Hugh Bicep tore off his shirt to reveal a torso that resembled the coils of a large rock python.

"What really scares you?" Mr. Hildebrand had then asked Hugh.

"What really scares me? That's an interesting question. Not having enough to eat, I guess. I have to eat five times a day to build muscle, see? Washing my hair. Chicken that hasn't been cooked properly. Switching on the television and finding nothing to watch. Losing my cell phone. Getting a wedgie. Running out of ketchup. Finding that the last candy in the box is a nutty one. Being bored. Lots and lots of homework. The thought that one day I might have to get a real job."

"Can your son do it?" Mr. Hildebrand asked Hugh's father. "Can Hugh pull it off and win the scary story contest?"

"Can he win?" Mr. Bicep laughed. "Of course he can win. My little boy is the most courageous person I've ever met. Let me tell you how courageous. Nothing scares my little boy. Nothing. You don't believe me? Then listen to this, Mr. Hildebrand. A few years ago we all went on a trip to Brazil, and a crocodile tried to eat him. What do you think of that? It crawled alongside him in the dark, while Hugh was in bed. Anyway, I guess my little boy must have rolled over in his sleep and crushed the croc to death. But was he scared?" Mr. Bicep chuckled loudly. "Not on your life. He just shrugged it off. Then, only last year, Hugh found himself in the sea with a shark. True, the shark was dead after my little boy jumped into the water and landed right on top of the shark's head and killed it, but that's not the point. The point is that being in the water alongside a shark, even a dead one, didn't scare him at all. In my opinion it'd be a pretty foolish ghost that tried to mess with my little boy. And as for a scary story. Well, this is the twenty-first century, not 1820. Besides, I can't see Hugh's bright enough to understand half the words they used back in 1820. You feel me?"

"Forget what I said about that other horrible boy," said Miss Wollstonecraft-Godwin. "*This* boy is the most ghastly, horrible little boy I think I have ever seen."

"He's not so little," observed Mercedes McBatty. "None of them are. The whole Bicep family looks like a truck with five tires."

Billy laughed. It was true. The Bicep family did look like five tires on a very large truck.

"It's even worse than that," said Mr. Rapscallion. "This muscle-bound ignoramus was another one of the so-called children who painted my mummy pink in the Curse of the Pharaohs room last Halloween. At least that's what the police seem to think." He nodded. "This is good, right? This is all part of the plan, right? This is what we wanted, right?"

Billy frowned. "There is one thing you might not care for."

"What's that?" asked Mr. Rapscallion.

Billy took Mr. Rapscallion, Elizabeth and Mercedes outside. He led them to a large trash can a few yards down from the front door of the Haunted House of Books. The can was full of books, many of them still in the paper bags supplied by the shop.

"There," he said. "That's what I mean."

Mr. Rapscallion shook his head. "Why would anyone throw away a new book?" he said, fishing one out and looking at the title. It was a horror novel entitled *Shadows Within Dark Landscapes* by the writer Ken Biro.

"Simple," explained Billy. "They're buying books—the cheaper books—not to read, but in order to qualify for the draw."

Mr. Rapscallion let out a weary sort of sigh.

"You try your best for people, Billy," he said. "But you can always depend on them to let you down. With all the books I've read, you'd think I would know that by now, wouldn't you?" He waved the book in his hand at Billy. "This isn't a great book. It might even be a bad book. But even a bad book demands our respect."

CHAPTER 21

UPLIFTING STORIES FOR BOYS

In spite of what Mr. Rapscallion had told him, Billy found it hard to respect *Uplifting Stories for Boys* and, at the very least, he believed that Mr. Rapscallion had been joking when he had recommended it to him. Far from being in the least bit scary, the book was full of sunny, happy stories about boys getting Christmas presents and going to summer camp with the Boy Scouts and receiving puppies for their birthdays.

"I'm more than halfway through this stupid book," he complained to Mr. Rapscallion, "and there's nothing remotely scary about it. The book is precisely what it says on the cover. A book full of uplifting stories for boys."

"Didn't anyone ever tell you?" said Mr. Rapscallion. "Never to judge a book by its cover?"

"Yes. But—"

Mr. Rapscallion shook his head. "Keep reading," he told Billy. "Take my word for it, kid. The book gets better. Much better."

And so, accepting what Mr. Rapscallion had said about the book, Billy read on; but if anything, the stories seemed to become nicer as he neared the end. And Billy was about to hurl the book aside in disgust when he got to the last story and thought he might as well read it and have done with the book forever, accepting his probable fate as the subject of Mr. Rapscallion's practical joke.

Billy read the last story in the book and it was so creepy that Billy had to read it again just to make certain that he hadn't imagined any of this. Because the last story in the book was completely different from all of the stories preceding it, Billy almost wondered if the editor of the book, who was called Octavian Girdlestone, had made a terrible mistake and included the last story in the wrong book. And he asked Mr. Rapscallion about it.

"I wondered that," said Mr. Rapscallion. "And then I discovered that before he was a book editor, Octavian Girdlestone was a disgraced schoolmaster at an English boarding school who was obliged to resign when it was discovered that he had gone around the school at night pretending to be a ghost, with the intention of scaring the boys witless. It's my belief that he hated boys because of their persistent misbehavior in his class and sought to be revenged upon them. And I think the book of stories was compiled with much the same motive, this being exactly the kind of book that a mother or a father might easily purchase for their son. You see, the book lulls you into a false sense of security that all is well with the world, and then *bam!* he hits you with the last story, which is a real shocker."

"Ingenious," admitted Billy. "So the last story becomes more frightening *because* of the twelve others that are before it."

"Exactly."

"What happened to this guy Girdlestone?"

"He won the Spanish lottery and spent the money opening an amusement park in Indianapolis that had the scariest roller-coaster ride in the Midwest," said Mr. Rapscallion. "Probably the world. The roller coaster was called the Indy 300 because it took three hundred seconds—or about five minutes—to complete. Most rides these days last around ninety seconds. The Indy 300 had two four-hundred-foot drops at a seventy-degree angle where the car actually traveled at more than a hundred miles an hour. And six three-hundred-sixty-degree loops. People on the ride were subject to forces that were almost four times that of gravity."

"Wow," said Billy. "Some ride."

"You bet it was. Apparently it went so fast the riders in the front car used to believe that the car had actually left the track. And people used to scream so loud they couldn't speak for hours after they got off. NASA used to send guys there to see if they were up to joining the space program; it was said that if you could get off the Indy 300 with a smile on your face, you were in. They had to have volunteers from the American Red Cross working full-time beside the ride to deal with all the people who fainted, or barfed."

"Gee, I'd love to go on a fairground ride like that," said Billy.

"Too late," said Mr. Rapscallion. "You see, a family of five all died of a heart attack while riding the Indy 300. And both the park and the ride were closed down, forever."

Billy winced. "Oooh," he said. "That's too bad."

"Girdlestone went bankrupt. And that was the last anyone ever heard of him."

[Author's Note: Space does not permit the inclusion in this book of all thirteen stories in Octavian Girdlestone's no-longer-in-print book, *Uplifting Stories for Boys;* however, the last story, which is entitled "New Shoes," is included here so that the reader who wishes to measure his or her bravery against that of Billy may get at least a taste of what he found so unsettling about this particular tale.]

"NEW SHOES"

There are few places in the world that possess as many churches as the ancient capital of Scotland and, of these, there are few churches that require such rigorous, unswerving devotion as the Free Church of Edinburgh. In truth, there is little or nothing about this church that is free, for it is a forbidding, granite-built institution of injunction, proscription and prohibition as opposed to one that is truly characterized by liberty of conscience, license and indulgence. Even in Edinburgh, which is not a city known for its good humor, the Free Church is a byword for small-mindedness.

Rare is the Sunday when the members of this strict Presbyterian sect are not rebuked by brick-faced pulpiteers for their worldliness, and sternly reminded of the many temptations in life that the devil has prepared for us and which must be avoided at all costs. Even the children are subject to thunderous, scary sermons on the eternal torments that await anyone who sins—perhaps them most of all, for in any normal child a natural lust for life outweighs a strict observance of rules and regulations.

Two such children were eleven-year-old Stephen Lang and his sister, Evelyn. They went to church on Sunday twice with their parents—morning service at eleven a.m. and evening service at six-thirty p.m.—and once by themselves to Sunday school at three p.m. Consequently, "the prince of the power of the air" and "the spirit that now worketh in the children of disobedience"—which was what the church minister, Mr. Redpath, used to call the devil—was never very far away from their youthful thoughts. And yet these two children were not without their jests and their diversions. They read books. They played games. Once a day, for an hour, they were even allowed to listen to the radio. But they were never allowed to watch television, which was generally perceived as the devil's favorite mouthpiece by all right-thinking members of the Free Church of Edinburgh. On Tuesday nights they went to church for what was called a "prayer meeting"; and on Thursday evenings they went to church again for Bible study. Secretly Stephen and Evelyn disliked going to church so much, but there were two events on the calendar they did enjoy: the Sunday school Christmas party, and the Sunday school summer picnic.

Of these Stephen Lang much preferred the picnic at Carberry Tower—paid for by one of the church elders, Lord Dull—for the freedom it afforded him to roam through the many beautiful acres of grounds without interference from his religious-minded parents. Later on there were races and, after prayers and Bible readings, of course, the picnic itself. But it was the races Stephen enjoyed most of all, since there were many prizes to be won. And win them he did. For Stephen Lang was a powerful and determined runner at almost any distance and it was generally held that he had the legs of a gazelle. Every Sunday school picnic, year in and year out, without fail, Stephen won all of the races he entered, and sometimes he would go home with so many prizes that he needed the help of his mother and father to carry the footballs, books, games, puzzles—there were even a few cups and medals in his haul of triumph. This did not meet with his father's approval, however, for although Mr. Lang was proud of his son's natural athletic ability, he was also a man who strongly believed in the virtue of humility.

"I think you've won everything that could have been won," exclaimed his sister as they carried his prizes to the car. "I've never seen so many prizes."

It was the wrong thing to say at that particular moment.

"'Pride goeth before destruction and a haughty spirit before a fall,'" Mr. Lang told his son. "Proverbs, chapter sixteen, verse eighteen."

"Yes, Father," said Stephen.

Mr. Lang opened the car trunk and placed the prizes on the neatly folded tartan rug that lived in there. "'And he said unto them, Take heed and beware of covetousness: for a man's life consisteth not in the abundance of the things which he possesseth.'"

As the months went by, the year ended and a new year began and Stephen forgot his father's words. But Mr. Lang did not forget and, the following summer, on the day of the Sunday school picnic, Mr. Lang took Stephen aside in order to speak to him.

Stephen was seldom invited inside his father's study. There was a large roll-top desk with a little wooden lectern on which a heavily underlined Bible lay open; and on the wall there was a fine print of a painting that depicted the temptation of Christ.

Mr. Lang sat down behind the desk and admonished his son solemnly.

"I think you should give one of the other boys a chance of winning something at this year's picnic races," he said.

"They have as much chance as I have myself," said Stephen.

"We all start from the same position. With that in mind, how can I give them what they don't have, which is the ability to run as fast as I can? It's not my fault if they can't run as fast as me."

"You don't understand," said Mr. Lang. "Your winning everything there is to win is beginning to look like greed. It looks as if you are seeking glory on this earth when we both know that real glory can only be had in heaven. You see, Stephen, we must always be on our guard against the devil's earthly temptations that are offered by winning things."

"But these things are prizes from the church," said Stephen. "I don't see what on earth the devil can have to do with those."

"On the face of it, that's true," admitted his father. "But the devil takes pains to hide or disguise the hoof. It may be that this is some kind of test, as Satan himself tested our Lord when he took him unto a high place in the desert and offered him the whole world if Jesus would kneel down and worship him." He nodded at the painting on the wall as if to emphasize the point he was making. "Yes, Stephen, even our Lord was tempted. So what I'm saying is that you should let one of the other boys win a race. That you should allow someone else to get a prize this year."

"But how will I do that?" Stephen asked his father, genuinely puzzled.

"Och, I mean just don't try so hard to win, laddie," he said, with great severity. "Surely that must be possible."

"Wouldn't that be dishonest?" objected the boy. "Not to try one's best is surely to deny what the Lord has given me, which is my God-given ability to run faster than anyone else." He shrugged. "For all you or I know, Father, I run for the glory of God."

It was a clever argument. His father seemed to reflect upon it for some minutes with an effort of mind.

"Aye, you're right," he said. "Perhaps it would be dishonest at

that. Ecclesiastes nine tells us, 'Whatsoever thy hand findeth to do, do it with all thy might.' And Colossians three reminds us that 'whatsoever ye do, do it heartily as to the Lord and not unto men.' It would be wrong to throw a race you have entered.

"So, I think it would be best, Stephen, if perhaps you simply did not enter more than half the races you did last year. By all means win the ones you're in, Stephen. But stay out of the others. For remember what the apostle Matthew tells us. That 'whosoever shall exalt himself shall be abused; and he that shall humble himself shall be exalted.' "

Stephen was about to make another point in his case, because as well as being a fine runner he was also tenacious in argument, but his father raised his hand and said, "I've said all I will say on this matter. You will do what you're told."

Stephen blushed with anger and somewhat hung his head, for he had been looking forward to carrying all before him on the sports field that afternoon as usual.

"Have I made myself clear?"

"Yes, Father," said Stephen, and regained his own room in brooding, resentful silence.

Now, for as long as Stephen could remember, it had always been his mother's habit on the morning of the day of the Sunday school picnic to take her son and daughter to the local shoe shop to buy them each a new pair of sandals. Stephen was looking forward to it because he liked the shoe shop. It was on the North Bridge and he loved peering over the bridge parapet at the many steam trains passing underneath in and out of Waverley Station. It looked like an infernal place, full of smoke and noise and far removed from the enforced quiet of home and church. It was like looking into the dark entrails of Edinburgh itself. Better than that, however, the trains went to places he had only ever dreamed of going. Places his parents hardly thought it fit to mention in pious company. Cities like Glasgow and London, which his father often described as "dens of iniquity." Stephen knew that "iniquity" meant injustice and wickedness, but that only made a place like London seem all the more exciting and attractive.

Stephen was also looking forward to sitting in the little blue wooden toy cars that were inside the shoe shop, where a boy might sit while he was waiting for his sister to have her sandals fitted. But most of all he was looking forward to visiting the shoe shop because he was keen to try out a large wooden cabinet that X-rayed your feet. Stephen had never had an X-ray before and he was anxious to see what the bones of his feet really looked like.

They went inside the shop, where a salesman approached unctuously. He was a small but handsome man with a high forehead and dark hair. He wore a little beard and a mustache that made him resemble a French king of the Renaissance.

"Can I be of assistance, madam?"

Evelyn went first. And while Stephen drove one of the wooden cars spiritedly—which was very unlike the way his father drove the family car—Evelyn's feet were measured, whereupon it was discovered that these had grown a whole size since the year before. A pair of brown leather sandals was produced and Evelyn put them on. Finally the moment came when Evelyn's feet in her new sandals were to be observed, scientifically, and the salesman moved Mrs. Lang and her daughter toward the shoe-fitting machine.

This was made by the Pedoscope Company of St. Albans, England, and in Stephen's eyes it looked more like something that belonged properly on a submarine. There were several knobs and switches and three viewing ports, like binocular cases, where the salesman, the customer and the customer's mother could all view an image of the customer's feet at the same time.

"There are twenty-six bones in the human foot," said the salesman. "And this machine allows us to make sure that none of them are squeezed by a pair of new shoes. Och, the wonders of science, eh? What could be more modern?"

When his mother had finished viewing Evelyn's feet, Stephen took her place and marveled at the milky green image of his sister's toes wiggling inside her new sandals.

"It's like looking at your skeleton," he told her. "In fact, I wish I was."

Evelyn checked that her mother wasn't looking and then stuck her tongue out at him.

At last it was Stephen's turn, and as soon as the black leather sandals were on his feet—black leather was essential so that he could wear them at school—he mounted the wooden step and shuffled his feet through the shoebox-size aperture on top of the X-ray tube. Excited, he pressed his face onto the viewing port and waited patiently for the salesman to switch on the Pedoscope. For several moments he stared into blackness. It was like looking down into the nether regions of the earth.

The man waffled on a bit to Mrs. Lang about how shoes that fitted well lasted longer and therefore SAVED MONEY—a very Edinburgh conversation—and then switched the Pedoscope on again.

Stephen Lang gasped with horror at the sight that greeted him, for his own feet seemed quite different from those of his sister. Indeed, they couldn't have seemed more different. He could hardly believe his own eyes. For there on the little X-ray screen was a perfect image not of two human feet with twenty-six bones each but of two perfectly shaped cloven hooves. It was as if he was looking at two feet that belonged to a goat or an antelope.

He straightened immediately before, thinking he must have imagined this—for his mother and the salesman were talking quite normally, as if they could see nothing unusual about the X-ray—he bent down to look again into the viewing port.

"Aye, there's plenty of room for growth," said the salesman. "Maybe an inch in front of the wee boy's big toe."

Stephen felt a cold sweat prickle on the back of his neck. There was no doubt about it. He was still looking at the feet of some animal.

"You don't think he needs the smaller pair?" Mrs. Lang asked the salesman.

"No, madam. Their feet grow so quickly at this age, what would be the point? After all, money for new shoes doesn't grow on trees, does it?"

"True enough," said Mrs. Lang.

"This is a joke," said Stephen. "Isn't it?"

Mrs. Lang frowned at her son. "Whatever do you mean, Stephen?"

"My feet," he said. "They don't really look like that. Do they?"

"They do," said the salesman patiently. "They do. What's under the skin may not look that pretty, son, but it's what we are, fundamentally."

Stephen shook his head. "But my feet aren't at all like my sister's. They look . . . horrible. They're hairy and, well, evil-looking. Yes, that's it. They're evil-looking feet."

"Everyone's feet are different," insisted the salesman. "That's why the Pedoscope was invented. There would be no need for a machine like this if everyone's feet looked the same."

But Stephen was hardly convinced. "No, this can't be right," he said, shifting one hoof and then the other. "Really, it can't. You can't be seeing what I'm seeing. It's monstrous."

"Of course it is," said Evelyn. "You're a monster. But every time you look in a mirror you ought to know that."

"That's enough, Evelyn," said Mrs. Lang. "And, Stephen, do stand still. You're spoiling the image."

"It's all right, madam," said the salesman. "Some people find the X-ray images of their own feet quite unnerving. It reminds some folk of our own mortal frailty. We had a woman from Corstorphine in here last week who fainted at the sight of her own feet. I was obliged to fetch a man from the St. John's Ambulance Service to give assistance."

Mrs. Lang nodded. " 'All go unto one place,' " she intoned gravely. " 'All are of the dust and all turn to dust again.' " She fixed her son with a gimlet eye. "Stephen. Can you tell me which book of the Bible that text is from?"

But Stephen wasn't listening. He was still transfixed by the image of his own feet, if feet they were. And now he felt a distinct chill come over him as he remembered the picture on the wall of his father's study. Surely these feet he was looking at now were the same as the ones in the painting of Christ's temptation in the wilderness. There was only one other human-like being with cloven hooves that he knew of. And even as this frightening thought passed through his mind, he also recalled something his father had said. Something about how the devil takes pains to hide or disguise the hoof. Was that what had happened to him? Might that be the explanation why no one else seemed to see what he could see? Was that why his own hooves were disguised? Because . . .

"Ecclesiastes," said his mother. "Chapter three, verse twenty." She tutted loudly. "You know that, Stephen."

As soon as the fitting was ended, Stephen sat down in one of the little wooden cars and quickly pulled off his new sandals and his socks to take another look at his own feet, which until now had seemed so familiar to him. He counted five toes on each foot and wiggled them all for good measure. He squeezed his heels and his Achilles tendons. He even nipped the skin on the upper part of his foot—hard enough to draw blood—to make sure his feet were real.

"Stephen, what on earth are you doing?" demanded his mother. "No one wants to see your bare feet. It's indecent. Put your socks and shoes back on immediately."

"I was just checking what my feet really look like," he said feebly.

"I know what they look like," said Evelyn. "But I can't tell you what they smell like. Unless it's Gorgonzola cheese."

Stephen sneered at his sister and started to put on his school socks again.

"An X-ray never lies, son," said the salesman. "It sees right through us, to what we really are." And he grinned a leering, sinister smile at Stephen as if he knew exactly what the boy had seen. "Sometimes I think it's fortunate that we wear shoes so that we might hide from the world what our feet really look like."

"Really?"

The salesman nodded. "Really. You can take my word for it. What you've seen is what's there."

The one o'clock gun had just been fired from the battlements of Edinburgh Castle when the coach carrying Stephen and Evelyn and the rest of the children from the Free Church Sunday School set off for the annual Sunday school picnic at Carberry Tower, in Musselburgh. Beset by uneasy suspicions as to who or what he was, Stephen sat by himself, moving grumpily away to another seat when any of his friends tried to sit beside him.

"What's wrong with him?" asked his best friend, Alec.

"New shoes," said Evelyn, and laughed as if that was really an explanation.

Stephen didn't answer his sister. He just sat there, prey to the most terrible imaginings. Every time he moved his feet or caught sight of them, the memory of the X-ray image in the Pedoscope inspired him with all manner of terrors. Soon the coach was driving through the Midlothian countryside and the sight of a herd of cloven-footed deer grazing peacefully on a green hillside convinced him that he was the center of obscure but infernal machinations. He closed his eyes, desperate to be rid of the one idea that now haunted him. That he was the devil himself. And where better for the devil to grow up than in the home of devoutly religious parents? Who would suspect such a thing was even possible?

A few minutes afterwards, worn out by sickening apprehension, Stephen fell asleep with his head on the coach window. He seemed to find the cold glass pillow soothing to his fevered speculations about who and what he was. And when he awoke to discover that the coach had reached Carberry Tower, he was calm again.

The tower was a castle keep built in 1547 and steeped in Scottish history. It faced the spot where Mary, Queen of Scots, had surrendered in 1567 so that her husband, the Earl of Bothwell—who was strongly suspected of practicing the black arts—might escape from the hands of his mortal enemies.

But upon his arrival at Carberry Tower, Stephen felt compelled to do something he had never done before. Instead of running off to play with his friends in the grounds, and much to his own surprise, Stephen decided to visit the historic house. Then again, he had a great deal to think about.

"Don't break anything," said the guide at the door to the mansion house. "And watch out for the ghost."

"What ghost?"

"The Earl of Bothwell's ghost," said the guide.

Stephen shook his head. "Believe me," he said. "There are plenty of things far more frightening than ghosts."

The guide frowned, for this was a curious answer for a boy to have given.

Stephen wandered through the old mansion house in a daze, ignoring the fine antique furniture and the many stained glass windows that distinguished the interior. He was feeling considerably put out by what had happened, although "cast out" might have been a more accurate description for his true state of mind. Cast unto the earth.

Eventually finding himself in the dimly lit chapel, Stephen knelt down to pray for guidance as to what to do. At home he usually prayed every night before he went to bed, as was his parents' habit, and, kneeling beside his bed, he had often felt the presence of God. But on this occasion it was not God's presence he felt, and, looking around, he saw a man sitting several rows behind him.

"I'm sorry, son," said the man politely. "I didn't mean to disturb your prayers."

Stephen sighed and shook his head. "That's all right. I don't expect he's listening anyway."

"You mean God's busy, is that it?" The man grinned pleasantly.

Stephen nodded.

"I wouldn't know," said the man. "I was never much on my knees myself. On the other hand, maybe you just need a better way of getting God's attention. Shall I tell you what my father used to do? When he wanted God to answer his prayers?"

"Is that really possible?"

"Oh yes," said the man. "I think so. My own father used to say that unanswered prayers were simply the result of absence from

fellowship with the Lord and his Word. And that all you had to do if you wished to regain his fellowship was to allow his Word to speak to us. Which would be the answer to our prayers. So what he used to do was get the Bible to answer the prayer on behalf of God, so to speak. He would say, 'Speak to me, Lord'; then he would close the family Bible, open it quickly, stab the first page with his finger and read the first text that caught his eye; and that would be the voice of the Lord speaking to him. And surely he would know then the answer to his prayer. After all, you imagine how busy God must be with all the prayers coming his way. It's a wonder he gets a chance to answer any of them."

The man sighed and leaned forward in the chapel pew. He was a very ordinary, typically Scots-looking man, with brown hair, a thin, wispy mustache, a florid, puffy face and shifty-looking eyes. He was wearing a yellow tracksuit top zipped right up to below his stubbly chin. His voice was much smoother than he looked.

"Yes, that's what I'd do. In fact"—he nodded at the Bible that lay on the chapel lectern—"if I were you, I'd go ahead and use that one there."

"Do you think they'd mind?" asked Stephen.

"Of course not," said the man. "And certainly not if you explain what you are doing." He shrugged. "Not that anyone will ask. It's always very quiet here on a Saturday afternoon. Especially in summer. On a day like this, most people have better things to do than speak to God. But I'll keep a lookout for you, if you like."

"Do you come here a lot, then?" asked Stephen.

"I'm pretty much here all the time," said the man, and stood by the door of the chapel. "Go on. Open it."

Stephen approached the big Bible.

"Speak to me, Lord," he said, and threw it open with a bang, stabbing his finger onto the first open page.

"That's it," the man said excitedly. "Now you read what's under that finger of yours, Stephen, and that'll be your answer, right enough."

Stephen nodded and read aloud the following text from the First Epistle of Peter, chapter three, verse twelve: " 'For the eyes of the Lord are on the righteous, And His ears are open to their prayers; But the face of the LORD is against those who do evil.' "

Stephen remained silent for almost a minute after that.

"Not the answer you were looking for, I dare say," observed the man.

"No," admitted Stephen. "Not exactly."

"In my experience of religion," said the man, "we seldom get the answer we most want to hear. Which is the story of my own life. But, as answers go, yours seemed quite clear enough, I should say."

"You think so?"

"Without question," said the man. "In truth, I imagine you already know what you have to do. Indeed, I suspect you've known it all along. And you just needed to have it underlined by what's in the Lord's book, eh?"

Stephen nodded. "I think you're right."

"I thought so. That's always the way with these things. It seems mysterious and then it's not."

"Thanks," said Stephen. "That's exactly how it seems."

The man shook his head. "Don't mention it. I'm glad to have been of help."

Stephen closed the Bible carefully.

"Now thank him," said the man. "Always thank him when you think he's spoken to you, Stephen. Even if you don't much like the message. Close your eyes and thank him in prayer."

Stephen shut his eyes and gave thanks in silence and when he opened them again the man had gone.

Now, as he made his way back through the old house, he began to discover strange things about himself that he was sure had not been there before. Curiously, his hair and fingernails smelled strongly of sulfur, as if he had been striking lots of matches. Then for a long time he stood in front of a large gilt mirror and, examining the space between his eyebrows, he formed the conclusion that it had become smaller, almost as if each eyebrow was reaching out to the other; and it was now he perceived how he was able to raise one eyebrow independently of the other, which he thought was very effective at conveying a certain intellectual disdain. The pupil in his amber brown eye he could dilate at will until it was a fathomless black hole. Moreover, there was now a somewhat wolfish aspect to the white teeth in his smile. And what with the smile and the raised eyebrow, he was able to make a scary, sinister face that might easily have frightened horses.

Satisfied with this clearer understanding of himself and now quite reconciled to exactly who and what he was, Stephen walked out of the mansion house and went to find his young friends at the Sunday school picnic. The weather was hot and they all enjoyed a perfect June afternoon: they played several games and caught tadpoles in the pond, and this was followed by a wonderful picnic tea where Stephen ate not just his own food, but several other children's as well, after which he dozed through prayers in the evening sun for half an hour. And later on, Stephen threw his new sandals into the lake and, in defiance of his father, he entered every race and, grinning fiercely, won every one of the prizes that there were to be won.

CHAPTER 22

THE THIRD KID(S)

The third kid's name to be drawn from the box was twelve-year-old Lavender Leapy. She was a pretty little girl with golden pigtails and a floral dress and a very sweet manner. She was good at schoolwork and played the flute and always kept her bedroom tidy and had a puppy called Sugar. The scariest thing Lavender had ever done was to ride a bicycle down a hill without holding on to the handlebars for all of five seconds.

Lavender was at home in Northwest Hitchcock when her next-door neighbor, Mr. Kaplan, called around to congratulate little Lavender on being one of the five lucky children who was going to hear the scariest story ever written. Mr. Kaplan told Mrs. Leapy that he had heard the announcement on a local radio news bulletin.

Lavender was in the shower when she heard the exciting

news from Mrs. Leapy. Immediately she became hysterical with fear at the very idea of hearing the scary story. She started to scream, and she kept on screaming for a full hour before her mother called an ambulance and had her taken out of the shower, to a hospital, where she continued to scream even after being sedated.

Mrs. Leapy was puzzled. She knew Lavender would never have entered herself in the contest at the Haunted House of Books. Lavender hated ghost stories. She always slept with the light on. She never ever went into the basement, even in the daytime, just in case something was hiding down there. Lavender was a very nervous girl and very easily scared.

But Mrs. Leapy wasn't stupid. And she soon guessed the truth, which was that the person responsible for entering Lavender's name in the scary story contest had been Lavender's nasty older brother, Biff, who disliked his little sister intensely.

Some brothers are just nasty. Biff couldn't have been a nastier older brother if he'd had a little brother called Joseph who owned a coat of many colors. And Mrs. Leapy had long and trying experience of Biff's behavior toward his sister. He was always amusing himself with new ways of annoying poor Lavender.

On one occasion Biff caught a harmless corn snake and placed it in Lavender's schoolbag. Another time Biff cut off one of her pigtails while Lavender was asleep. But perhaps the worst thing Biff had done to his sister—at least it had been the worst thing Biff had done until entering his sister's name for the scary story contest—had been to lay a trail of honey between a mound of fire ants in the garden and the sun lounger where his sister was lying quietly reading a schoolbook. The ant bites took weeks to heal completely.

The record for the loudest-ever scream is held by a woman from Kent, England, who hit 129 decibels in October 2000. The record for the longest and loudest scream is now held by Lavender Leapy. After Mr. Kaplan told her the news about the scary story contest, Lavender screamed without interruption for an astonishing eight hours. The story was on the front page of the *Hitchcock Hard News*.

The headline read: HITCHCOCK BLONDE GOES PSYCHO IN THE SHOWER.

When Lavender's father, Norman, returned from work and heard what had happened, he ordered his son into the car, drove for twenty miles into the middle of nowhere and told the boy to get out and walk home. Then he telephoned the Haunted House of Books and explained to Mr. Rapscallion that his daughter would not be taking part in the contest.

Mr. Rapscallion said he understood and agreed with Mr. Leapy's decision. He said he was sorry that such a thing could have happened and expressed the hope that Lavender would stop screaming soon.

And then he prepared to draw another name from the box.

Meanwhile, several more newspapermen turned up at the Leapy home in Northwest Hitchcock to get another angle on the story of why Lavender had chickened out of the contest.

Mr. Leapy, who ran a thrift shop, had never had any dealings with the world's press before and, foolishly perhaps, told them about the punishment he had inflicted on Biff. As soon as this was reported on local TV, the Hitchcock Children's Welfare officer, Miss Demeenor, showed up at the house with the state police and had Mr. Leapy arrested and put in jail for being cruel to his son.

The newspaper headline read: HITCHCOCK BLONDE'S PSYCHO DAD, NORMAN.

No one ever said it was easy being a parent.

Meanwhile, Mr. Rapscallion drew another name from the box. And this time the trouble was that he couldn't read the handwriting on the sales receipt. He was about to throw this latest name away when one of the newspapermen who were in the shop said that to do so might be illegal. And poor Mr. Rapscallion was obliged to consult a lawyer, Mr. Stoker, who then suggested he consult a handwriting expert in order to read the third child's name. So he was particularly irritated when, several hours and several hundred dollars in legal and graphologist fees later, it was revealed that the name on this sales receipt was that of Mickey Mouse, Disneyland, California.

"Someone's idea of a joke," said Mr. Rapscallion. Muttering crossly, he bit his lip and drew yet another sales receipt from the box and this time was relieved to announce that he had what looked like a genuine name and address.

"And the third child to hear the scariest story in the world will be V. Capone." He shook his head. "V. Capone. Is that a boy or a girl? You tell me. Even when I actually see the kids in front of me, I find it hard to tell one from the other."

While the identity and whereabouts of this third winning child were investigated by the press, Mr. Rapscallion was informed that Wilson Dirtbag and Hugh Bicep were now in training for the forthcoming contest and had already consulted hypnotherapists in order to conquer their fear of almost anything.

"Well, that's just great," said Mr. Rapscallion. "It's always gratifying to realize that, as always, our fellow citizens are approaching this humble little contest in the true spirit of American fair play."

But the world's press weren't listening. Most of them were running excitedly out of the shop.

"What's all the commotion now?" Mr. Rapscallion asked Billy.

Billy, who had been eavesdropping on the conversation of two of the journalists, explained:

"V. Capone is Vito Capone," he said. "It seems that Vito is the fourteen-year-old son of the infamous Hitchcock gangster Don Cesare Capone, who is himself a relation of the infamous Al Capone. One of the reporters said Cesare Capone is the toughest man in Hitchcock. That's his stretch limo pulling up outside the shop now."

Mr. Rapscallion, Billy, Elizabeth Wollstonecraft-Godwin and Mercedes McBatty followed the world's press onto the sidewalk outside. There, parked right in front of the Haunted House of Books, was an enormous bulletproof black stretch limo. And from it was emerging a small, dark-haired man in a shiny gray suit and a large hat. The man was accompanied by a smaller, identically dressed version of himself. The two of them were surrounded by burly-looking men with sunglasses who looked like bodyguards.

"No pictures," snarled one of the bodyguards, and, grabbing a photographer's camera, he hurled it onto the ground angrily.

Cesare Capone waited for the press to fall silent and then spoke quietly:

"Let me say right away that my son Vito is pleased and

honored to be taking part in this contest of manly courage. And I have high hopes for him. I've brought up all my sons to be law-abiding citizens, to be men of honor, but, above all, to fear nothing. *Nothing.* I've heard this man Rexford Rapscallion is a serious man, to be treated with respect. And I flatter myself that I understand what his purpose is here. I suspect he thinks as I do: that the children of today are greedy and they have no manners. They speak when they should listen. They have no learning. And they have no respect. I suspect this Rapscallion guy thinks that if the children of today have no character of their own, then perhaps they should be shown how to get it. At first I did not approve of my youngest son, Vito, taking part in such a contest as this. But I have a sentimental weakness for my children. Consequently I have decided to allow him to participate. So that he can prove his courage to me. And to the American public. That's what you want, isn't it, Vito?"

"Yes, Papa."

"So I say, good luck to everyone taking part and, as we say in the old country, *maggio il miglior uomo vincere,* eh, Vito?"

"Yes, Papa."

Besieged by questions, which they ignored, Hitchcock's most fearsome gangster and his son, and their menacing entourage, got back into the stretch limo and drove away with a loud squeal of tires and an even louder squeal from a reporter whose foot got driven over.

"That's a very frightening man," observed Elizabeth.

"Very," said Billy.

"I should say that he's not the forgiving sort," said Mercedes. "I mean, you wouldn't want to make an enemy of a man like that."

"Did you see those bodyguards?" said Billy. "I bet they were all carrying guns."

"Holy Toledo," said Mr. Rapscallion. "Do you think I need to be reminded of that?"

"I wonder what would happen if that kid doesn't win?" said Billy.

"Yeah, let's think about that," said Mr. Rapscallion. "What if his kid is scared witless? What if young Vito ends up in the loony bin? What's his father going to do to me then? Answer me that." He shook his head sadly. "I'll end up in the river, that's what'll happen. I'll end up in the river wearing a pair of cement slippers. I mean, that guy's not called Capone for nothing."

He went back into the Haunted House of Books, muttering loudly: "Why did I have to do this? I must have been crazy."

CHAPTER 23

BILLY'S DILEMMA

Redford had never seen so many people in the Haunted House of Books. Billy was handing out sales receipts for books like bus tickets. The box was full of them, and with all of the people who were in the store, he almost didn't see the boss's daughter. Seeing Redford walk in through the door of the Haunted House of Books ought to have made Billy feel happier, but on this particular occasion it didn't.

"Your dad just went out to get a cup of coffee from the shop across the street," he told her glumly.

"I know. I watched him leave." Redford realized that she was just a little bit disappointed that Billy didn't look pleased to see her. "I figure he'll be in Fool of Beanz for at least twenty minutes. He always likes to shoot the breeze with the guy who owns that place. So I figure we've got fifteen minutes to talk before I have to make myself scarce."

"Sure. Whatever."

"You really think this'll work?" she asked. "The contest?"

"It is working. Just look around. Sales are through the roof."

"Given where they were before, that can't have been too difficult."

Ignoring her, Billy rang up another sale on the till.

"What's the matter with you, Billy?" asked Redford.

"Me? I'm fine."

"You don't look fine. As a matter of fact, you never look fine. You always look a bit pale, and like you could use a good meal, and maybe a bit more of the sun. And sometimes I wonder about those clothes you're always wearing. Do you really only have the one shirt? But today, today, you look like the man who lost a dollar and found a cent. Are you okay?"

Billy shrugged silently.

"If you don't want to talk about it, that's fine," said Redford. "I hate it when people make me talk about things I don't want to talk about. Which is pretty much all the time. My mom is always telling me that I need to open up a bit. But, you know, if you did want to talk, then maybe I could help."

Billy sighed and nodded.

"Well, it's this," he said. "According to the terms and conditions of the contest, employees of the Haunted House of Books are not allowed to take part. Does that mean me, do you think?"

"I don't know," said Mercedes. "*Are* you employed by my dad?"

"To be honest, I really don't know," admitted Billy.

"Well, does he pay you any money?"

"No. I'm an intern."

"Nothing at all?"

"Nope."

"Not even a few bucks for bus fares?"

"I prefer to walk. It's good exercise."

Redford smiled wryly. "That sounds like my dad, all right." She shook her head. "Do you pay any tax?"

"No."

"Do you have a Social Security number?"

"No."

"Then you can't possibly be an employee of this shop, or any other," said Redford. "You know, it beats me why you bother coming here at all."

"I come because I like coming here," admitted Billy. "I like being around books. I like your dad. And I like you, too. If I hadn't ever started hanging out in this bookshop, I wouldn't ever have met you. Would I?"

Redford colored with embarrassment, just a little. "That's nice to know," she said coolly; but she was secretly pleased to discover he still liked her.

"But not working here leaves me with another problem," said Billy. "I don't know if I ever told you how poor my family is. We really don't have any money at all. My father isn't working right now. Nor is my mother. If I went through my father's coat pockets, I would find nothing at all. Thin air, I guess. So we certainly don't have money for books. Books are expensive. Very expensive."

"That's because people don't buy as many of them as they used to," said Redford. "And they buy even fewer now because they're expensive. It's what Dad calls a vicious circle. Pretty soon they won't buy any books at all and then the country will be as dumb as it deserves to be. That's what Dad says, anyway."

"That is kind of scary," said Billy. "Which is saying something in a place like this, don't you think?"

"Yes, I do."

"Tell me, Redford. How come you picked that name?"

"I like the color red. But, I don't know, somehow it didn't seem enough of a name on its own. I thought about Red Cloud, for a while—like the Native American chief—but I was worried people might think I was trying to make a political statement, so I chose Redford. Besides, *Out of Africa* is one of my favorite movies."

Billy looked blank.

"Redford is the star of *Out of Africa,*" explained Redford.

Billy nodded. "You know, Redford, I'd very much like to be one of the five kids who gets to hear the scariest story in the world. But the plain fact of the matter is that I simply don't have the money to buy a book so that I could even enter the draw, according to the terms and conditions and all the small print, et cetera, et cetera. Even the cheapest book in the shop is, like, ten bucks. So here's my question: Where am I going to get ten bucks?"

Billy smiled nervously and wiped a tear from his eye. Just talking about all that had made him feel quite upset.

"You should have said something before, Billy," said Redford. "I'll buy you a book."

"You will?"

"Of course. That's what friends do. Friends buy each other stuff. Even books. So. Go and choose one. And let me pay for it. It'd be my pleasure."

"Redford? Are you sure?"

"Sure, I'm sure. Just don't tell my dad. He'd be bound to

disapprove on the grounds that all my money comes from him, so strictly speaking it'd be him who's buying a book from his own shop. I mean, you can see how that would bug him, can't you?"

Billy grinned. "Yes. I can."

Billy went to the shelves and came straight back with a reputedly terrific ghost story called *A Thin Wisp of Ectoplasm*.

Redford handed over ten dollars and, carefully, Billy rang up the sale on the Brown Bomber. The bell rang and the cash drawer came out of the corner like Mike Tyson, only by now Billy had become ring-savvy in dealing with it.

With the precious sales receipt in his hand, the boy wrote out his name and address on the back and was about to put it in the shoebox with all the other hundreds of sales receipts for the day's draw when Redford said, "Of course, there's no guarantee that you'll get drawn." She was anxious not to get Billy's hopes up too high in case they were disappointed. Now that she'd seen real tears in his eyes, she realized just how sensitive he was, and how much it pained her to see him upset.

"You have to be in it to win it, right?" said Billy. "Are you coming? To the reading?"

Redford was silent.

"You are going to come, aren't you?" said Billy.

"Are you kidding?"

"You mean you're not?"

Redford shook her head. "Look, Billy, you read 'The Pocket Handkerchief,' didn't you?"

He nodded. "It was kind of creepy, yes," he admitted. "But—"

"Creepy?" Redford gasped. "I told you, Billy. That story totally freaked me out. After I read it I was a gibbering wreck for days. If Rexford wasn't my dad, I'd probably sue him for post-traumatic stress. I mean, that stupid story has left me emotionally and psychologically scarred. Quite possibly I'll never read another book as long as I live. Which is a considerable disadvantage for someone who wants to go to college and study journalism, I can tell you. I have to sleep with the light on. Even in summer. Just being near that horrible book is enough to give me a nightmare about dead mothers and premature burial. I have to steel myself just to walk through that door. And only in daylight. The day you read 'The Pocket Handkerchief'? I was worried sick about you."

"You were?" Billy smiled.

"Of course I was." Redford glanced around fearfully. "It's true. Just coming in here scares me. This whole place gives me the heebie-jeebies. Really. So do you really think I'm going to sit through a reading of the scariest story ever written?" She shook her head and grinned ruefully. "I don't think so. I'd rather poke needles in my ears."

"Ouch," said Billy. "You know, maybe you should talk about this with your father."

"No way. I couldn't, ever."

"Why not? I mean, he thinks you don't come in here because you hate him. It's kind of unfair that you don't tell him the truth about the way you feel about this place."

Redford shook her head. "I love my dad. I really do. And it would break his heart to sell this shop, which is what he'd probably do if he ever found out that this shop is the only reason I don't see more of him. That's why I don't ever want him to know the way I feel about it. Understand?"

Billy nodded. "I understand. But you know, there are many more unpleasant things in this world than what's in a few scary books."

"Maybe," allowed Redford. "But I don't want to find out what those are either."

"And you want to be a journalist?"

"Meaning?"

Billy shrugged. "Isn't that what journalism is all about? Reporting on the unpleasant things in the world?"

"You sound like my dad."

"I don't mean to. But even if I did, what's wrong with that? Your dad is a great guy. And by the way, Altaira is a much better name than Redford. You're lucky you've got a dad who gave you a name like that."

"You really think so?"

"Sure. I looked it up. Altaira means a star of the first magnitude, the brightest star in the constellation Aquila. Redford is probably a nice guy. But let's face it, he's no longer the big star he used to be."

Redford nodded. "Maybe you're right. I dunno. Thanks, Billy."

She turned and started to walk toward the door.

"And you should come to the contest," he called after her. "Your dad would like it. And more importantly, so would I."

Later on that day, the world's television cameras and news reporters turned up at the shop to film Mr. Rapscallion drawing the fourth name from the box. They were hoping to witness something unpleasant. And they did.

The name on the sales receipt wasn't Billy's. The receipt belonged to a girl called Lenore Gas and she and her family were there, like many other Hitchcock children and their families.

Billy tried to hide his disappointment. Surely he had no chance of taking part in the contest now.

Lenore Gas whooped loudly like a train and jumped up and down like a pogo stick. When she'd finished doing that, she punched the air several times until she accidentally managed to punch one of the reporters, and knocked him out cold. This was hardly surprising, as Lenore was a tall, athletic girl with bright red hair and legs as long as telephone poles. The girl was only fifteen years old but her parents had fed her too much meat and she had kept on growing when it might have been more sensible to have stopped. She wore retainers on her teeth, glasses and a sort of collar around her neck that was meant to stop her from scratching her eczema.

When the reporter had been safely carried outside, the cameras pressed around Lenore Gas for her instant reaction to being in the contest. You would think she had already won the thousand dollars, because every so often one of her even taller family would lean over and hold out a hand that Lenore would slap loudly and triumphantly.

"All right," one of them said loudly.

"All right," Lenore replied.

"How do you feel about being one of the lucky five kids who are going to hear the scariest story in the world?" asked the woman from CNN.

"Pretty psyched," admitted Lenore.

Her brother Tod leaned over and held up a hand for another high five and Lenore took a swing at it, missed and caught another reporter on the cheek, and knocked him out as well.

"No fears of fainting with fright when the scary story gets read out?" asked the man from XYZ TV.

"No fears of *anything,*" yelled Lenore. "Whaddya take me for, buster? A wimp?" She punched the man on the shoulder, who fainted with pain and had to be carried out of the shop with a broken arm.

"Do you read much, Lenore?" asked the lady from the BBC.

"Read?" Lenore sounded astonished. "Do I look like I'm a reader? I play hard and train hard, and books don't figure in my life at all. I like soccer and tennis, and running and gym work. The last thing I read was what was written on my breakfast cereal box. Books are for people who sit around on their butts all day, and I've never done that in my life. Don't intend to start neither. Scariest story I ever heard was when I heard a rumor I was going to miss the cut on the softball team. It wasn't true, though. They aren't stupid. I'm their best player, by a country mile. Without me they have nothing."

"And if you won a thousand dollars," asked a man from the *New York Times*. "What would you do with the money?"

Lenore laughed. "You make it sound like that's a lot of money. Mister, I'm not in this for the money. A thousand dollars wouldn't keep me in sneakers for six months. You'd better believe it, I'm in it to win it. *To win it,* ya hear? Same way I always do. It's the honor and the glory I'm after."

And, so saying, she let out another whoop that was so loud it made a cameraman from CLUNK TV jump several feet in the air with surprise; his camera caught the lady from the BBC with a hard blow on the forehead, knocking her out; she collapsed like a felled tree onto the man from the *New York Times,* and when he fell several others fell, too, like a row of dominoes.

"That is the clumsiest girl I think I have ever seen," Elizabeth told Mr. Rapscallion.

"I quite agree," said Mr. Rapscallion. "It's hard to imagine her being frightened of anything except perhaps an atomic bomb in her gym bag." He shook his head. "I really am wishing I had never started this contest."

But that same evening worse was to come. Much worse.

CHAPTER 24

MR. RAPSCALLION IS SCARED

It was a dark and stormy night.

Billy was downstairs in the stockroom of the Haunted House of Books with Mercedes McBatty the ghost hunter and Elizabeth W-G when they heard Mr. Rapscallion cry out with fright, and straightaway they ran upstairs to see what had happened.

"Perhaps he saw the ghost," Mercedes said hopefully. "It'd be just my luck if he saw it when I wasn't there."

They found the bookseller in the Reading Room, sitting upon the leather armchair that had possibly once belonged to Edgar Allan Poe with the leather-bound book containing the scariest story ever written open on his lap. Mr. Rapscallion's eyes were like glass and there was a look of extreme horror on his face. His mouth was hanging open and he had turned a whiter shade of pale.

"Mr. Rapscallion," said Billy. "Speak to me, sir. Are you okay?"

"Goodness gracious," exclaimed Elizabeth. "Whatever possessed the man to do it?"

"What's happened?" asked Billy.

"Isn't it obvious?" said Elizabeth. "Contrary to the explicit warning that is printed very clearly on the title page that the scary story should never be read alone, it's quite clear that Mr. Rapscallion has read the scary story *alone*."

A flash of lightning lit up the Reading Room like a fairground, and this was followed by a loud clap of thunder.

"Not only that," said Billy. "But it's a dark and stormy night."

"Gosh, you're right, it is," said Elizabeth. "Why did he do it?"

She bent down beside Mr. Rapscallion and took hold of his hand. "Are you all right?" she asked anxiously. "Speak to me, dear Rexford. Speak to me."

Mr. Rapscallion didn't answer. Mr. Rapscallion didn't move. It was as if he had been paralyzed, struck down by some unseen, supernatural hand. His eyes stared straight in front of him like he had been turned into a waxwork in some horrible Chamber of Horrors.

"You warned him," said Mercedes. "You couldn't have stated it more plainly. Could you?"

"His hand," said Elizabeth. "It's as cold as ice."

"Look at his eyes," whispered Mercedes. "The way they're staring straight ahead. It's like they're made of glass."

"It was exactly the same with my late father," said Elizabeth. "We found him just like this. With a look of extreme horror on his face. As if he'd seen something truly fiendish and ghastly." She took out her handkerchief and bit the corner for a moment. "I fear we shall never see dear Mr. Rapscallion like himself again." And she started to weep. "Now I shall never be able to make him understand how much I love him. Poor Mr. Rapscallion. He looks quite dumbstruck."

Mr. Rapscallion stood up. Which gave everyone, including Billy, a bit of a shock.

"Of course I'm dumbstruck," he said. "I had no idea you felt that way, Elizabeth, my dear. I feel the same about you. But enough of that for now. Yes, I'm horrified. But not for the reason you think. And I *have* seen something really ghastly."

"What happened?" asked Billy. "Tell us."

"I'll tell you what happened," said Mr. Rapscallion. "I read the story, that's what happened. I thought I had better read it before the actual contest. Just so that I could be sure that it wouldn't actually injure anyone, or put one of those horrible kids into a loony bin. And guess what? The scariest story ever written? *It isn't in the least bit scary.*"

"What?" said Elizabeth. "But that's impossible. Are you sure?"

"Of course I'm sure," insisted Mr. Rapscallion. "I own a bookshop that specializes in ghost and horror fiction, don't I? After thirty years I think I know what's a scary story and what isn't. And this isn't. Maybe it *was* scary, back in 1816. Or in 1820. But it isn't anymore. Not really. After the creaking door noise and the sound of someone banging on the floor, which is still a bit creepy, that's about it for freaking you out with fear." Mr. Rapscallion pulled a face. "The fact is, I actually fell asleep while I was reading it."

"But what about the poor boys of the workhouse in All Hallows Barking by the Tower?" asked Elizabeth. "What about my poor father?"

Mr. Rapscallion thought for a moment.

"Elizabeth, exactly how old was your dear father when he passed away?" Mr. Rapscallion asked her.

"He was one hundred and five," she said. "Give or take a few weeks."

Mr. Rapscallion groaned. And so did Mercedes McBatty. And so did Billy.

"Are you kidding me?" said Mercedes.

"One hundred and five?" said Mr. Rapscallion. "So it's just as likely that he died of extreme old age as it is from his having read the scariest story ever written."

"I suppose it's possible," admitted Elizabeth. "But Daddy was always a man who was in excellent health."

"Since he lived to such a ripe old age, I don't doubt it," said Mr. Rapscallion.

"I expect he was the healthiest man in the cemetery, when he died," said Mercedes.

"And the events at the workhouse in All Hallows Barking by the Tower, in London," said Mr. Rapscallion. "I don't suppose there could be another explanation for what happened back in 1820, could there?"

"Yeah, how old were *those* kids?" said Mercedes.

"It was almost two hundred years ago," said Elizabeth. "And if there was another explanation, I never heard of one."

"I think I might just have thought of a *possible* explanation," said Billy. "Maybe they were just pretending. They were pretending to go mad just so that they could get out of the workhouse. From what I've read, in *Oliver Twist,* for example, most boys wanted to escape from those places *really badly.* So maybe that's what they did. They faked it just to get out of there."

"Of course," said Mr. Rapscallion. "Billy's right. That's exactly what must have happened. They faked it to get out of there. Brilliant. Devious but brilliant."

"I must say I never thought of that," confessed Elizabeth. "But it does make a lot of sense when you think about it."

Mr. Rapscallion sighed loudly. "Billy. Ladies. I don't mind admitting to you all right now that I'm scared. *Really scared.* In fact, I'm terrified. I'm terrified because in two days' time I have to read a story to a bunch of kids who are *expecting* to be scared witless. Only they're not going to be scared in the least. In fact, they're probably going to laugh. They're going to come out of my shop laughing and I'm going to look like an idiot. That is always supposing that they don't take it out on the shop and try to destroy it, like they did before. Well, three of them, anyway."

"I'm sorry," said Elizabeth. "I don't know what to say. I feel awful. It's all my fault."

"It's not your fault, Elizabeth," said Mr. Rapscallion. "It's mine. I should have read the story before I went and told the world's press all about it."

"What are you going to do?" asked Billy.

"You could cancel the contest," said Elizabeth. "In the terms and conditions and all that small print and very small print there must be something that gives you the right to pull out."

"I'm not a quitter," said Mr. Rapscallion.

"So what are you going to do?" asked Mercedes.

"Draw the last name, ham up the story in the telling and hope for the best," said Mr. Rapscallion. "There's nothing else I can do."

"Couldn't you read them a different story?" suggested Mercedes. "You must know plenty of good ones that would scare those kids."

"Yes," said Billy. "You could read them 'The Pocket Handkerchief.' Or 'New Shoes.' One of those scary stories might do the trick."

"Nope," said Mr. Rapscallion. "That would be cheating. I won't fix a problem by cheating kids."

He started to laugh his mad, careering laugh, which sounded like a car that was out of control. It was Mr. Rapscallion's way of cheering himself up.

"Even if they are the kind of awful kids who belong in a zoo."

CHAPTER 25

THE RETURN OF HUGH CRANE

The shoebox used for the draw in the Haunted House of Books was no longer big enough. So many sales receipts containing the names and addresses of children who wanted a chance to hear the scary story and to win a thousand dollars had been stuffed inside it that they were now spilling onto the shop floor.

Next door to the Haunted House of Books was a shop selling washing machines. The man who owned the shop, Mr. Thornhill, gave Mr. Rapscallion a large box that had once contained a tumble dryer, so that all of the names and addresses could now fit comfortably inside it. But by the time of the last draw, even this bigger box was full. In fact, it was so full it looked like there might actually have been a tumble dryer hidden underneath the top layer of paper. Or some kind of surprise for a children's party.

Billy looked at the box full of names and addresses without

much optimism that his was going to be the fifth and last name chosen. At the same time he felt glad for Mr. Rapscallion, because with so many sales receipts in the box, it was clear that the scary story contest had probably restored the fortunes of the Haunted House of Books.

That became even more obvious when the very last book in the Haunted House of Books was sold three whole hours ahead of the scheduled time for the draw. Which, of course, meant that no one else could enter. Since most of the world's press were already there in preparation for the last draw, Mr. Rapscallion decided to bring the time of the final draw forward.

And he was just about to pick the last name from the box when there was a dreadful commotion in the shop: a man and his son who had just arrived in Hitchcock after having flown all the way from Japan to take part in the contest now stood weeping loudly by the front door. Both of them.

Mr. Rapscallion tried to explain to the man—who was called Hideo—that his son Mikimoto could only take part if he bought a book, but that there were no books left to buy.

It was Billy who solved the problem. Despite the fact it meant that he was shortening his own chances of winning the draw by one, Billy selflessly went out to the garbage bin down the street, retrieved a copy of Ken Biro's book thrown away by another customer and sneaked it back into the shop so that Mr. Rapscallion could resell it to the visibly delighted Hideo.

As soon as Mikimoto's name was on the very last sales receipt, Mr. Rapscallion rolled up his sleeve, showed off his empty hand like a magician in case there should be any suggestion of a fix and, with flashbulbs going off all around him, plunged his arm into the deepest depths of the paper-filled box.

There it stayed for several seconds while he made a big show of fishing around for a piece of paper with a fifth name.

Billy closed his eyes. Elizabeth took hold of one of his hands. And Mercedes took hold of the other.

Finally Mr. Rapscallion's arm, which had a tattoo of a ship's anchor on it, came out holding one sales receipt. He held it up for all to see and then opened it up to read the name.

"And the fifth child to hear the scariest story in the world will be . . ."

There was an electric hush in the shop. Cameras started flashing. Mr. Rapscallion grinned.

"Billy Shivers! 320 Sycamore, Southeast Hitchcock!"

Billy leaped for joy and was promptly hugged by Elizabeth and then by Mercedes.

"Now all I have to do is to persuade my dad to come through with those consent forms," said the boy. "Not to mention asking him to put in an appearance."

"Well done, Billy," said Mr. Rapscallion.

"You take my advice you'll get out of here for a while," murmured Mercedes as she hugged Billy to her shoulder. "That is, unless you want the press asking all sorts of nosy questions about you."

"Mercedes is right, Billy," said Elizabeth. "Just look at all those awful things they've already written about poor Mr. Leapy."

Billy nodded. He could see they were right. It was time to make himself scarce.

"Just a minute," said a voice that sounded like a piece of gnarled wood. "Isn't Billy Shivers the kid who works in this shop?"

It was Hugh Crane, the local lawyer and tycoon. He walked

into the shop, the lenses in his blue-tinted glasses shining like two tiny fishing holes cut in an ice floe. Under the surface of the blue glass, Hugh Crane's white eyes were two hungry polar bears. His bald head had been recently polished and shone like a cue ball. Everyone in the Haunted House of Books went silent.

"It seems to me," said Crane in his crusty old voice, "that this can hardly be called a fair draw if one of the people who works in this bookshop of yours, Mr. Rapscallion, is allowed to enter it. And not merely to enter, but to win one of the five places to hear the scary story. I should think that any one of these people who've paid good money to have their name in this draw would feel rightly aggrieved to discover something like that. In fact, they might even feel inclined to take legal advice—my legal advice, perhaps, since I am also the most important lawyer in town. And my advice would be that they should band together and sue you and this preposterous bookshop of yours for a million dollars. Yes sir. That's what I'd do if I'd been dumb enough to put my name and address on one of those sales receipts and put it in that box."

"I know what you're trying to do," said Mr. Rapscallion. "You're trying to get the Haunted House of Books for yourself in order that you can turn it into some stupid shop selling very expensive shampoo. Well, you won't do it."

"Won't I? We'll see about that. But we're straying from the subject here, Mr. Rapscallion. Why don't you simply answer the very serious charge I've just put to you in front of all these people? That Billy Shivers works for you. And is therefore disqualified from entering the contest. Answer that, if you can, sir."

Mr. Rapscallion shook his head. "As a matter of fact, Billy's an unpaid volunteer," he said. "An intern. I pay him no salary and I flatter myself that he helps out around here because of his great love of books and me and this shop." He raised his voice above the clamor of reporters' questions. "Which means, according to the terms and conditions and all the very small print on the sign in the window, that perhaps you ought to have read, Mr. Crane, before you go around accusing people of cheating, that Billy's free to enter the contest like anyone else. Isn't that right, Billy?"

But, keen to avoid the crush of television cameras, reporters and photographers, Billy had wisely disappeared.

"I can vouch for that," said Mercedes. "And I'm sure the bookshop accounts will bear out what Mr. Rapscallion says. Billy is not an employee of the Haunted House of Books."

Mr. Rapscallion reached under the counter and produced a heavy-looking ledger. "I have the shop's accounts right here. These will prove beyond all reasonable doubt that the only person who gets paid by this shop is me."

Hugh Crane growled irritably.

"Since you are here, Mr. Crane," said Mr. Rapscallion, "perhaps this would be a good time for me to pay you back the money I owe you. Just so that you don't ever have to come in here again. In fact, for that reason alone, I insist on it."

Mr. Rapscallion put his hand into his coat and took out a thick wad of banknotes that he handed to Crane, who counted them crossly and thrust them into his hip pocket.

"What about the interest on the loan?" he demanded. "What about that?"

"Whatever you think is right, Mr. Crane," said Mr. Rapscallion. "There's the cash register. Please. Help yourself. It's full of money."

Hugh Crane went over to the cash register and stood squarely in front of it.

"Help myself, eh?" Crane chuckled meanly.

"By all means. Whatever you think is the right amount, Mr. Crane."

"And it's full of money, you say?"

"Full of money."

"Well then, how about I take all of it?" said Crane. "I might think that's right, for the length of time this loan has been in existence. Yes, indeed. I might think that every dollar and cent in this here cash register would be a fair sum for you to pay, Rexford, after all this time."

"Take whatever you can get," said Mr. Rapscallion. "Be my guest."

Crane pointed at the world's press, who were watching closely. "You heard him. All of you are witnesses. Whatever I can get. He said it."

And, so saying, he hit one of the keys on the Brown Bomber.

The drawer of the Brown Bomber shot out like a bullet and hit Hugh Crane squarely in the chest. The impact carried him flying across the shop and out of the door, which, fortunately for him, was open.

Several people cheered and clapped their hands, as it was clear to everyone that in common with a great many lawyers and tycoons, Hugh Crane probably had it coming. And, in fact, he was never seen again.

CHAPTER 26

MR. RAPSCALLION GETS SOMETHING OUT OF HIS SYSTEM

The night before the day of the reading, Mr. Rapscallion was feeling very nervous and a little bit depressed about what would happen the next day.

So he telephoned his psychiatrist, Dr. Stundenweise, for some mental health advice.

"I feel very *tense,* Dr. Stundenweise," said Mr. Rapscallion. "*Tense*. Like something awful is going to happen. Very *tense*. If only there was some way of getting this feeling out of my system. Then I might be able to relax. And stop feeling so *tense*. And if I could relax, then I might not be so *anxious* about reading the story tomorrow. And who knows? If I can relax, then I might even be able to make the scary story sound a lot more scary than it seems to me right now."

Dr. Stundenweise, who was from Austria and spoke with a

strong Austrian accent, gave Mr. Rapscallion the same useful shrink-wrapped advice he always gave him:

"When you're feeling *blue,* this is what you *do;* you write a little *song,* which might just fix what's *wrong.* Music soothes the savage *breast,* and gives your anxious mind a *rest,* from everything that ails and *bothers;* and, my fee is fifty *dollars.*"

"Of course," said Mr. Rapscallion. "Why didn't I think of that before? That's what I did when those hooligans destroyed my mummy. That's what I'll do now. I'll write a little song. Thanks a lot, Dr. Stundenweise."

So Mr. Rapscallion went to the piano and spent the whole night with pencils and music paper, composing a new song to help get himself into the best frame of mind for what was to come.

The next morning Elizabeth and Mercedes found Mr. Rapscallion asleep, with his head resting on the piano lid. Mercedes thought he looked a bit like Beethoven after a hard night on the staves, and so she took a picture of him with one of her cameras.

The camera flash awoke Mr. Rapscallion, who yawned and stretched for a while. And after a reviving cup of coffee and a muffin, he sang his new song to the two young ladies.

"Scaring the Kids,"
a song by Rexford Rapscallion

If there was one thing I did enjoy
When I was just a little boy
It was my dad telling me a story
About something very gory

And a creature who was vile.
When I shrieked it made him smile,
Yes, it's fun scaring the kids.

Now, a tale about a ghost
Was the thing I loved the most.
My dad was quite a storyteller
For a nervous little fellow.
He might sound a crazy coot,
Because my screaming made him hoot
But, you know, it's fun scaring the kids.

Please don't ever look under the bed,
Or check out things that go bump in the night.
They can really mess with your head
And give you a terrible fright.

At six I wanted to see a ghost.
At ten what I wanted most
Was a haunted house to call my home.
And while it might sound gruesome,
My parents did the next best thing,
And hung up some sheets with bits of string,
To have some fun scaring the kids.

I'm older now but just the same
When I hear a kid exclaim
I'm spooked, I get a kick.
Please don't think me sick
If I hide and then say "Boo!"

For me it's like a how d'you do,
I'm just a guy who likes to scare the kids.

Wake up, hush, d'you hear that moan?
And what is this coming up the stair?
Did you see it move, the tombstone?
D'you think there's something here that isn't there?

Now the message of this little song,
Is that there's nothing really wrong
With inflicting harmless terror.
Yet some think it an error
And want to wrap their kids in cashmere wool
They just don't get the fact it's cool
To have fun scaring the kids.

There are some kids who like to say
That nothing scares us anyway,
It's all a yawn, a waste of time,
Stories really are not worth a dime,
There are no mysteries anymore,
This modern world is such a bore.
It's no fun scaring those kids.

There are no ghosts, there are no ghouls,
This is what we're told in schools.
It's sad to say but education
Shows a failure of imagination.
If the world is just a scientific place
We take the magic from the human race.

There's more to us than meets the eye.
And if I'm forced to specify
My argument's hypothesis,
It's the wisdom of scaring the kids.
Yes, and if I'm forced to specify
My argument's hypothesis,
It's the wisdom of scaring the kids.

CHAPTER 27

THE CONTESTANTS ARRIVE

It was a dark and stormy night. Again. For which Mr. Rapscallion was very grateful to whoever was in charge of Hitchcock's weather. Scary weather is useful stuff for making a story seem a lot more scary than it is. Thunder makes children jump. And lightning makes even a kind face seem frightful. Wind can moan like a ghost. And rain on a windowpane can sound like the fingers of a skeleton. All in all, it was a fine night for fear.

It was almost midnight. The evening of the reading had arrived. Mr. Rapscallion had forbidden all the reporters and television cameras entry to his shop so as to try to make sure there was what he called a proper "atmosfear" inside. Which would have been impossible with lots of people milling around, not to mention camera lights. In Mr. Rapscallion's expert opinion, light created the polar opposite of an "atmosfear." So the world's press were camped on the sidewalk outside the Haunted House of Books to see what would happen. Some of the regular customers were there, too: Father Merrin, Mr. Stoker, Miss Maupassant, Miss Danvers. Each of them was giving an interview about what kind of man Rexford Rapscallion really was. Even Redford had turned up to wait on the sidewalk and wish her dad and Billy good luck.

Apart from the five contestants and their families, the only people Mr. Rapscallion was planning to allow in the shop were Mercedes and Elizabeth, and a local doctor called John Henry Holliday, just in case there was some sort of frightful accident during the actual reading.

Dr. Holliday was a tall man, with blond hair, a mustache as big as a roll of wallpaper and a large black bag that was full of all sorts of medical equipment.

"Holliday," said Elizabeth. "That's an interesting name. For a doctor."

"Yep," said Dr. Holliday.

"Do people ever call you Doc?" she asked. "Like the famous gunfighting doctor of dental surgery from the O.K. Corral."

"Some," admitted Dr. Holliday, who was a man of very few words.

"I didn't mean to be rude or anything," said Elizabeth.

"Nope. T'weren't rude." Dr. Holliday smiled. "As a matter of fact, Doc Holliday was my great-great-granddaddy," said Doc Holliday. "My family have always been doctors to make up for all the people he shot. Now if you don't mind, ma'am, I'd like to get set up."

"Of course," said Elizabeth.

Mr. Rapscallion had set a little table beside the piano

for the doctor, and without further ado, Doc Holliday took off his coat, rolled up his sleeves and donned a leather apron. Then he opened his bag and laid out some surgical equipment on the piano lid: a couple of large saws, several scalpels and curettes, a largish hypodermic and a drill. Last of all he poured lots of sawdust onto the floor around the table.

"What's that for?" asked Mercedes.

"It's to mop up the blood," explained Doc Holliday.

"Don't worry," said Mr. Rapscallion. "It's just a little bit of 'atmosfear,' a joke to help unsettle our contestants. I don't want these little thugs thinking this contest is going to be a piece of cake. Especially now that I can't rely on the actual story to be as scary as I'd originally hoped."

There was a knock at the front door.

"I expect that will be one of them now," he said excitedly, because, despite his pessimism as to the scariness of the story, Mr. Rapscallion was in a good mood. Mostly this was due to the effect of singing his song, which Elizabeth and Mercedes had appreciated very much.

Mr. Rapscallion opened the door to reveal his daughter on the sidewalk outside. He motioned for her to come inside but she shook her head.

"Good luck, Dad," she said.

"Thanks, Redford."

"Altaira," she said. "Call me Altaira." She looked rueful. "I'm cool about my real name again, Dad. Honest."

"What changed your mind, Altaira?"

"Billy. Who else?" And she gave her father a warm hug, which was the first time she'd hugged him in a while. "Looks like the first contestant is here," she said, and pointed along the street.

The first contestant was Wilson Dirtbag and he was accompanied by his mother, Fedora.

"Wilson," said Mr. Rapscallion. "Welcome back to the Haunted House of Books. Come in, come in. Let us hope it is a happier experience for all than the last time you were here."

"I had nothing to do with that pink mummy," insisted Wilson.

"No matter. Water under the bridge, eh? Now then. This delightful lady must be your mother, Fedora. What a beautiful name. Tell me, do you spell it like the hat?"

"Hat?" Fedora Dirtbag looked at Mr. Rapscallion, uncertain as to what on earth he was talking about. "What hat?" she said, and looked around uncertainly as if she expected to see a sequined Stetson spinning through the air toward her. "Don't tell me I should have worn a hat."

It was clear she'd never heard of a fedora hat.

"Never mind, never mind," said Mr. Rapscallion. "A hat is not necessary, even for a woman with a head as small as yours. The main thing is, you're here. And what a pleasure to meet you. I trust you've brought all the appropriate consent forms for young Wilson here."

Wilson was busy inspecting the shiny-looking scalpels. Instead of them unsettling or scaring the boy, they appeared to fascinate him.

"Don't touch, sonny," said Doc Holliday. "If you know what's good for you."

"Forms?" Mrs. Dirtbag looked blank, which was quite normal for a woman with her modest intellectual gifts.

Mr. Rapscallion's heart gave a leap. Was it possible, he wondered, that he might be able to immediately disqualify Wilson—a boy he considered to be a troublemaker, and with good reason—on the grounds that he had forgotten to complete his consent forms?

"Forms. Yes, the forms. Pieces of paper with writing on them. Like the ones you use to claim Social Security. The boy can't take part without all the appropriate forms. Says it quite clearly in the terms and conditions of the contest."

"You mean these papers?" Mrs. Dirtbag handed several sheets of paper to Mr. Rapscallion, who inspected them quickly and then nodded, trying to conceal his disappointment.

"Well, everything seems to be in order," he said, ushering the woman to the door. "We'll see you later, Mrs. Dirtbag. Wilson? You're the first. Mercedes will show you to your seat. Won't you, Mercedes?"

Wilson sneered an ugly sneer. "Mercedes? What kind of a name is that? I guess your daddy must have liked cars, huh?"

Mercedes bit her lip and considered making a similar remark about tennis rackets until she decided that Wilson did not look like the kind of boy who even knew how to spell "tennis racket." And instead she smiled sweetly and took Wilson to the Reading Room, where the reading was scheduled to take place.

As Mr. Rapscallion ushered Mrs. Dirtbag out of the shop, Hugh Bicep and his father came in, two abreast. For a moment they almost got stuck in the door, they were so large and in such a hurry.

"Hugh! You're here!" said Mr. Rapscallion. "And your father. You're here, too. Hard to miss either of you, really. I expect they can see you both from space. But excellent. An honor to see you both in such obviously muscular good health. Which reminds me. You did bring the forms, Mr. Bicep. No entry to the contest is possible without those all-important consent forms."

"Of course," said Mr. Bicep. "Do you take me for an idiot?"

"Well, now you come to mention it . . ." Mr. Rapscallion paused. "No, I don't."

Mr. Bicep delved into his pocket, removed a protein shake and a banana and, finally, found the forms.

Mr. Rapscallion held the forms up to his keen nostrils and sniffed. "Hmm," he said. "I smell eggs, Canadian bacon, sausage, tomatoes and mushrooms, wheat toast. Delicious. Do I take it that these forms were signed on this morning's breakfast table?"

Mr. Bicep smiled sheepishly. "Must have been." Handing his son the banana, a packet of sandwiches and the protein shake, he said, "There you go, son. To keep your strength up."

"This is an in-store event, Mr. Bicep," said Mr. Rapscallion. "A reading of an important and historical story. Not a Sunday school picnic."

Mr. Bicep shook his head. "Best let him have it," he said. Lowering his voice, he added, "You wouldn't want to see my little boy when he's hungry, Mr. Rapscallion. You wouldn't like him at all when he's hungry."

"I find that only too easy to believe," said Mr. Rapscallion. "Elizabeth, take our young friend to the Reading Room, while I see his father OUT."

At the shop door, which opened and closed with its customary hollow, wicked laugh and a blast of cold air, they were met by Lenore Gas and her parents. Mr. Rapscallion ushered the big man out, and the Gas family in.

Mr. and Mrs. Gas were an odd-looking couple: Mr. Gas was at least seven feet tall and had to duck as he came through the door, which was when Mr. Rapscallion saw that his hair was an even more livid shade of red than his daughter's. Mrs. Gas was exactly half as tall as her husband, even in the diamanté heels she was wearing on her doll's feet. But the thing Mr. Rapscallion noticed most about her was her fingernails. These were six inches long, like those of a Chinese emperor, and painted gold.

"Greetings, greetings," said Mr. Rapscallion. "Welcome, Lenore, welcome to our humble in-store event. That's what we booksellers call a reading. Unless I'm very much mistaken, these two delightful people with you must be your parents."

Mr. Gas loomed over Mr. Rapscallion like a giant sequoia tree. "Consent," he said.

"Oh, I do, I do," said Mr. Rapscallion. "Whatever you say is fine with me, Mr. Gas."

"I mean, these here forms," said the tall man, handing over Lenore's consent forms. "Unless the game done changed."

"The game's the same, Mr. Gas," said Mr. Rapscallion. "Same as it always was, Mr. Gas."

Mr. Gas raised a heavily ringed fist in the air, and for a moment Mr. Rapscallion thought he was going to find himself on the receiving end of a punch. Instead, Lenore raised her own fist and pressed it against her father's in a gesture that appeared to Mr. Rapscallion to be a substitute handshake.

"I'm gonna win this, Daddy," she said.

"No doubt," said her father sternly. Then he turned on his

heel and walked out of the shop, followed closely by his small but perfectly formed wife.

Mercedes had returned from the Reading Room and Mr. Rapscallion asked her to take Lenore there, even as the door opened again to reveal Mr. Capone and his son Vito. The two were dressed in sharp suits with dark shirts and loud ties. And they were accompanied by several nervous-looking bodyguards who kept their hands inside their coats and their eyes on the rooftop of the building opposite.

"Vito," said Mr. Rapscallion. "We've been expecting you, of course. And how's the rest of the mob? I mean the family."

"This doesn't apply to my family," said Mr. Capone. "Just Vito."

"We're here for the sit-down, bookseller," said Vito. *"Capisce?"*

"With the greatest respect, I know why you're here, Vito," said Mr. Rapscallion.

"I certainly hope so, old man," said Vito. "I certainly hope so."

The young Vito had a curiously rasping voice. It was like the sound of charcoal coming out of a paper bag. Mr. Rapscallion wondered if the boy had a heavy cold and, for a moment, he considered offering to fetch him some cough syrup. But time was getting on, he told himself. And besides, he had no wish to be accused of favoritism. Not that Vito Capone would ever have been Mr. Rapscallion's idea of a favorite outside a dog race. Mr. Rapscallion already disliked the boy intensely, especially after the "old man" remark.

"I trust you have brought young Vito's consent forms, Mr. Capone. Because I'm afraid our intimidating little friend here can't take part without them."

"You speak of friends," said young Vito. "And you speak of respect. But if you really came to me with your friendship, your loyalty, your respect, then your enemies would become my enemies and then, believe me, Mr. Rapscallion, they would fear *you*. Not some stupid scary story."

Mr. Capone nodded gravely, as if he approved of his son's speech.

Mr. Rapscallion bent down to speak to Vito at his level. "Well, that's right handsome of you, Vito," he said. "You know I bet you could talk my ear off, sonny, given the chance. But right now I'm not interested in you being my friend. Or your daddy. All I'm interested in is that he has the correct paperwork."

Mr. Capone put his hand in his breast pocket and Mr. Rapscallion hoped there would only be some papers in it and not a gun when the hand emerged again.

To the bookseller's relief, the gangster handed him the consent forms, and Mr. Rapscallion had Elizabeth take Vito to the Reading Room to wait with the other kids.

Then he looked at his watch. "Where's Billy?" he said when Mercedes returned to his side. "I thought he'd be the first. Not the last. It's not like him at all."

"Oh dear," said Mercedes. "He said something about having to persuade his dad to sign the forms and put in an appearance."

"What?" Mr. Rapscallion frowned. "You mean he didn't ask him before he put his name in the box?"

"He never expected his name to be selected," explained Mercedes. "Not with so many other names in that box."

"Maybe you have a point." Mr. Rapscallion looked anxiously at his watch again. "I really should have taken the precaution of drawing a sixth name as a backup. Just in case there was a no-show."

"I'm sure he'll come if he can," insisted Mercedes. "Billy will be so disappointed if his father refuses to allow him to take part."

"Is that likely, do you think?"

"I don't know," admitted Mercedes. "But surely you've met Mr. Shivers."

"Ah, no," admitted Mr. Rapscallion. "He wrote to me once to give his permission for Billy to accompany me to Kansas City. Odd sort of letter, really."

"In what way?" asked Mercedes.

"The handwriting. It was very faint. As if the pen was running out of ink. The letter couldn't have been harder to read if it had been written in lemon juice."

"From what Billy's told me," said Mercedes, "his family has had a pretty tough time of it. There's not much money in that house."

Mr. Rapscallion looked at his watch for a third time in as many minutes. "It's almost midnight. Look, if he's not here in two minutes, we'll have to start without him."

Two minutes passed. The town clock started to strike the midnight hour.

Mr. Rapscallion shook his head and did his best to contain his disappointment. He had been counting on Billy.

"Too late, we'll have to start without him. Mercedes? If you could lock the door, please? We don't want anyone coming in and spoiling the 'atmosfear' after I get started. It's going to be hard enough to scare these four brats as it is."

CHAPTER 28

BILLY IS LATE

Mercedes knew there was no point in arguing with Mr. Rapscallion. She went to the door and was actually reaching for the large brass key that was sticking out of the lock when, hearing a knock on the other side, she opened the door to reveal Billy and a man she assumed must be his father.

"Hey," said Billy. "Dad, this is Mercedes. Didn't I tell you how nice she was?"

"How do you do?" said Mr. Shivers. "Mercedes. That's a lovely name."

Mercedes hurried them inside the Haunted House of Books and called out after Mr. Rapscallion.

"Thank goodness you're here," Mercedes told Billy. "For a moment there I thought we were going to have to start without you."

"Glad you could make it, Billy," said Mr. Rapscallion. He cocked an ear at the town clock, which had almost finished striking midnight. "Only just, by the sound of things."

"I'm sorry we're late," said Billy. "I saw Redford outside and stopped to say hello. I'm so glad she's here."

"Me too, Billy," said Mr. Rapscallion.

"She's calling herself Altaira again. Isn't that good news?"

"It sure is, Billy, and thanks."

Mr. Rapscallion smiled at the man behind Billy. "I guess you must be Billy's father."

Mr. Shivers was a tall, thin man with not much hair. There were shadows under his eyes and his clothes were old and threadbare. He wore a rather unfashionable pair of widely flared jeans, and a Windbreaker that wouldn't have broken the breeze from a fan-assisted oven. On his feet were a pair of work boots and in his hand was a lunch pail, as if he had just come straight from physical work of some kind. But he had a lovely, kind smile, as if he didn't have a care in the world.

Mr. Shivers held out a thin hand. "Fenton Shivers," he said. "I'm pleased to meet you, sir. Billy's told me so much about you. How kind you've been to him. You and your shop have been the best things to happen to Billy since his accident."

"It's been a pleasure, Mr. Shivers," said Mr. Rapscallion, shaking the other man's hand. "Billy's a credit to you. Polite, thoughtful, hard-working, diligent and a keen reader. Need I say more?"

"That's good to hear." Mr. Shivers glanced around the shop. "What a great place this is. I can see why Billy likes it here." Then he sighed. "But I'll be honest with you, Mr. Rapscallion. I was of two minds about allowing Billy to join in something like this."

"You were?"

"We're not like most people, Mr. Rapscallion. Me and my wife. We don't do much socializing, sir. We keep ourselves to ourselves. Let me ask you something. This scary story. What's it about?"

"Dad," protested Billy. "Please, you're embarrassing me."

"Billy, I'm your father. It's my job to look out for your spiritual welfare."

"Ghosts." Mr. Rapscallion shrugged. "Apparitions. Specters. The usual kind of stuff."

"Oh, that's all right then." Mr. Shivers smiled. "So you're saying there's nothing unpleasant or unholy about this story of yours."

"Are you a religious man, Mr. Shivers?"

"Yes sir, I am. Is that a problem for you?"

"No, not at all. I respect you for wanting to look out for your son's spiritual welfare. Not many parents do, these days." Mr. Rapscallion pulled a face and lowered his voice. "Between you and me, Mr. Shivers? The so-called scariest story in the world is not half as scary as I'd hoped. In fact, I'm kind of worried about what's going to happen. To be honest, I've kind of oversold it. The other four kids are not exactly what you would call shrinking violets."

"So I hear from Billy," said Mr. Shivers.

"I'm a bit worried what they're going to do when they realize they've not been scared at all," said Mr. Rapscallion. "Putting it mildly, they're rather less forgiving than your son."

Mr. Shivers smiled again. "I can believe that," he said. "Billy's an unworldly sort of boy, Mr. Rapscallion."

"Nothing wrong with that, Mr. Shivers. Nothing wrong with that. We all need our dreams. Our own idea of heaven."

"I'm sure everything will work out for the best," said Mr. Shivers.

"I sure hope so," said Mr. Rapscallion.

"I know so," said Mr. Shivers. He reached for his back pocket and pulled out a couple of folded sheets of paper. "There you go. The consent forms. Like you asked."

"Thanks, Dad," said Billy. "Thanks for letting me do this."

Mr. Shivers turned and went out of the door.

Mr. Rapscallion went down to the Reading Room accompanied by Billy, Mercedes and Elizabeth.

CHAPTER 29

LITTLE RASCALS

In addition to the six chairs that had been bought from the old Edgar Allan Poe Club, in Boston, the Reading Room had some oak paneling on the walls that had come from a haunted castle in Scotland. All the thick purple drapes had been pulled and there was a small coal fire and a clock ticking loudly on the mantelpiece to help with the "atmosfear." A large tank of tropical fish added a surreal blue light to the room.

Not that this "atmosfear" was having any effect on the four kids who were in there. Not yet, anyway.

Wilson Dirtbag, Hugh Bicep, Lenore Gas and Vito Capone were hardly the kind of kids to wait patiently for the arrival of their host, Mr. Rapscallion. In the absence of a television set or a cell phone, they were easily bored. And when they were bored they became . . . mischievous, which is a nice word covering a whole multitude of sins that any one of the four was capable of committing.

Wilson Dirtbag was disappointed that there were no books on the empty bookshop shelves. Not because he would have read one but because he would have liked to burn one. Wilson loved to start fires. He thought about burning the stuffed raven on the bust above the door, and only the thought that this might have disqualified him from winning the thousand dollars deterred him from tossing it onto the coals. So he took out a marker pen and amused himself by writing several rude words on the oak-paneled walls.

Hugh Bicep, no less badly behaved than Wilson, ate his banana and threw the skin onto the floor in the hope that someone else would slip on it, the way they did in cartoons. Next he unwrapped the large packet of sandwiches his father had given him and ate two in as many minutes. Then he peeled the buttered bread off another and tossed it up at the ceiling to see if he could make it stick there. And when it did, he tossed another and then another, until the ceiling was tiled with squares of white bread. At this point he sat down to admire his handiwork and thought it very funny when one of the slices of bread fell, buttered side down, onto Lenore's head.

Lenore had been amusing herself by testing her own not inconsiderable strength. She had picked up the poker from beside the fireplace and, in an effort to test her strength, managed to bend it several inches when the slice of buttered bread fell onto her head. At first she didn't notice since she had so much hair on top of her head it looked like a bird's nest, and it was only when Hugh Bicep started laughing at her that she guessed what had happened. So she peeled it off her head and smacked the buttered slice onto Hugh's face, which at least stopped him laughing. Although only because as soon as Hugh had peeled it off his face, he put the slice in his mouth and started to eat it. Hardly satisfied with the effect that her retaliation had had on her muscular fellow contestant, Lenore took another of his sandwiches, peeled it in half and slapped the two slices hard against his ears.

Upon entering the Reading Room, Vito Capone sat down in a chair and closed his eyes. But the light from the tank was too bright for him to doze. And not to be outdone by the juvenile delinquency of the other three, he got up and looked more closely at the tropical fish, to see if there was any havoc that could be caused in the tranquil blue underwater world of the tank. He decided he didn't like the fish because they reminded him of a dentist's waiting room, and he hated dentists almost as much as he hated policemen and judges and the feds. So, first of all, he heated the poker in the fire and then doused it a couple of times in the water, just to see what effect it might have on the fish. Not a good effect, it has to be said. But that didn't appear to bother Vito. In fact, it seemed to give him an idea. He took two of the fish now floating on the surface of the water, folded them in the brown paper that had been wrapping Hugh's sandwiches and laid the little parcel on Mr. Rapscallion's chair.

"That's a Sicilian message," he told Wilson and the others.

"Meaning what?" asked Hugh.

Vito realized he had only a vague idea what the message meant.

"I'm not exactly sure," he admitted. "I think it means you can't get any sleep when there are fish in the room."

When Mr. Rapscallion came into the Reading Room he did his best to ignore the graffiti on the walls, the slices of bread sticking to the ceiling, the bent poker and the parcel of dead fish that had been laid on the chair that had once belonged to Edgar Allan Poe. There seemed little point in making things worse by trying to confront the culprit(s). Besides, he was still rather hoping against hope that the story might deliver a real scare to these unpleasant brats. Even if that did mean he might also scare Billy.

And yet. As he watched the boy take his seat, for some reason he couldn't quite explain, he wasn't worried about scaring him. Not anymore. Not since speaking to Mr. Shivers. There was a strength in Billy he hadn't perceived before. And a realization that, in his own way, Billy was actually every bit as tough as the other four. Perhaps tougher. How could Billy not be tough? It was obvious that Billy's family circumstances were very hard. His father had been wearing the oldest clothes Mr. Rapscallion had ever seen.

"All right, settle down," he said to no one in particular. "Right, then. If everyone's ready?"

He glanced over at Mercedes and Elizabeth, who were going to observe the proceedings from the edge of the room.

"Ready," said Elizabeth.

"Ready," said Mercedes.

"Are you all sitting comfortably?" Mr. Rapscallion asked the five kids.

"I'll be a lot more comfortable when I've got that thousand bucks in my hand," said Wilson Dirtbag.

"Dream on, Dirtbag," said Hugh. "The green stuff is as good as mine."

"The only green stuff you're leaving with," said Lenore Gas, "is the salad in your sandwiches."

"I'll take care of the muscle boy's green stuff," said Vito Capone. "Out of my share."

"All of you be quiet," said Mr. Rapscallion. "The next person to talk will be disqualified."

He opened the cover of the book by Mary Shelley and John Polidori, which creaked loudly like an ancient wooden door in a remote Romanian castle, and a rather damp, musty smell filled the air, as if a coffin had been opened.

Mr. Rapscallion read the title aloud he found on the first page: "*The Modern Pandora,* or *The Most Frightening Story Ever Told*. By Mary Shelley and John Polidori."

The second that Mr. Rapscallion finished reading out the title and before he could read any more of what was printed there, the very peculiar thing happened. Once again. The book seemed to produce a knocking, hollow sound, like someone banging the tip of a walking stick on the bare wooden floor of an empty old house.

Wilson Dirtbag gulped loudly. "What was that?" he said. "That weird sound?"

"It seemed to come from inside the book," said Hugh.

"It did," said Mr. Rapscallion, and carried on reading from the title page: " 'Let the reader beware. The story contained in these pages is not to be trifled with. Frightful it is. And supremely frightful is the effect of that which lies herein. Under no circumstances should this story ever be read alone, or on a dark and stormy night. No more should this story ever be read aloud to children, to the mentally infirm, or to those of a nervous disposition. You have been warned. M.S. Villa Diodati. Italy. 1816.' "

"You never said it was an Italian story," said Vito, making a fist. "And in case anyone hasn't noticed, it *is* a dark and stormy night."

"Relax, will you?" Lenore Gas shook her head and whispered. "He's just trying to scare you."

"Shh," said Billy. "I want to hear."

"Yes, Billy's quite right," said Mr. Rapscallion. "Shh." And, turning over the page of the old book, he began to read the story itself.

CHAPTER 30

IN-STORE EVENT NUMBER ONE

Mr. Rapscallion did his best to make the story seem more frightening than it was. He read it in his deepest, scariest, most sepulchral voice, with full expression, as if he had been an organist sitting in front of a church organ, pulling out all the stops to make the organ come alive. By doing this he hoped to inject some more "atmosfear" into the story.

Mr. Rapscallion was an excellent reader. Billy thought he sounded professional, like an actor onstage. Vincent Price could not have read better, and he was an actor whom many people thought an expert in the delicate art of sounding sinister.

After ten minutes it was already becoming clear, however, what had been clear to Mr. Rapscallion from the first time he read the story himself: that the words in the story were too long and the ideas too complicated for young minds to grasp. Kids reared on cheap cartoons and comic books had little or no understanding of the proper English used by Shelley and Polidori. He might as well have read them a dictionary. In short, the scariest story ever written was too old-fashioned to be scary anymore.

Wilson's eyes were closing. Hugh was yawning. Lenore was shifting impatiently in her chair. Vito was scratching his butt. Only Billy looked as if he was at all interested in something other than the possibility of winning a thousand dollars.

And then something strange happened. The clock on the mantelpiece stopped ticking. Of course, mechanical clocks stop ticking all the time. That is why they must be wound up with keys. But it was the way that the clock on the mantelpiece stopped ticking that made this seem a little more strange than it might otherwise have been. This particular clock stopped ticking and instead it started tocking. Only it couldn't properly be called tocking so much as *talking,* because the noise the clock started to make sounded much less mechanical and much more human, as if someone inside the clock was actually repeating the word "tock" over and over again:

"Tock-talk-tock-talk-tock-talk-tock," said the clock.

"Excuse me," said Wilson Dirtbag. "I'm very sorry to interrupt you, dude, but, like, is it my imagination, or is the clock actually talking?"

Billy shook his head. "I can't hear anything."

Mr. Rapscallion paused for a moment and looked up at the mantelpiece. "Perhaps it does seem to be making a slightly different sound to the one it usually makes," he admitted. "What of it?"

"Tock-talk-tock-talk-tock-talk-tock-talk," said the clock.

"Hello-oh," said Lenore. "They're just trying to scare you, birdbrain."

Ignoring the insult—which was hardly an insult, since his mother was always calling him "birdbrain" and he was quite used to the name—Wilson Dirtbag got up to investigate the timepiece. It was a large, rectangular wooden clock with an unusual mechanical feature. In a little arched window above the actual dial was the tinplate model of a small, dwarfish man wearing a brown suit and a black bowler hat. The man held a large, lethal-looking ax and was chopping at another dwarfish man's neck in time with the clock's movement.

For a moment or two, Wilson looked closely at the clock. "Cool clock," he murmured. Then he pressed his waxy ear against the clock face and listened closely.

"Hear anything?" asked Billy.

"Shut up," hissed Wilson. "I can hear something."

A second or two later, all of the color drained from Wilson's spotty face. He took a step back and looked gravely at the mantelpiece. For it seemed to Wilson that a dark, almost spectral voice had spoken directly to him from inside the clock.

And this is what the voice said to him: "Wilson. Yes, I *am* talking. I'm talking to *you,* sonny, you evil little creep. You're a very naughty, horrible, disgraceful boy, Wilson. Even worse than those kids back in the London workhouse, in 1820. I've seen rabid dogs I liked better than you, Wilson. Who were better behaved than you, too. And if you don't mend your ways soon, I'm going to leave this clock and come after you and chop off your head with an ax. Don't think I won't. Because I will."

No one else in the room had heard what was said to Wilson, but everyone else in the room couldn't help but notice that all his greasy, straw-colored hair was now standing on end. Billy thought Wilson's hair looked exactly like a wheat sheaf.

"It's a trick." With fumbling fingers Wilson opened the door on the front of the clock and peered inside. "There must be some kind of transmitter inside the clock." But there wasn't. All he could see were sprockets and wheels and weights and pulleys. All of which stopped moving quite suddenly. Even the little man with the ax stopped moving.

Wilson closed the clock and, expelling a deep, unsteady sort of breath, he moved away from the mantelpiece and was about to sit down when the voice spoke in his ear again.

And this is what the voice said to him: "It would be a grave mistake to think that I'm inside the clock. And I mean a *grave* mistake. That's where you'll be if you're not careful, you mongrel. So. You can't get away from me. I'm going to be watching you from now on, Wilson."

Wilson squealed and spun around on his heel, as if looking for someone. But there was nothing there. All he saw was everyone else looking at him strangely.

"Stop fooling around and sit down," said Hugh.

"Didn't you hear it?"

"They can't hear me," said the voice. "Only you can hear me, Wilson. And just in case you think you're imagining this, here's a little reminder that you're not."

Wilson squealed again as something invisible squeezed his elbow and pinched his earlobe. This was too much for Wilson and, screaming with fright, he ran from the Reading Room, out of the Haunted House of Books and into the street, where he was pursued by his mother, Fedora, and several news reporters keen to buy his exclusive story. Because good news doesn't sell newspapers.

CHAPTER 31

IN-STORE EVENT NUMBER TWO

Back in the Reading Room, everyone was astonished, most of all Mr. Rapscallion.

"That's very odd," he said.

"Very," agreed Billy.

"What's wrong with him?" said Mr. Rapscallion. "I haven't even gotten to the frightening part of the story yet."

"No kidding," said Lenore.

"You haven't gotten to the interesting part either," yawned Hugh.

"And then there were seven," said Vito.

"Seven?" said Hugh. "What do you mean, seven?"

"Seven," repeated Vito. "What, are you blind? Mr. Rapscallion, you, me, Billy, Lenore and the two ladies observing. That makes seven people in this room."

"No, no," said Hugh. "There are eight of us here, surely. All of the above. And the baby."

"Baby?" Vito laughed. "Are you crazy? There's no baby in here. Who would bring a baby to hear some old man read a scary story?"

"So-called scary story," said Lenore. "Let's be accurate here."

"Less of the 'old man,' please," said Mr. Rapscallion. "If you don't mind."

"Of course there's a baby," said Hugh Bicep. "Can't you hear it? It's on the other side of that door, in that room." He was pointing to a small door in the oak-paneled wall behind him.

Everyone listened closely for a moment. Lenore Gas shook her head of red hair very slowly.

"You're losing it," she said.

"That's just a closet," said Mr. Rapscallion. "Where I keep a mop and the vacuum cleaner. There's no room there. And certainly no baby."

Hugh shook his head and laughed. "You can't fool me," he said. "I know a baby when I hear one. And I don't believe anyone would keep a baby in a closet." He got up and moved toward the door in the paneling. "Look, I'll prove it to you."

As he put his hand on the little handle, Lenore said, just a little nervously, "I don't think I'd open that door if I were you."

"Why not?" said Hugh. "There's nothing scary about a baby. For Pete's sake, what's wrong with you people?"

"Nothing's wrong with us," said Lenore. "We're not the ones who are crazy enough to believe there's a baby in that closet."

"Perhaps I've just got better hearing than anyone else," said

Hugh, and threw open the door, to reveal a mop and a vacuum cleaner and, on the floor of the closet, a pile of old blankets.

"If you ask me," said Vito, "he's got indigestion. Too many cheese sandwiches."

Hugh knelt down and, placing his hand on the blankets, he leaned into the closet, which appeared to be empty. For this reason, he was surprised to find that the blankets under his hand were warm, exactly as if someone had been lying on them. There was a baby smell, too. Milk and baby powder and diapers. And then he saw something at the back of the closet.

"Wait a minute," he said. "There's movement."

In spite of all his muscles, Hugh wasn't a courageous boy. It was the idea of proving the others wrong that made him reach all the way back into the closet.

"There's a baby in here, all right," he said firmly, although he still couldn't actually see a baby. "I've got its little hand in mine. I can feel its other little hand, tickling my forearm."

"What on earth are you talking about, Hugh?" demanded Mr. Rapscallion. "Of course there's no baby in that closet. You know what? I think this is just a tactic to delay my telling the rest of the scary story, and scare the others."

"Agreed," said Vito.

"Except that we're not scared," insisted Lenore, although her voice was more than a little scared.

Hugh recognized that it wasn't normal to keep a baby in a dark closet beside a vacuum cleaner and a mop. He also recognized that the baby wasn't tickling his arm; it felt more as if the baby was writing on his arm. All of this took just a few seconds, and, slightly unnerved by this last realization, he withdrew his large paw from the back of the closet and stood up again. And that was when he perceived that his forearm was now covered with tiny, neat handwriting. Writing that would have taken any adult—let alone a baby—several minutes to have completed.

The fright of seeing this writing was quite enough to remove Hugh's desire to remain at the in-store event and, screaming, he ran from the Reading Room, out of the Haunted House of Books and into the street, where he was pursued by his father and several more news reporters keen to buy his exclusive story. Because good news doesn't sell newspapers.

Hugh hadn't even read the message written on his arm. But when, several hours later, he did read the message—and, it must be said, this was the first thing Hugh had read in a long, long time—this is what he read:

> *"Hugh Bicep. You're a very naughty boy. Greedy, barbarous and cruel. I've seen goats who were more civilized than you. With better table manners, too. And if you don't mend your nasty little ways soon, I'm going to leave this closet and crawl after you and cry underneath your bed at night so that you won't ever be able to get any sleep. Not ever. Don't think I won't, because I will. I'll lie there crying every night, and drive you mad until you start behaving yourself like a normal boy. What's worse, only your ears will hear me. And just in case you think you're suffering from indigestion and that you've imagined any of this, you haven't. Which is why this message, that only you can see, Hugh, will remain on your arm for three whole months, or until your behavior improves, noticeably."*

CHAPTER 32

IN-STORE EVENT NUMBER THREE

"Well, I wonder what scared him?" said Mr. Rapscallion.

Lenore snorted. "As if you don't know, pal," she said. "Some trick or other. I bet you got someone on the other side of that closet." She shook her head. "We're not stupid."

"Really, I'm as mystified as you are," confessed Mr. Rapscallion.

"Yeah," said Vito. "Sure, old man." Vito put some gum in his mouth and began to chew furiously. He was nervous. He was so nervous he offered a stick to Lenore, who nodded and took it without a word of thanks, which was only typical. "Lenore's right. It's a con, like in a carney. What do you think, Billy?"

Billy shrugged. "I think I might be the only one who wants to hear the end of the story," he said.

"Aw no," said Lenore Gas. "You don't get us like that. We're here. And we're staying for the end of the story. No one's gonna cheat me out of winning this game. Not to mention a thousand dollars."

"That's right," said Vito. "So read on, old man. Read on. We can take it."

Mr. Rapscallion did as he was asked and continued reading the story aloud.

Once again Mr. Rapscallion did his very best to make the story seem more frightening than it was. He read it in his deepest, scariest voice, with full and sinister expression. Indeed, the sound of his voice was almost hypnotic.

So hypnotic did it seem to Lenore Gas that she spent a full minute telling herself that she must only have imagined that the bust above the door had been occupied by a stuffed raven. Because it was no longer there. Nor was there any sign of a raven in the Reading Room.

Another ten minutes passed.

And Lenore closed her eyes for a moment.

And while she nodded, nearly napping, suddenly there came a tapping, as of someone gently rapping, rapping at the chamber door that made Lenore get to her feet instinctively, because she was always the first to answer the door in her house. Indeed, it was a source of pride to her that she was always quicker getting to the front door than any of her brothers. And before she had quite registered where she was and what she was doing, Lenore had gotten up out of her seat and opened wide the door of the Reading Room, thinking that one of the boys—Wilson, or Hugh—must have recovered his nerve and returned.

She found only darkness. Nothing more. And, peering into

the inky black, she tried to make out what might have tapped upon the door. The silence was unbroken. Not a word was spoken. Although oddly, it seemed to Lenore, Mr. Rapscallion kept on reading and no one else seemed to have noticed either the gentle tapping on the door or, for that matter, Lenore herself answering it.

She closed the door. And went back to her chair. But even as she started to sit down again, she heard a tapping at the windowpane behind the purple curtain. Once again, no one else seemed to have noticed either the gentle tapping on the pane or, for that matter, Lenore herself going to the window, and, pulling aside the curtain, she opened the shutter and then the window to reveal a handsome black raven.

The raven stepped neatly through the window and flapped off over Lenore's head.

Lenore closed the window and returned to her seat. Had anyone noticed her getting up from her chair? It seemed not. At the same time, she observed that the raven was now sitting back on the bust above the door.

"That's a good trick," she said. "I mean, I could have sworn that crow was a stuffed bird."

Mr. Rapscallion stopped reading and looked over his yellow-tinted glasses at Lenore. Then he looked up at the raven.

"It's a raven," he said. "And it *is* stuffed."

"No, it's not," said Lenore. "It flew in the window, just now. I should know, I just let it in."

"No one's opened that window since I've been in this room," said Vito.

"Get outta here," exclaimed Lenore. She looked questioningly at Billy.

Billy shook his head. "Sorry," he said. "But Vito's right."

"I saw your eyes close a few minutes ago," Vito told Lenore. "If you ask me, you must have nodded off for a moment and dreamed the whole thing."

"No, no, no, no, no," said Lenore, jumping up from her seat. "Whatever you fools are trying to pull here, it isn't going to work. Ya feel me?" Standing on a footstool, she reached up to touch the raven. "This is a real bird. Has to be. I just saw it fly in here."

Experimentally, she flicked the bird on the perch with her forefinger and discovered, to her astonishment, that it was indeed stuffed.

And just as she began to wonder what had happened to the raven she was sure she had let into the room at the window, Lenore felt something shift and stir on top of her head. She let out a shriek and reached on top of her head to grab the bird that was now nesting in her hair. Something pecked her hand and then her head hard, and she shrieked again.

"Only you can hear me, Lenore," said a loud and rasping voice that Lenore was certain had to be that of the raven. "Listen to me, or I'll peck a hole in the top of your thick skull. And don't think I can't. It's the larger and heavier beak that makes us ravens differ from mere crows. You are a very bad girl, Lenore. Selfish, rude, intolerant and cruel. It's time that you turned over a new leaf. And if you don't, I'm going to lay my eggs in your hair and take up permanent residence here in this very comfortable nest of red hair on top of your ugly red head. Which could be for evermore. Quite a while, anyway. You see, we ravens are very long-lived. There are individual ravens in the Tower of London who have lived for as long as forty years. So unless you want to hear my voice for evermore, you'll mind what I say and improve your behavior."

Lenore shrieked as once again, the raven in her hair pecked her skull hard for good measure.

This was more than Lenore could bear and, screaming with fright, she ran from the Reading Room, out of the Haunted House of Books and into the street, where she was pursued by her parents and several more news reporters keen to buy her exclusive story. Because good news doesn't sell newspapers.

CHAPTER 33

THE TIEBREAKER

"I wonder what scared her?" said Mr. Rapscallion, genuinely mystified. "I don't think it could have been the story. I mean, I don't think she was really listening. Do you, Billy?"

"That makes two of us," said Vito, and yawned. But the yawn did not mean he was relaxed. The truth was, he was feeling anything but relaxed. Given that three kids had already run screaming out of the shop, Vito was finding it hard to feel anything but terror.

"I think it had something to do with that raven," observed Billy.

"Yes, I think you're right, Billy," said Vito. "Although it's a little hard to believe that anyone could get spooked by that old bird."

"Especially an old bird that's stuffed," said Billy.

Mr. Rapscallion sat up straight for a moment and turned to Elizabeth and Mercedes. "Tell me, ladies," he said. "Has either of you actually seen or heard anything at all scary tonight?"

"I'm afraid not," said Mercedes.

"Not a dickey bird," said Elizabeth. "Nor, for that matter, a raven."

"I suppose it is a *bit* scary when someone runs screaming from the room," admitted Mercedes.

"For no apparent reason," added Elizabeth. "Yes, that is *quite* scary. But apart from that—" She shook her head.

"Nothing," said Mercedes.

Billy sensed Vito's nervousness and gave him an encouraging smile. "Take it easy," he said kindly. "Don't be scared."

"I can take care of myself," snarled Vito, who had quite misunderstood Billy's remarks and was judging the other boy according to his own low standards. "Lemme tell ya something, Billy. Don't think that you can out-psych me here, my friend. I can't be got, okay? Not by anyone. Least of all by you. Because you don't look so tough. Matter of fact, you don't look tough at all. You look like you could use a good meal. You know what? You look weird, too. I mean, where did you get those clothes? From the local thrift shop? I seen homeless people who are better dressed than you, pal."

"That's enough of that, please," said Mr. Rapscallion. "Let's mind our manners and get back to the story, if we can."

"Why not?" said Vito.

Mr. Rapscallion started to read again, continuing with the story, which was now nearing the end. As before, he did his very best to make the story seem more frightening than it was. He read it in his deepest, scariest voice, with full and sinister expression. Indeed, the sound of his voice was almost hypnotic. Which perhaps it was.

Vito Capone tried to look like he was listening without hearing anything. He figured that was the best way to get through the remainder of the story and win the contest. So that he could prove to his father that he was a tough guy, just like him, and fit to inherit the family crime business.

Biting his lip hard, Vito did his best to ignore the two fish on the sheet of brown paper that lay on the floor where Mr. Rapscallion had placed them. Vito was feeling bad about that, and not just because the sight of the dead fish had evidently upset Mr. Rapscallion. Vito was feeling bad because he was also feeling scared. He was scared because the fish now appeared not to be dead at all. They were jumping in the air and flapping on the paper as if gasping to get back into the tank of water. And yet Vito had been quite sure they were dead when he left the Sicilian message on Mr. Rapscallion's chair. Could it be that they hadn't been dead at all? In which case, why didn't someone else pick them up and put them safely back in the tank before they really did expire, or suffocate, or whatever it was fish did when they were left out of water on a sheet of brown paper? Why did it have to be him that put them back in the tank? And what might happen to him if he did pick them up? Would something scary happen that might make him run screaming from the shop, just like the others?

Vito closed his eyes for a moment and stayed put in his chair. So that when Mr. Rapscallion said "The end" loudly and snapped the storybook shut, Vito almost jumped out of his skin.

"That's it?" he exclaimed. "You mean I've won?"

"Er . . . not exactly," said Mr. Rapscallion. "Billy is still with us, after all."

"Hmm." Vito sneered. "But the so-called scary story is over, right?"

"Yes."

"So what happens now? Do we fight for the dough?"

"First of all," said Mr. Rapscallion. "Congratulations to you both for hearing the scariest story ever written without being scared witless."

"You ask me," said Vito, growing in confidence again, especially now that the two fish had stopped moving, "it wasn't scary at all." He sneered again. "I've had bigger scares with the feds."

"I enjoyed it," admitted Billy.

"You would," said Vito. "So what happens now, pop?"

"A tiebreaker," said Mr. Rapscallion. "In the form of an ordeal, so to speak. It's number nine on the terms and conditions: 'In the event of a tie, then the remaining contestants will be asked to spend ten minutes proving that they're really not scared by entering the Haunted Cellar.' "

"What's that?" said Vito.

"It's our newest little horror," said Mr. Rapscallion.

With Mercedes and Elizabeth following at a distance, Mr. Rapscallion led the two boys out of the Reading Room and back into the entrance hall. There he opened a door to reveal a set of descending stone steps, and then lit the large candelabra.

"I keep all the antiquarian books down here," Mr. Rapscallion told Vito.

"Best place for that old junk," said Vito.

Their footsteps echoed as they went down into the basement.

At the bottom of the stairs they entered the old cellar that Billy remembered from his first days at the Haunted House of Books. In the farthest wall was a heavy wooden door that led to the canal, and beyond the creature of the black canal were the subterranean library and the phantom organist with the fiery head.

But instead of going through this door, Mr. Rapscallion lifted a heavy trapdoor in the floor and handed each boy a single candle.

"What now?" asked Vito.

"Down there," said Mr. Rapscallion, "is the Haunted Cellar. The loser is the person who comes out first."

"That's it?" said Vito, full of bravado.

"That's it," said Mr. Rapscallion.

Billy peered down into the cobwebby darkness. "Kind of creepy down there," he said uncomfortably.

"That's why we call it the Haunted Cellar," said Mr. Rapscallion.

"Chicken," said Vito, and, with his heart in his mouth, led the way down some more stairs into the darkness.

After a second, Billy followed.

"They're very brave," said Elizabeth. "I don't think I'd have the nerve to go down there."

"No one's forcing them," said Mercedes.

"Exactly," said Mr. Rapscallion.

"I hope it's Vito who comes out first," said Elizabeth. "I don't much like that boy at all."

"Amen to that," said Mr. Rapscallion.

"Exactly what *is* down there?" asked Mercedes.

"The wine cellar," admitted Mr. Rapscallion.

"That's it?" asked Mercedes.

"That's it," he admitted.

"Nothing else."

Mr. Rapscallion shook his head. "No, I'm afraid not," he said. "You see, there simply wasn't time to build something new. The Haunted Cellar is just darkness, some old wine bottles, a lot of dust, a few rats and, I expect, their own imaginations."

Mercedes nodded thoughtfully. "But sometimes," she said, "your own imagination is the creepiest thing there is."

CHAPTER 34

LIGHT AT THE END OF THE TUNNEL

Vito Capone and Billy Shivers advanced cautiously into the darkness of the cellar, which was hardly diminished by the flickering light from two small candles. And it was only too easy for one boy to mistake the enlarged and wavering candle-lit shadow of the other for some kind of shapeless black cellar-dwelling monstrous creature.

"I wonder why we're afraid of the dark?" whispered Billy. In the cavernous cellar his whispered voice sounded distinctly ghost-like.

"Speak for yourself, wet fish," said Vito.

"I guess the dark just makes everything seem scarier," said Billy, answering his own question. "Even when it's not."

"What does that mean?" demanded Vito.

"Only that just about anything in daylight will seem a lot less scary than it does at night."

"Says you, hero," said Vito. "How long do we have to stay down here, anyway?"

"Ten minutes," said Billy.

Vito sat down on an empty wine crate and looked at the luminous dial of his expensive sports watch. Then he glanced around nervously.

"Mr. Rapscallion must have something hidden down here," he said. "Someone dressed in a sheet, maybe. Or . . . I dunno. Any minute now I just know that someone or some*thing* is going to leap out and try to scare the heck out of me." Vito made a fist and hit himself on the thigh. "But I won't be scared off, do you hear? Not by him. Not by you. I'm going to win. Just see if I don't."

"I really don't mind if you do win," said Billy.

"You don't?"

"I've learned that there are worse things in life than losing."

But Vito wasn't having any of this. "Speak for yourself. My dad didn't raise me to be a loser."

"Perhaps if we were to explore the cellar and find it before it found us," suggested Billy.

"You mean go and look for it?" Vito sounded appalled at the very idea. "Whatever *it* might be?"

"That way we might scare it first," said Billy. "Don't you see? We'd be taking away the element of surprise."

Vito nodded. "Yes, I suppose that's possible," he said reluctantly. "But you go first, okay?"

And so they began to edge their way around the pitch-black cellar, with just their candles to illuminate their search.

"You're a lot more courageous than you look, Billy," said Vito grudgingly.

"Thanks," said Billy. "I'm scared of a lot of things. But I'm not scared of the dark. I used to be. But not anymore."

They were just about to conclude the search when, low down on the dampest, farthest wall, the two boys came upon what appeared to be the opening to a dark tunnel. A cool breeze emanated from the tunnel opening, although it wasn't quite enough to extinguish the candles.

Billy stepped into the tunnel and peered ahead. The tunnel was a black void but, oddly enough, it didn't make him feel afraid. Indeed, he thought that there was something reassuring and even pleasant about the tunnel. It seemed to beckon him on.

"You're not serious," said Vito.

"Funnily enough, I am," said Billy, going a bit farther into the tunnel.

"You're crazy," said Vito. "It's like someone's tomb in here." He put his hand on the wall and then pulled it quickly away. "Gives me the creeps."

"I think that was the general idea, don't you? Only it's really not all that creepy in here. It's just like any other cellar: dark and cold and a bit damp."

"What else do you want from a creepy place?"

"Wait a minute," said Billy. "There's something there."

Vito held his breath for a moment. "What is it?" he whispered.

"I think I might be able to see it if it wasn't for this candlelight. The flame moves around so that it's impossible to make out whatever it is. I'm going to blow mine out."

"Are you mad? Then we'd only have the one candle."

"We could always relight the other candle."

"Not if that one blows out, we can't. Please, Billy, don't blow your candle out."

But it was too late. Billy had already blown out his candle.

"Yes. There *is* something," said Billy. "There appears to be a light at the far end of the tunnel. It's like the light from a brilliant gemstone. It's getting bigger, too. And yes. I think I can also see the silhouette of a figure coming toward us. Don't be scared, Vito. I think it's something quite benign."

But Vito had heard more than enough. Leaving Billy in the darkness, he ran back up the stairs as quickly as he could without extinguishing his own candle, up through the trapdoor and into the upper cellar, where Mr. Rapscallion, Mercedes and Elizabeth were waiting for him and Billy to return.

Vito didn't say anything. He was too busy screaming. He went up the stairs, three at a time, and into the entrance hall. Then, still screaming with fright, Vito ran out of the Haunted House of Books and into the street, where he was pursued by his father and several more news reporters keen to buy his exclusive story. Because good news doesn't sell newspapers.

CHAPTER 35

THE WINNER

After several moments had passed, Mr. Rapscallion said, "I wonder what scared him so much?" Mr. Rapscallion sounded genuinely mystified. "It certainly wasn't the story. And I don't think it could have been the cellar. I mean, there's nothing down there except a few bottles of wine. Some of them are actually quite drinkable, too."

Mercedes peered anxiously down through the trapdoor. "I can't see any sign of a light down there," she said. "It's pitch-black. Do you suppose Billy's all right?"

"It's only a wine cellar," said Mr. Rapscallion. "Not a wicked troll's dungeon."

"Perhaps he's dropped his candle," said Mercedes, "and can't find his way out in the dark."

"I never thought of that," said Mr. Rapscallion, and, leaning through the trapdoor, he switched on an electric light that lit up the Haunted Cellar like an airport terminal.

And, seeing the look of surprise on the faces of Mercedes and Elizabeth, he said, "Like I said, it's a wine cellar, not a dungeon."

The moment the electric light went on, they heard a shout from deep inside the cellar and everyone smiled with relief.

"Billy," said Elizabeth. "I expect he just realized that he's won."

Mr. Rapscallion called out to him through the trapdoor of the cellar.

"You've won, Billy," he said. "Vito's run away. So you can come up now."

A few moments later, Billy's head and shoulders appeared through the trapdoor. He was smiling in a way none of his three friends had ever seen before. Like he had lost a cent and found a hundred dollars. Or maybe even a thousand.

"Jolly well done, Billy," said Elizabeth, and kissed him on the cheek. "I'm so pleased for you."

"Yeah," said Mercedes. "You did all right, kid. Nothing scares you, that much is clear."

"Congratulations, my boy," said Mr. Rapscallion, shaking him by the hand.

"Thank you, sir," Billy said. "Thank you all."

"Who'd have guessed it?" said Mercedes. "Billy. The one kid who looked like he wouldn't say boo to a goose. The winner." And, not to be outdone by Elizabeth, she kissed Billy on the other cheek.

"Where's Vito?"

"He took off," said Mercedes. "Like a bat out of you know where."

"Something spooked him," said Mr. Rapscallion. "The same as the others. Any idea what it was?"

Billy shrugged. "A trick of the light, I think. I thought I saw a light and then a figure." He smiled bravely. "But it was probably just my imagination. Anyway, I've come to the conclusion that there's nothing to fear except fear itself. For some reason that kept on running through my mind while I was down there. There's nothing to fear except fear itself."

"That's all?" Mr. Rapscallion sounded disappointed. "A pity."

"A pity?" Billy laughed. "What do you mean?"

"The way he ran out of the shop, I thought that Vito Capone might at least have seen the famous Haunted House of Books ghost," said Mr. Rapscallion. "It would have been very good for business if I could have reported one sighting, anyway."

"I really don't believe there *is* a ghost," said Mercedes. "Not in this shop, anyway. Maybe not anywhere in the whole world. I'm seriously thinking of giving up the ghost-hunting business."

"Oh, please don't say that," said Mr. Rapscallion. "At least don't say it to all those newspapermen and television reporters. After all, who's going to buy books of ghost stories if you go around saying sensible things like that?"

"That reminds me," said Mercedes. "There are hundreds of them out there. Reporters, that is. Simply hundreds. What's poor Billy going to do? They'll eat him and his father alive."

Mr. Rapscallion shrugged. "Maybe Billy wants to sell his story to a newspaper. Why not? How I survived listening to the scariest story ever told. Something like that."

Billy shook his head.

"I'm tired," he admitted. "I think I've had enough excitement for one night. It is very late, after all. Besides, I don't think my dad would approve of us selling our story to a newspaper."

"Your father is obviously a very sensible man, Billy," said Mr. Rapscallion. "And a man of strong moral fiber. That much was very clear from our conversation. I admire a man of principle." He nodded. "But Mercedes is right. It might be easier if you were to slip out of the back door. I'll speak to your father, Billy, and tell him where you are."

"I expect he'll have disappeared off home by now," said Billy. "I can't imagine he'll have stayed throughout all this fuss. He doesn't like crowds of people at all. He's really a very shy person. Shy and retiring, that's what he says."

"Of course," said Mr. Rapscallion. "But look here, it's late like you say, Billy. And you're just a kid. Maybe someone should go home with you."

"It's okay," said Billy. "The thunderstorm's over now. I'll find my own way back. I always do."

"Very well," said Mr. Rapscallion. "If you're sure. Meanwhile, I'd better go and face the world's press. I know I'm not going to get any sleep until I've told them something of what happened here tonight." He smiled. "If only I understood a little more about that myself."

"If you are going out there," said Billy, "then perhaps you could tell Altaira to meet me around the corner."

"I can't tell you how happy I am she's calling herself Altaira again instead of Redford," said Mr. Rapscallion. "I owe that to you, of course."

"Me?"

"You're the reason she's been coming back to the shop, Billy," said Mr. Rapscallion.

"You think?"

"I know."

Billy Shivers sneaked out of the shop into the alley and, to his surprise, he found Altaira already waiting there.

"I won," he said modestly.

"I heard. Billy, I'm so glad."

Billy shook his head. "Only I didn't really feel like speaking to all those newspapermen. So I slipped out the back way."

"I thought you might."

"I don't really like crowds of people," he confessed.

"That's why I'm here," she said. "Because I'm not crowds of people. Just a friend come to walk you home."

CHAPTER 36

320 SYCAMORE

Mr. Rapscallion awoke late and with a sore head. He'd taken a couple of old bottles from the wine cellar and had celebrated a little too enthusiastically. But almost immediately after he was out of bed, he realized that in all the excitement of the previous evening he had quite forgotten to give Billy his prize money.

"How could I be so careless?" he asked Mercedes when, eventually, she and Elizabeth showed up at the shop. "And him and his family so poor and everything. You know, I bet a thousand dollars is really going to make a lot of difference to those people."

"It's probably just as well you didn't give it to him last night," said Mercedes. "A twelve-year-old boy walking home at night with a thousand dollars in his pocket? That wouldn't have been such a good idea."

"He didn't walk home alone," said a voice. "I walked him home."

They looked around as the door announced a customer in the usual spooky way. It was Altaira.

"Altaira," said Mr. Rapscallion. "How wonderful. I'm so glad you came by. And while I was here."

"I just dropped in to congratulate you," she said. "On the success of the contest. I think you must be in every newspaper and on every TV show in the country. I guess now you'll be able to keep the shop."

"Yes. Elizabeth? Mercedes? This is my daughter, Altaira."

"Hi," said Altaira.

"What a lovely name," said Elizabeth.

"Thanks," said Altaira. "It's from *Forbidden Planet,* the movie."

"Oh, I love that movie," said Mercedes.

"Me too," said Altaira.

"I wonder where Billy is," said Mr. Rapscallion. He looked at his watch. "Frankly, I thought he'd be here. He usually is, by now."

"We did have a very late night," said Altaira. "I can't stop yawning."

"Isn't it supposed to be the other way around?" said Mr. Rapscallion. "Him walking you home?"

"I can look after myself," said Altaira. "I'm street-smart. He's not."

"That boy is rather unworldly, it's true," admitted Mr. Rapscallion. "So what happened?"

"Dad." Altaira looked away. "Please. It's private, *if you don't mind.*" She found herself coloring as she remembered how

they had sat on his porch in front of Billy's house and Billy had held her hand in his. Nothing had been said. Nothing needed to be said. But she certainly didn't want to tell her dad any of *that.*

"You know what we should do?" said Mercedes, quickly changing the subject. "We should take a taxi over to Billy's house and give him and his family the prize money right now. We could all go. The four of us. It might be a nice surprise for them."

"You think they'd mind?" asked Elizabeth. "Us turning up unannounced like that?"

Mercedes shrugged. "When did people ever mind someone turning up to hand them a thousand dollars in cash?"

"You've got a point," said Mr. Rapscallion. "I think it's a terrific idea."

He went to the drawer in the cash desk.

"Now where's that proof of purchase he filled in with his address?"

"It's 320 Sycamore, Southeast Hitchcock," said Altaira.

"What if he's already on the way here?" said Elizabeth.

"Sycamore is off Potter Road," said Mr. Rapscallion. "If he's already on his way here, we're bound to see him. Potter Road is the quickest way to get here."

Carefully, Mr. Rapscallion took a thousand dollars in cash from the Brown Bomber and put it in his coat pocket.

"What kind of place is it?" he asked his daughter.

"Oh, a big old house. It was nice. A real family home, you know."

Then they went outside onto Hitchcock High Street and found a cab.

Mr. Rapscallion told the taxi driver, "320 Sycamore."

The cab driver looked at them strangely. "*320* Sycamore?"

"That's what I said," said Mr. Rapscallion. "Off Potter Road."

The driver shrugged and did as he was told. They drove southeast for about ten minutes, along Potter Road, and then left onto Sycamore. The houses along Sycamore were big, brick-built, three-story homes for large, wealthy families, with high mansard roofs. Some of the houses looked at least a hundred years old. Finally, the driver pulled up in front of the very last house on the road.

"Is this the place?" asked the driver.

"Of course it is," said Mr. Rapscallion without really looking at the house.

"Well, this house ain't been lived in for forty years," said the driver.

"Oh, my Lord," said Altaira, and covered her mouth.

320 Sycamore was a large, heavy block of a house with a big, square central tower that was sort of standing guard over it, and at least a dozen blank, staring windows. It was also badly neglected—a dreary, creepy-looking ruin. The front door was gone and most of the window shutters were hanging off their hinges. The front garden was badly overgrown and full of discarded tires and broken timbers.

"Are you sure this is 320 Sycamore?" Mr. Rapscallion asked the driver.

"Mister, I've been a cab driver in Hitchcock for thirty years and I know every inch of this town."

"This is the house," Altaira said quietly. "Only it was kind of different last night. Everything was. The house. The garden. Everything."

Shocked and puzzled, Mr. Rapscallion paid what was on the meter and followed Mercedes and Elizabeth up to the ruined porch. Altaira stayed on the sidewalk for a moment and then walked after her father, who kept on glancing at her with a look of concern.

"It's all right, Dad," she said. "I'm okay."

They stepped across a large hole in the floor and paused in front of the open doorway. This was shrouded with hundreds of spiders' webs as if no one had crossed the threshold in at least ten years.

"It's like something out of 'Sleeping Beauty,'" said Elizabeth.

"Except there's no sign of any beauty," said Mercedes.

Mr. Rapscallion cleared the webs away with the forearms of his coat and went inside. Broken glass cracked under the soles of his shoes. Inside, the house was dark and forbidding, cold and damp and, most of all, unwelcoming, as if some terrible, unspeakable tragedy had affected it.

"Billy?" he called. "Mr. Shivers. It's me. Mr. Rapscallion. Is there anyone at home?"

But there was no answer. Just the sound of the wind moaning through a broken window, and a loose shutter tapping gently against the casement.

"I'm getting a bad feeling about this," admitted Mercedes.

"Think how I feel," said Altaira. She shook her head. "Maybe I made a mistake. I must have. I mean, just look at this place."

Mr. Rapscallion stuffed his hand into his pocket and took out the sales receipt that had brought them there. "No," he said. "There's no mistake. 320 Sycamore. That's his handwriting. He wrote the address out himself."

"Great," said Altaira. "That's just great."

They went into the front garden, where a man with a hard hat and a roll of plans under his arm was getting out of a small truck. He looked surprised to see anyone coming out of the old house.

"Can I help you folks?" he said.

"We're looking for the owner of the house," said Mr. Rapscallion.

"I'm the owner," said the man. "My name's Burt Erney, and I'm planning to restore this house and live in it myself."

"Then I really think we have the wrong address," said Elizabeth.

"We were looking for the Shivers family," said Mr. Rapscallion. "Fenton Shivers and his son, Billy."

"Sorry," said Mr. Erney.

"Our mistake," said Mercedes.

Mr. Rapscallion, Altaira, Mercedes and Elizabeth started to walk back along Sycamore.

"Wait a minute," said Mr. Erney. "Did you say Shivers?"

"Yes," said Mr. Rapscallion.

Mr. Erney went back into his truck and took out his briefcase. "I have the deeds to the house with me," he murmured, searching through some old papers. "I thought I recognized that name. Yes. Here we are. A Mr. Shivers was the previous owner of the house."

Mr. Erney showed them the deed.

"Only I didn't actually buy the house from him. I bought it from his lawyers, just a few weeks ago."

"There's something attached to the back of the deed," said Elizabeth. "It appears to be a newspaper clipping."

"So there is," said Mr. Erney, and, removing the paper clip that attached the clipping to the deed, he handed it to Mr. Rapscallion.

Mr. Rapscallion glanced at the clipping and sighed. "It appears to be dated forty years ago," he said, and then read the clipping aloud:

> *Hitchcock: Monday. Three members of a family, including a six-month-old baby, were killed and one was seriously injured when a truck lost control and ran into the back of a car on Hitchcock High Street, outside the public library on Sunday morning. The victims were traveling in the car. They have been identified as Fenton Shivers, 38, his wife, Agnetha, 34, and their daughter Fiona, age six months. The Shiverses' son, Billy, 12, has been admitted to the Walden Pond Hospital, Potter Road, in critical condition but is not expected to survive. The family, residing at 320 Sycamore, in Southeast Hitchcock, was on its way to the Hitchcock Baptist Chapel when the accident happened. Fenton Shivers was at the wheel at the time of the accident. The driver of the truck was not injured.*

Mr. Rapscallion was quiet for a moment.

Altaira took a deep breath and tried to stop herself from screaming. "Well, I guess that explains why his hand was so cold," she muttered.

"You held hands with him?" said Mr. Rapscallion.

"I thought I did. Now I'm not so sure."

"Yikes," said Elizabeth.

"That's what Billy used to say," said Altaira.

She sat down on the sidewalk for a moment and wiped a tear from her eye.

"Are you okay?" asked her father.

"I think I'm going to barf."

Mercedes and Elizabeth sat down as well and put their arms around her.

"She's had a bit of a shock, that's all," Mr. Rapscallion told Mr. Erney. "We all have. May I borrow this clipping, please?"

"Of course."

After a few moments, Altaira started to feel a bit better.

"Come on," said Mr. Rapscallion. He started to walk back along Sycamore.

"Where are we going?" asked Mercedes.

"The Walden Pond Hospital," said Mr. Rapscallion. "On Potter Road."

The Walden Pond Hospital, which was now called the New Walden Pond Hospital, was a large building on the edge of a small lake. There was an old part and a new part. The old part looked better than the new part.

They went inside and asked to see the person in charge and eventually they were all admitted to the office of a Dr. Price, who was a tall, fair-haired man in a white coat with large bright eyes.

Mr. Rapscallion explained their mission: "We're making inquiries about a patient who was brought here forty years ago."

"Forty years?" Dr. Price took a deep breath. "That's quite a while."

"Yes, I know it's a long time. The boy was called Billy Shivers and he was age twelve. This may sound strange to you,

Doctor, but we were hoping to find out when he died. Presumably it wasn't long after the car accident that killed the rest of his family. I brought this newspaper clipping along to help us find out a bit more."

He handed over the clipping, but Dr. Price did not read it.

"You're asking me about William Shivers?" He looked surprised.

Mr. Rapscallion nodded. "I know it's a lot to ask."

"Look, I don't know what this is about. Or who you people are. But William Shivers was, in a way, this hospital's most famous patient. When I say famous I actually mean infamous. You see, William Shivers was in a coma here at Walden Pond for forty years."

"A coma?" said Altaira.

"Yes. That's a profound state of unconsciousness, miss," the doctor told Altaira. "Or what's also sometimes called a persistent vegetative state. It just means that the person's brain died a long time before their body."

"I know what a coma is, thank you," said Altaira.

"Then you'll also know that people can remain in a coma for a very long time before they die. That's what made Billy—I mean William—so famous. Until he died, just about a month ago, William Shivers had remained in a coma for almost forty years. That's what made him infamous. Forty years is the longest coma in American medical history."

"Crumbs," said Elizabeth.

"And the house?" asked Mr. Rapscallion. "320 Sycamore?"

"After his family died, it belonged to William. But of course no one could buy it, because he couldn't sell it. Not until he himself died."

"I see," said Mr. Rapscallion.

"Do you mind telling me what this is about?" asked Dr. Price.

"If I told you," said Mr. Rapscallion, "you'd never believe me." He sighed. "Can I ask you one more thing? Where is Billy buried?"

"He was cremated," said Dr. Price. "And his ashes were spread on the lake out there. It's what usually happens when the deceased person has no relations to decide these things for us."

"Thank you." Mr. Rapscallion's voice was now little more than a whisper.

Altaira had already started to cry.

"Don't cry," he told his daughter.

"Why not?" she said. "I mean, it's not every day you fall in love with a boy who's been dead for a whole month."

CHAPTER 37

QUOTH THE RAVEN

They went back to the Haunted House of Books.

But on the way, they stopped in at L. B. Jefferies Photographic on Hitchcock High Street to collect the films Mr. Rapscallion and Mercedes had left there for processing.

They took the prints into the Reading Room to take a look at them.

But none of the pictures taken of Billy by either of them in Kansas City or Hitchcock had come out properly. Sometimes there was a sort of blurred figure that was almost there, but mostly there was nothing at all.

Elizabeth selected one of the pictures. "Is that a picture of a ghost, do you think?" she asked.

"It is, as far as I'm concerned," said Mercedes. "As far as I'm concerned, this picture seems to put the matter beyond dispute.

Billy was a ghost." She laughed. "There was me thinking they didn't exist. And all the time I was hanging out with one."

"Me too," admitted Mr. Rapscallion. "I thought I would never see a ghost. And it seems I've been seeing one for four whole weeks."

"Looks like this shop was haunted after all," said Mercedes.

"I used to think this shop was the scariest thing," said Altaira. "But I guess it doesn't look so scary now. Not in view of what's happened. Last night I walked a ghost home. I had coffee with his dead family and then he and I sat out on the porch and watched the moon. If Billy was a ghost, and I think he must have been, he was the nicest ghost anyone could hope to meet."

She smiled bitterly. "How do you like that for luck? The first boy I fall for and he turns out to be a ghost."

"Him being a ghost would certainly explain his old clothes," said Elizabeth. "And his father's. Those are the clothes people were wearing forty years ago. And it probably also explains why they looked so thin and pale in themselves. They were dead, after all."

"But it doesn't explain everything," said Mr. Rapscallion. "It doesn't explain why Billy told me that he was so afraid of ghosts. How can you be afraid of ghosts if you are a ghost? And it certainly doesn't explain why those four horrible children, Wilson, Hugh, Lenore and Vito, were so scared of a story that wasn't scary. I don't suppose we'll ever have the answers to all those questions."

"I'm not so sure," said Mercedes. "Look." And she pointed up at the stuffed raven that was sitting on the bust of Pallas just above the chamber door. "Is it my imagination, or is there a piece of paper in the message capsule attached to its leg?"

"Good grief, you're right," said Mr. Rapscallion. He leaped up from his chair and, fetching a stool to stand on, reached up, removed a small piece of paper from the raven's leg and read out loud what was written there: "*The Modern Pandora,* page sixty-six."

"The book!" yelled Elizabeth. "The scary story."

She ran to the shelf where Mr. Rapscallion had placed it carefully after the reading and, ignoring the loud creak as it opened, hurriedly turned to page sixty-six. A sheet of very thin, almost transparent paper floated to the floor like some ethereal thing.

They all looked at it for a moment, hardly daring to pick it up, afraid of what it might say.

"I'm scared to touch it," admitted Elizabeth.

"Me too," admitted Mercedes.

"And me," admitted Mr. Rapscallion.

Altaira bent down and retrieved it from the Reading Room floor. And this is what it said:

Dear Mr. Rapscallion,

Thanks very much for the last few weeks in the shop. I've had a terrific time haunting the place, and you and Mercedes and Elizabeth and the lovely Altaira / Redford have all been very kind to me. As you have probably gathered by now, I'm a real ghost. Yes, we do exist! I decided to hang around after my recent death because the fact is that I was just a little bit scared about moving on into the next world, so to speak.

I think it had something to do with being in a coma for forty years. I'm not sure. After forty years of being neither one thing nor the other, it's easy to get a bit confused. My dad did his best to talk me around to the idea of the afterlife, or whatever you want to call it, but, for a long time, there was something about the idea of being dead and moving on that I didn't like. I suppose I was scared of ghosts because I was a ghost, if that doesn't sound too pathetic. And that was partly why I hung around the shop. I suppose I thought that if I read enough stories about ghosts, then I might not be afraid of being one.

Anyway, I've gotten over all that now. In fact, I got over it just last night when I went down to the so-called Haunted Cellar. You see, there was this tunnel down there, and there was a light at the end of it. Not just any light, you understand, but a really fantastic light that made me feel wonderful. Better than I've felt in a long while. And there was something pulling me toward the light, too. It was about then that I noticed my body wasn't there anymore and that felt just fine. Also there were all these amazing colors, and flowers and stars and galaxies, and yes, it sounds a bit corny, but I sort of knew that I was at one with the universe. My dad was there, too, to help guide me over to the other side. And I wasn't in the least bit afraid. He was a bit reluctant to let me go back again, but I simply had to return for just a few minutes to say goodbye to you in person last night, to write this note and to say goodbye to Altaira of course. Tell her I'm sorry I have to leave her like this just as we were becoming good friends. I'll never forget her. You can also tell her that now that she's met a real ghost, there's no need to be afraid of anything and certainly not some stupid ghost story about a pocket handkerchief.

My dad got the idea of how to bring me through to the other side when I told him about the contest. And from talking to you, Mr. Rapscallion. I expect you've guessed by now, but, of course, it was Dad who assisted you with the reading of the scary story last night. He did all that creepy ghost stuff. He was very grateful to you for helping me out and decided to do the same for you. And to help those other kids, too. He only scared them a bit, just enough to make them behave themselves a bit better from now on. Which I'm sure they will.

Perhaps we'll see each other again one day—in this world, or the next—I don't know. I'm not sure how this ghost thing works yet. My only regret is the way you all had to find out that I'm dead. Sorry about that. I know it must have been a bit of a shock for you all. Especially Altaira.

Well, that's all for now. I'd best be going. My dad will be thinking that something dreadful has happened to me. Not that anything dreadful could really happen to me. Not anymore. But you know what I mean. You can't stop a father from worrying about his son, I guess. Especially when that father loves me as much as mine does. Remember me, if you will, but always try to remember this: that Love is always stronger than Life and Death.

Take care.

Your affectionate friend,
Billy Shivers

p.s. Tell Elizabeth I really enjoyed the story. And Dad says the kids were a lot more scared by it than you'll ever know. They were just pretending they weren't. The way kids do, right? Scaring kids—for that matter, scaring anyone!—is a lot easier than you might think, Mr. Rapscallion. Take it from one who knows.

Everyone was silent for several minutes.

After a while Altaira said, "That was the nicest boy I think I never met." She smiled tearfully. "If you know what I mean."

"Absolutely," said Mercedes.

Altaira looked around the air in the room as if Billy might still be there, unseen. "I'll never forget you, Billy," she whispered. "Not ever."

Mr. Rapscallion took off his glasses and wiped a tear from his own eye. "Odd that it should have taken someone who was dead to show me the true meaning of life," he said.

"Gosh, and me," admitted Elizabeth.

"All of which means just this." Mr. Rapscallion took hold of Elizabeth's hand and kissed it. "It means I'm going to write a love song, on the piano. And then I'm going to sing it to you, dear Elizabeth. And if you like it, then perhaps you might do me the inestimable honor of consenting to be my wife."

"Yikes!" exclaimed a blushing Elizabeth. "This is all a bit sudden. A bit scary. I really don't know what to say."

"I do," said Altaira.

AUTHOR'S NOTE

THE GHOST OF MRS. BETTE C. WARD

Twice in my life I have seen a ghost. Or thought that I did. And in both cases I also believed that the ghost wanted to scare me.

The first time was when I was a child of about ten or eleven years old. I would like to be able to describe this incident as a hallucination, except for the fact that I remember it so vividly. It was the look of sheer malevolence on the apparition's face that alarmed me the most and caused me to jump six or seven feet, from one side of the room to the other.

That night, I slept with the light on.

The second time was in the autumn of 1975 and I was nineteen years old. I was standing in front of a dressing table and unloading my pockets of wallet and keys, and as I glanced up at the cheval mirror in front of me, I saw someone step away from behind me. I could not have said that it was a man or a woman with any degree of certainty any more than I could have said that there was someone there at all, for I knew the room to be empty of anyone but me. But the strong sense that I had seen *something* in the blink of an eye was underlined by the fact that at the very same moment, the electric light fused with a loud bang, the fan heater stopped working and the flame on the gas fire died out. In the same moment, I felt something very cold behind me, as if someone had opened a refrigerator door, and, with my hair standing on end, I felt quite sure that if I turned around, I would see a ghost—moreover, a ghost that wanted to scare me. So I ran out of the room and into the drawing room, where the friend I lived with looked up from the book he was reading and said, "What's the matter? You look as if you have seen a ghost."

That was another night I slept with the light on.

Do ghosts exist? I don't know. No one does; however, for a number of reasons, I prefer to think that they do. But mostly, the reasons boil down to this: I'd hate someone to prove that they really don't exist. Life is dull enough as it is without ghosts going the way of the Loch Ness monster and Santa Claus.

A poll of two thousand people in August 2009 showed that 40 percent of people believe in ghosts; this compares with a 1950s Gallup poll in which only 10 percent of the public said they believed in ghosts.

Clearly, there are more people who want to believe in ghosts than there used to be. After all, where would Christmas be without a good ghost story?

It goes without saying that I have met several people who claim to have seen a ghost. My own mother was one of these. And I believe her father told her he once saw a ghost, too. Neither of them strikes me as the kind of person who would make up a ghost story. That's my job.

The best ghost story I ever heard was the one in Kansas City, in 1987, which informs the scene in chapter fourteen of this book, in which Mr. Rapscallion and Billy go to stay at the Savoy Hotel. Because it was there that I met an old man who told me the following tale.

I have no idea if it's true or not. But I'd like to believe it is.

I once met Harry Houdini. I was a kid at the time, about eight or nine years old. He was staying at the Savoy Hotel on Ninth Street, where my dad was the manager, and—I'm not sure how this happened exactly, because Houdini was incredibly famous—Houdini agreed to keep an eye on me for half an hour while my dad went outside to run an errand for him. Houdini was the most famous escape artist in America, and he couldn't walk around the streets like normal people or else he'd have been mobbed. So, anyway, he showed me some magic tricks and looked at my toys and games, and noticing a Ouija board among my possessions, he laughed and told me that spiritualism was nonsense.

"All mediums and psychics are frauds," he said. Houdini had a Hungarian accent that was almost as broad as his face and his shoulders. "And there are no such things as ghosts."

With the precocity of youth, I contradicted him and told Houdini that the Savoy Hotel had a ghost in Room 505. "That's what my pa says, anyway."

"Have you seen it?" he asked me gravely.

"No, but I've heard it," I told him.

"Tell me what you heard," said Houdini.

"Well, there's someone who turns on the faucets in the bathroom," I told him. "When there's no one in there. And then afterwards you sometimes hear the sound of someone running along the corridor."

"And has your pa heard this, too?"

"Oh yes. Lots of people have. That's why 505 now stays locked."

"If that really happened, then wouldn't the room flood?" he asked, very sensibly.

"That's the curious thing. It doesn't. Someone turns the faucets off, too."

"So if we went in there now," said Houdini, "do you honestly think the bath would be full of water?"

"Well," I said. "It's possible. I dunno. I haven't been in there for a while. To be honest, sir, I'm not allowed. But I overheard my pa telling my ma that the last time he went in there, the bath was full."

"Why don't you go and get me the key to 505?" Houdini smiled kindly. "And we'll put a stop to this silly superstition."

"I dunno," I said. "My pa wouldn't like it. He's pretty strict about me not going in there."

Houdini nodded and rubbed my hair vigorously. "Yes," he said. "Yes, you're absolutely right. Always obey your parents. If I had done this, I might have become a rabbi like my father. But I was headstrong. At your age, I was a trapeze artist in a circus and calling myself 'Ehrich, the Prince of the Air.'"

"But you're Houdini," I told him. "The Handcuff King. You're famous. Surely you have no regrets."

"Fame isn't everything," he told me. "Believe me, I know what I'm talking about."

When my father returned from performing the errand, Houdini told him about our conversation and told him that he should very much like to see inside Room 505. My father gave me an exasperated look, at which point Houdini begged him not to be cross with me and said that really it was all his fault for leading me on. I think cash may also have changed hands at this point, and the upshot was that all three of us went upstairs with the key to 505, and my father unlocked the door.

We paused in the room for a moment, my father drawing a large, nervous breath, and then opened the bathroom door. He could hardly bring himself to look at the bath, which of course was full of water and perfectly still, at least until Houdini rolled up his sleeve and placed his muscular arm in it. I never saw a man more muscular than Houdini.

"Freezing cold," he said. "Unusually so, perhaps."

"It would be cold," said my father. "It's at least a month since anyone was in here."

"And the bath was empty when you left?"

"Yes," said my father. "Quite empty."

"And no one else has been in here?"

"I keep the key in my safe."

Houdini moved his arm around in the water for a moment and then pulled out the plug. We watched the water drain noisily down the plug hole, and even before he said it both my father and I knew what he was going to say.

"I should like to spend the night in this hotel room," he said. "I should like to observe exactly what happens—if anything—for myself, as, ever since the death of my mother, the subject of the supernatural has been of great interest to me. I have considerable experience in these matters and it may be that by a great effort of concentration—I will not call it anything more, as I have formed the opinion that most psychics and mediums are charlatans—that

in this way I may gain some insight into what happens in this room and, perhaps, I can offer you some kind of reasonable explanation in the morning. We may even lay a superstition to rest, which will enable you to rent this particular room again."

"Your pardon, sir," said my father, "but suppose something happened to you? What then? You are a famous man, sir, and no doubt a wealthy one. We should not be able to resist a suit brought by your family that held us contractually responsible for an injury to your person."

"I am very well insured against all manner of injuries," explained Houdini. "In my line of work, that is only prudent, yes? But as in all things where there is some risk, I am always properly prepared, both physically and mentally. I assure you that I am as equal to this particular feat of endurance as if it had been a straitjacket or a sealed casket in a grave."

He stood squarely in front of my father as he said this. My father was taller by a head than the great man, but there was no question of Houdini not getting his way. He wasn't very tall, but he was built like a small boxer, with thick, curly black hair and bright, piercingly blue eyes—not to mention a smile that could have charmed the birds from the trees. If my father had any doubts about letting Houdini have his way, these were overcome by the great man's smile, which was the most charismatic smile I ever saw. He put his hand on my cheek and patted it gently, which only served to endear him to me even more.

"Very well, sir," said Pa. "It shall be as you wish. And I ask but one thing of you in return, Mr. Houdini. That if you do discover there is any substance to our superstition, that the room is indeed haunted, then you might please keep this matter to yourself beyond what you tell us. I should not like this hotel to become the subject of

idle gossip and newspaper speculation. It would not be good for the reputation of this hotel."

"It shall be as you ask," replied Houdini.

My father handed Houdini the room key and said that he himself would bring Houdini's bags along to the room, as it was certain that neither the hall porter nor the maid would set foot in the room; and then we left him alone until the morning.

That night, I hardly slept at all and I confess I was more than a little worried about the little man, which manifested itself in a nightmare. What if some terrible accident happened to him? Having escaped from handcuffs, and mail sacks, and safes, what if he was unable to escape from whatever it was that haunted 505?

My mother was obliged to come into my room and calm me.

"Rest assured, son," she said, "if anyone can discover the truth of Room 505, it is the great Houdini. He's not called the master of mystery for nothing."

The following morning, we did not go up to the room but waited for Houdini to come down for his breakfast. The previous day, he had breakfasted at eight o'clock exactly, so when nine o'clock came and went, we began to grow a little anxious that some unfortunate fate had befallen America's hero. My father was just about to go upstairs with the only other key to 505 and to knock on his door when Houdini appeared in the dining room.

The look on his unshaven face was enough to tell us he had not enjoyed an untroubled night. But worse than that was the color of his hair, which had been black and curly all over and now was distinctly gray around the ears. Or had we imagined that? I don't know, but Houdini sat down and ordered black coffee and a brandy to be brought to him immediately.

"Did you see anything?" I asked excitedly. "Did you see a ghost?"

My father gestured at me to pipe down, and I did, although I could hardly restrain my curiosity.

Houdini was quiet for what seemed like ages. He raised the glass at us and toasted our health. Then he downed the brandy, sipped the coffee and spoke rather sadly. This is what he said:

"First of all, I must ask you to accept what I say without question. For what I know, I can offer no explanation that would not itself require further explanation, perhaps several explanations. And while what I say to you now might, you feel, insult your intelligence and hospitality, I may only plead in mitigation that what I now know goes beyond all normal methods of reason and inquiry. The most important principle of my life has always been: never lie, always tell the truth. So when I say that everything I am going to tell you now is the truth, you may know that I am speaking from the bottom of my heart.

"Many years ago, there came to the state of Missouri a woman by the name of Miss Bette C. Onions. Originally, she was from England and a schoolteacher, not to mention a Presbyterian. She settled in Hanover, New Hampshire, where, for a time, she worked in a local Indian school, one of many that had resulted from the Civilization Fund Act of 1819, which provided money for the education of American Indians to European standards.

"In 1840, Miss Onions married Mr. Ward, who was also a teacher, and having obtained a grant of government money, they came west to Kansas City and founded a school for Indians of their own on the site of what is now this hotel. They were both strong in the Lord, which meant that the Indians who were obliged to attend the school—mostly displaced Cherokee from Alabama and Georgia—were forbidden to speak their own native language, denied the right to practice their own native religions and taught Christianity and the English language.

"Mrs. Ward, who had lacked all maternal affection herself, was not a loving or even a caring woman. No more was Mr. Ward the fatherly type, and the Ward Indian Mission School was a brutal place. The hair of the Indian pupils was cut short, their names and clothes were taken away and they were forced to wear uniforms. The children were given new, Christian names and, in addition to book learning, they were assigned hard physical work, which left many of them little better than slaves. The punishments for neglecting work were severe, but none were so severe as the punishments handed out for speaking the Cherokee language or venerating the old gods.

"One day, Mrs. Ward caught a Cherokee boy named Col Lee, the son of a great chief, in possession of a medicine bundle. This was a collection of closely guarded sacred objects believed to contain the magical essence of the spirit that the objects represented—in this case, an evil spirit monster called Nunyunuwi. Now, possession of a medicine bundle was a very serious infringement of the school rules, and Col Lee was brutally whipped by Mr. Ward while Mrs. Ward took the bundle and told him she intended to toss it into the Kansas River.

"Almost hysterical with fear, the Cherokee boy begged her not to throw away the bag, and warned them both of the terrible consequences that might attend anyone who treated it, and by extension what it represented, with disrespect. He explained that the only reason he hadn't thrown away the bundle himself was that he was more afraid of the spirit monster than he was of Mr. and Mrs. Ward. But it was no use. The Wards were not disposed to listen to anyone unless they had a white face. Mrs. Ward threw the bag into the river the very same day. And that was when their troubles began.

"First, I ought to say something about the Cherokee idea of evil. Interestingly, they believe that evil spirits are female and invisible

to everyone except a medicine man and the human victims they have offended. In this case, the poor Wards. For however uncaring and neglectful they had been to their Indian pupils, neither of them surely deserved what befell them. No one would.

"Within days, both of them had developed a strange hydrophobia, which is to say they became desperately afraid of water, however it was to be consumed—either as something to drink, something to cook with or something to wash in. In those days, the Kansas River—the very place where Bette Ward had thrown the medicine bundle—was the source of all the city's water.

"But it was not the water itself they feared like some mad, rabid dog, but what came with it. For every time each of them poured a glass of water, or filled a ewer with a jug to wash, or drew a bath, or watered a plant, the figure of a terrible-looking woman would appear somewhere close at hand. In the garden outside the window, at the top of the stairs, or even in the same room.

"Mrs. Ward drew a picture of the woman she saw and showed it to a doctor whom she had consulted for help. The doctor reported that the drawing was most curious, being a skillfully rendered drawing of Mrs. Ward herself, albeit in a state that could best be described as her having been dead for several months.

"The doctor prescribed laudanum, which was a powerful drug that killed pain but also produced powerful hallucinations. Which was probably the last thing they needed.

"Soon after this, the Wards stopped sleeping, they stopped washing, they stopped drinking water and drank only alcohol. The Indian school fell into disrepair and closed. Mr. Ward died first. His body was found floating in the river. His heart had been eaten by eels, it is said, but the Cherokee will tell you that Nunyunuwi always ate the heart of her victims.

"Bette Ward lasted a few months longer than her late husband before throwing herself out of the fifth-floor window of the now-derelict school, although not—the report stated at the time—before running herself a bath, which police officers entering the bathroom in what is now Room 505 found to be still warm. Soon after the autopsy, her heart disappeared and was never found."

My mother shook her head. "That is the saddest story I ever heard," she told Houdini.

"Indeed," said my father. "So it is poor Bette Ward who runs the bath in Room 505." He shook his head. "But why would she do that if she was going to throw herself out of the window?"

Houdini shook his head gravely. "No," he said. "It's worse than that."

"Really, I don't understand; what could be worse than that?" asked my mother. She looked anxiously at me, obviously full of regret that my young ears should have heard the telling of such a terrible story, even if it had been told by the great Houdini himself.

"I sat in the darkness of Room 505 for several hours without anything odd happening," said Houdini. "I must have fallen asleep for ten or fifteen minutes, I'm not sure, but I suddenly awoke with the strong feeling that there was something in the bathroom. And when I went in there to investigate, the bath was full of hot water, as if it had just been drawn, when I was certain beyond all contradiction that it had been empty before."

He shook his head.

"It was quite impossible that the water could have ended up in there by itself. For one thing, I had tightened the taps and made sure that the bath plug was hanging on the chain over the side. Either I had drawn the bath in my sleep or something else had done it for me. I say 'for me' because the temperature was perfect and the level

of water in the bath ideal and, thinking that my understanding of the phenomenon in 505 might thereby be enhanced, I took off my clothes and got in."

My mother let out a gasp. "Oh, Mr. Houdini," she said. "I don't know how you found the courage to do that. I should have been much too afraid."

"Me too," I said. "I'm scared just listening to this."

"Fear is something I have learned to control," said Houdini. "With fear comes panic and with panic death. Once, in California, I was buried alive, without a casket, in six feet of earth. The weight of the earth was much more than I had expected and I panicked. It was the panic, not the earth, that almost cost me my life. I had to control the panic first, in order to control my breathing. And only then was I able to force my way out of the grave to the surface."

"Wow," I said, impressed.

"I tell you this not to solicit your admiration, merely to illustrate how it was that I was able to witness and tolerate what happened next. For as I lay in the water, frankly enjoying the bath, the water started to run from the taps again. I sat bolt upright and saw the figure of Bette Ward standing beside me—and, it seemed, desperately trying to turn off the taps on the bath—with such a terrible look of fear on her face that I never hope to see on another human being as long as I live. But no matter how hard she tried, she could not turn them off, and suddenly I knew it was not she who had turned them on but something else. At which point I tried to get out, but could not.

"For even as she tried to stop the flow of water into the bath, the water around me turned suddenly brackish and then foul, and something came up from under me, through my legs, and stood up in the bath. It was like no creature I have ever seen. A long-dead thing that seemed only vaguely human and smelled strongly of

decay and death. I did not see the face, for which I have to say I am eternally grateful. But Mrs. Ward did, and, seeing it, she let out a silent scream that must have shattered the peace of the next world, only I could not hear it in this one. She ran out of the bathroom, followed by the Cherokee evil spirit. I call it such because there was an aspect to it that seemed vaguely Indian.

"Compelled to witness the end of this horrific visitation, I ran, still naked, out of the bathroom into the bedroom and then out of the door of Room 505, where I caught sight of Mrs. Ward standing at the end of a corridor in front of a window that is no longer there, with the creature advancing upon her, inexorably. Then Mrs. Ward shrieked her silent shriek once again, turned and threw herself out of the window. At which moment the creature disappeared."

"Do you mean to say that it is not Mrs. Ward who turns on the faucets, but this awful creature?" asked my father. "And that all of this precedes the continuing torment of this poor woman by some dreadful Indian apparition?"

"I do mean that, sir," said Houdini. "I most sincerely do."

"But what are we to do?" asked my father.

"My advice, sir," replied Houdini, "is to do nothing except what you have always done. To keep the door to Room 505 securely locked. And never to allow anyone in there." He smiled at me. "In particular, the boy here. I hope I didn't scare you, little man?"

"Me? I'm not scared," I said.

Houdini continued to offer no logical explanation for how he knew any of this and, given his previous instructions on the subject, we did not feel able to press him on the matter; indeed he was gone, returned to New York the same day, the same morning even, and with an alacrity we might have found almost disturbing. Such was his haste to leave, he even carried his own bags downstairs.

As he left the hotel to climb into a large Rolls-Royce that was parked outside the front door, I noticed he seemed to be in a little pain. His hands were trembling and he kept on looking over his shoulder as if he thought death itself had tapped him on the shoulder.

Perhaps it had at that.

My father thanked Houdini for his efforts on our behalf, and he in turn thanked us for allowing him to stay in Room 505.

"You have afforded me a fascinating glimpse of something I felt sure I should never see for myself," he said. "Really, it was quite, quite fascinating. And I am eternally grateful. Perhaps I shall come back here one day and investigate the matter further."

But Harry Houdini never, ever returned to Kansas City. Because he died the following month, of acute appendicitis, at the age of just fifty-two.